Bridge of Sighs

Bridge of Sighs

Jane Lane

THE JOHN DAY COMPANY

NEW YORK

Library of Congress Cataloging in Publication Data

Lane, Jane, 1905–
   Bridge of sighs.

   1. Mary, of Modena, consort of James II, King of
Great Britain, 1658–1718—Fiction.   I. Title.
PZ3.D1512Br4   [PR6007.A237]   823'.9'12   74–9360
ISBN 0–381–98277–7
   2 3 4 5 6 7 8 9 10

First United States Publication 1975

Printed in the United States of America

Contents

1	The Story Opens	1
2	Garland for a Lamb	8
3	A State of Innocence	27
4	Farewell Content	46
5	The Night of Judas	72
6	St Martin's Summer	107
7	The King My Son	138
8	The Story Closes	183

Bridge of Sighs

I

The Story Opens

1

For some moments after she woke, she remained the child Mary Beatrice of her dream, whimpering with terror, cowering from the sight of chimney-sweeps with blackened faces. The shots they were firing to bring down the soot deafened her; she could not move, for a firm hand held hers. A voice admonished:

'You will stay here, daughter, until you show no more fear.'

From high in the convent tower the great bell, Henriette-Marie-Phillipe-Augustus, swung over woods and valleys and winding Seine in the morning Angelus, dispelling her nightmare; and she smiled to think how vivid it had been. But it was always so lately; her dreams were not jumbled and meaningless, but faithful re-enactments of some trivial little happening in her past. Perhaps the infusion of hemlock leaves she must drink before she went to bed was responsible; it fulfilled its function of dulling pain, and one must be thankful for that.

The convent was awake now. She could sense the Community stirring as the Caller went round the dormitories with a horn lantern, whispering *Benedicamus Domino* at each cell door. On previous visits she had risen with them, observing all the conventual routine, but when last he examined her, M. Fagon had prescribed staying in bed till eight, and one must obey one's physician. The hideous thing that had taken up its abode in her breast had to be treated warily; it disliked cold and must be kept warm with layers of fur and flannel; it was beginning to emit a faint sickly odour, corrected by poultices of grated carrot and sweet herbs. To propitiate it entailed a mercurial pill once a week, a strict diet, a careful avoidance of contact, and periodic lancings.

The sound of a broom quietly sweeping, and a smell of polish, made from the ends of unbleached candles and turpentine, told her that the lay sisters were at work in her apartments. Presently the

1

two members of her Household who were with her here, Lady Strickland and Lady Sophia Bulkeley, would come to help her put on the widow's dress she had worn for the past sixteen years. She must rouse herself to repeat the prayers she always said before attending Mass.

When Mass was over, she stayed on for a while in the chapel, her nerves soothed by the plain-chant as the Community recited None behind the grille. She scarcely heard them leave for their morning's work in farm, orchard and little carpet factory; they took such small even steps that they glided almost noiselessly over the worn stone floors. Lady Strickland had preceded her to her own apartments to superintend the making of coffee; something of a martinet, she scolded her mistress.

'M. Fagon has told your Majesty over and over again that chills must be avoided, and the chapel here is like a vault. A note has been brought for your Majesty from Reverend Mother, but be pleased to drink your coffee before reading it.'

Panic, for ever lurking in ambush, rushed upon the Queen. Notes, couriers, the particular bell which summoned the Portress to the outer gate, each brought her heart into her mouth. She tore open the missive; written on cheap paper in accordance with holy poverty, it began as usual with 'Praised be Jesus Christ' under a small cross; it begged permission to wait upon her Majesty at eleven o'clock on a private matter of importance; and it concluded with the assurance that the writer was her Majesty's most humble servant *in Christo*, Charlotte Agnes Bouchare, *Supérieure*.

'She has received some news about the King my son which she must break gently!' wailed the Queen.

'Now what could she have heard, dear madame,' soothed warm-hearted Lady Sophia, 'which would not have come to you direct, either from his Majesty himself or from your advisers at St Germains?'

The Queen bit back an obvious retort; enclosed these nuns might be, but they were allowed visits to the parlour. Ashamed of her recurrent panic, she forced down some coffee while her ladies set out her work-table. For years she had been engaged on a set of seat-covers, in which the gifts of the Holy Ghost were symbolized by

2

flowers, but so far she had completed only Wisdom, Understanding and Counsel. She was to make a start on the honeysuckle which typified Fortitude, but as usual she had forgotten where she had put her spectacles, and there was an interval while her ladies searched for them. Even with them on, her fingers shook so uncontrollably that it was hard to thread a needle with yellow silk, and she could not concentrate on the *Spiritual Conversations of St Francis de Sales*, read aloud to her by Lady Sophia.

The cloister bell began to ring, warning the sisters who worked outdoors to come to the refectory for dinner at ten.

'I have not yet said the Rosary,' exclaimed Mary Beatrice, laying down her needle. 'I shall be too distracted to say it after Reverend Mother's visit.'

In her little oratory, she knelt at the prie-dieu, took out her beads, made the sign of the cross, and tried to concentrate on the Joyful Mysteries. *Acce ancilla Domine* . . . behold the handmaid of the Lord, be it done unto me according to thy word. She had been taught to make that the motto of her life; and here she was, nearly sixty, with the lesson still unlearned. While her lips formed the Paters and Aves, her thoughts flew hither and thither like the pigeons wheeling out there in the cloister garth. They reminded her of the famous carrier pigeons of Modena, the ancient Mutina of the Romans, where she was born. How much more real was the past than the present! Before her closed eyes she could see the lion-coloured walls of her home, the eighty full-length windows, the gigantic statues of Hercules and Cerberus guarding the Courtyard of Honour . . .

Her fingers felt for the next bead, and she discovered with shame that she had recited all five Mysteries without meditating upon one of them. And now a gentle knock on the door of her apartments, a voice saying *Benedicamus Domino*, and her ladies' murmured response, warned her that Reverend Mother had arrived.

'You have some news to disclose to me, *ma mère*,' she began, after the customary exchange of kisses on both cheeks. 'The King my son is——'

She could not frame that question which had haunted her for so many years: Is he dead?

Sitting bolt upright on an armless chair, Mère Bouchare began at once to withdraw from an old piece of linen the threads for use in mending, a practice of holy poverty. She made no excuse; the Rule enjoined that a nun's hands must never be idle except in prayer and sleep. St Francis de Sales had astonished the world when he founded an Order in which widows, the aged and the infirm could be received; but Mère Bouchare was a brisk and healthy virgin in middle life, recently elected *Supérieure*. Though said to be a masterpiece of spiritual perfection, she was formidably practical and slightly cold; her face within the black veil and white wimple, downbent now over her task, gave nothing away.

'I have received no news of the King your son, madame. The matter on which I desired this private talk with your Majesty concerns our house. Upon your Majesty's arrival here at Chaillot last week, I called a council of four senior sisters to ask their advice. After supper yesterday they came to tell me they were agreed it was my duty to remind your Majesty that your rent for these apartments is in arrear to the extent of 18,000 livres.'

Merely the old question of being in debt! Yet it was painful enough, especially when dear Chaillot was concerned.

'Did these senior sisters include Mère Priolo?'

'Surely your Majesty remembers our Rule? When her term as *Supérieure* ended, she became *Mère Déposée*, and now takes the lowest place that she may learn again to obey. The sisters I consulted were the Bursar, responsible for our temporal affairs, the Arcaria, in charge of our archives, Mother Vicaress and the Novice Mistress. In addition to your Majesty's arrears of rent, there are the 46,000 livres for which your Majesty was good enough to give us a promissory note.'

There was silence while Mary Beatrice calculated these formidable sums in English money. Italian by birth, exiled in France for nearly thirty years, still she turned everything into the English of her marriage. Something in the nature of £2000. She could not remember having given this promissory note; but there it was, whipped from Mère Bouchare's pocket. Looking round in vain for her spectacles, the Queen flushed and apologized.

'My memory grows so bad, dear mother; twice this morning I

went to wind my watch, though I had done so as usual when I woke. And yet I remember the most foolish trifles from my youth. It is, I suppose, a common affliction when one approaches one's sixtieth year.'

Mère Bouchare inclined her head; and waited.

'Among the greatest misfortunes of my life is to see for how many years I have been lodging with you without payment. You must attribute it to the unhappy state of my affairs, and to that necessity which has no law. Perhaps you could move me into some cheaper apartments; I do not care how narrow they are, so long as I have a little corner where I may be near the hearts of my dear husband and my poor daughter, enshrined in your tribune.'

The tears had sprung into her large dark eyes, but in childhood she had acquired an art of not permitting them to fall. Royalty, she had been taught, did not weep in public. Mère Bouchare unbent.

'The whole Community, I assure you, madame, is truly grateful for having your Majesty among us, for your example has inspired us with a new zeal for the performance of our duties in Religion. It gives us great pain when the poverty of our house compels us to mention anything that is due to us.'

She withdrew several threads from her linen before she continued:

'On many occasions since your Majesty has done us the honour of lodging with us, we have petitioned you for the history of your life. This we much desire to include in the Annals of Chaillot, chronicled by successive Reverend Mothers since the foundation of this convent by Queen Henriette Marie. Upon your Majesty's first visit here in 1689, you graciously consented to be our Patroness; we long to hear from your own lips all you can relate to us, for it is the opinion of many of our sisters that we entertain a saint.'

Colour flushed the Queen's pale skin. She said vigorously:

'My enemies have accused me of the most odious crimes; my friends impute to me virtues I do not possess; but God will be my judge!'

At once, in a familiar gesture, her hand sprang across her mouth.

'I beg your pardon, *ma mère*. Never have I overcome my natural impulsiveness. But as for what you have suggested, I have no faculty for writing histories, and moreover my little malady has robbed me of strength.'

'I was not for one moment proposing that your Majesty should give yourself such fatigue. It is for me to assign the sisters their duties, and since Mère Priolo has the honour of your particular friendship, I am willing that at a time convenient to your Majesty, and when she is not employed in our spiritual exercises, she takes down these memoirs at your Majesty's dictation. The tragic events in which your Majesty was involved as Queen Consort of England, and the misfortunes which have befallen his present Majesty, your son, would be of surpassing interest if related from your Majesty's personal knowledge.'

Mary Beatrice was silent. She was ashamed to admit that the realm of public affairs had remained a mystery to her, that causes meant little in comparison with persons. Mistaking the reason for her silence, Mère Bouchare brightly encouraged her.

'Only just now your Majesty was saying that the memories of your youth are very clear to you. For the many years your Majesty has been in exile, we have between us rich material for a memoir. You have been good enough to confide to me, madame, that here in these apartments you treasure in a special cabinet the letters of your husband, your son and your daughter. Then there is the correspondence your Majesty has kept with Mère Priolo. You know our Rule; we must not use the word "mine" about anything here; the cell, the rosary-beads, the habit, all are "ours", and such letters as we are permitted to receive are no exception.'

It was all unanswerable. And what a small favour to grant to those to whom she was in debt for such formidable sums.

'As for the painful matter which I have been obliged to bring to your Majesty's notice,' said Mère Bouchare, as though guessing her thoughts, 'we shall be most willing to await your Majesty's convenience. Perhaps the hour before Vespers would be most acceptable to your Majesty, when you have rested after dinner. May I order Mère Priolo to come to you for dictation at that hour?'

2

'*Eh bien!*' chirruped Mère Priolo, bustling in next afternoon with a sheaf of cheap paper. 'We begin our little history, madame!'

All the Sisters of the Visitation were required by their Rule to cultivate the virtue of cheerfulness; Catherine Angélique Priolo was sunny by nature. It was supposed by the Community that her Italian blood had made her from the first the Queen's special friend, but rather it was herself. She had the rare quality of listening to what was said to her; she never betrayed a confidence; and she shared the Queen's keen sense of the ludicrous. On more than one occasion the Community had been startled by peals of laughter issuing from her Majesty's apartments when Mère Priolo was there.

'We go very slowly,' encouraged the old nun, setting out her quills and paper. 'Your Majesty is not returning to St Germains before September, and please God you will visit us again next year. I set down nothing without you first approve it, and at the least fatigue, we stop!'

She was one of the very few who knew that 'my little malady', as the Queen called it, was an incurable cancer, terribly advanced. Mary Beatrice began obediently, as one reciting a lesson:

'My father was Duke Alphonso d'Este, and my mother was born Laura Martinozzi, niece of Cardinal Mazarin. My birth took place in the ducal palace of Modena on October 5th, 1658, and that of my only brother, Francesco, two years later, not long after our father's premature death of consumption. We were left under the guardianship of our uncle, Prince Rinaldo, though our education and welfare were in the hands of her Serenity, our mother, who loved us devotedly, though it pleased her to keep us at an awful distance, and never to excuse our faults. When I was old enough to leave the hands of my nurse, I went daily to receive instruction from the Sisters of the Visitation in their convent founded by my mother, and connected with the ducal palace by a bridge of sighs . . .'

Her voice continued to recite dull facts, but before her mental

7

vision the scenes of childhood began to pass, so vivid that she ceased to be the exiled Queen Mother of England, old and sick, and became again the Princess of Modena, aged fourteen, running across the bridge of sighs to her true home.

2

Garland for a Lamb

1

Lent was over; only on Fridays now would she be obliged to eat that horrible *soupe maigre*, with the all-seeing eyes of her Serenity watching until the bowl was empty. Tomorrow the ducal family were going to their summer palace at Sassuolo, a place she loved. She ought to be happy; instead she felt as miserable as the criminals who had been led across this bridge of sighs to their execution in what was then the prison. But one day soon she too would be crossing it for the last time, and then it would be a bridge of smiles.

Vespers were not yet finished, the Portress told her; perhaps she would like to say a prayer in the chapel. Mary Beatrice took her usual swift glance at a door, locked and bolted on the inside, at the end of the Great Cloister. In eighteen months' time, it would open to receive her; she would hear Reverend Mother say, 'Come in, dear child,' and in her honour there would be a garland hung over the entrance to the Novitiate. Henceforth for the rest of her life she would be snug and safe.

In the chapel she carefully did not look at the statue of Our Lady of the Visitation on its bracket. It dated from the original Rule of St Francis de Sales, when much of the nuns' time was spent in visiting the sick and poor. But when St Francis bowed to the wishes of his Archbishop that his Institute become an enclosed Order, the statue had lost its meaning. It portrayed the young Virgin, arms outstretched, hastening towards the homes of the unfortunate. Suddenly today this statue, hitherto so dear, had become something the child dared not look at. She knelt with down-cast eyes until she heard a combination of notes, struck with a rod on a small triangle of metal, which told her that Reverend Mother was being 'tinged to the parlour'.

She waited there in a frenzy of impatience while someone unseen hooked back the shutters, opened wide the grille. Then she was in that motherly embrace she never experienced at the ducal palace.

'I declare you grow more beautiful every day, my child. You have a new dress for Sassuolo, I see, but if you were in rags, you would look enchanting. Your beauty is a great gift from God, for which you must be grateful, though of course without vanity. Why are the tears standing in your eyes? Let them fall, and tell me what is amiss.'

'Her Serenity chides me when I weep. And this morning she beat me! She said she feared for my soul, but truly I did not think I was seeing visions, truly I did not!'

'Tell me, little one, but tranquilly,' soothed Reverend Mother.

'I remarked to her Serenity that I was going to make my temporary farewells at the convent, and to Our Lady of the Visitation who has such a gay smile. Her Serenity beat me; she said that the sculptor who carved that statue had too much reverence to portray the Blessed Virgin with a gay smile, and that if I was pre-sumptuous enough to imagine that it smiled for my benefit, I was guilty of mortal sin. But ever since I first saw her, I always thought she smiled. Her Serenity is so harsh with me! She never kisses me except to brush my cheek; I must never call her "mother". Oh I do so long for my sixteenth birthday when I shall be admitted here as a postulant. It is so warm with affection here! And I shall be with you, dear mother; I know that until I take my perpetual vows and go up to the Community, I shall be in the charge of Mother Mistress, and see you only at a distance, but——'

'Hush, child, you must be tranquil. Regarding the punishment inflicted on you by her Serenity, you must understand that she con-sidered it her duty. As for the smile you think you see upon Our Lady's statue, perhaps it is some effect of the light, though I am sure that when she was on earth, she smiled often and gaily. Now you are quieter, and can attend to what I say.'

She released herself gently from the clinging arms, and launched into a little homily on vocation.

'We do not come here to seek security, but to be crucified in spirit, and to offer our prayers and sacrifices for all mankind, as Our Lord offered His body on the cross. You have been present at a clothing; do you remember the words of the Responsory? "The kingdom of this world, and all the ornaments of time, have I despised for the love of Jesus Christ my Lord." Ponder them, little one; you must not come here for the love of any creature, nor to make a warm nest for yourself. You cannot be admitted until you are sixteen, and that is eighteen months distant. It may be that in the meantime you will discover that God has other designs for you.'

She kissed the innocent, bewildered face, and said cheerfully:

'Now be happy at Sassuolo. And if you are going to say good-bye to the Princess your aunt, I will not keep you, for there is but an hour before the Angelus, when our Great Silence begins.'

2

There were two Aunts Leonora, though they inhabited the same body. When Mary Beatrice visited the Princess in the apartments she rented in the convent, she never knew which of the two she would find. If she was met with eyes turned heavenwards and hands joined at the finger-tips, if *The Dark Night of the Soul* lay open on the table, then it was the Aunt Leonora who was much given to visions and ecstasies. If on the other hand the table was strewn with the Gazettes of the principal capitals of Europe, and letters in many different scripts overflowed on to the floor, it was the Aunt Leonora who doted on gossip, and who, through friends and agents, gleaned the most intimate details of what was happening in the outside world. There was no doubt which Leonora was present this afternoon. Her plain face was alight with excitement, her mantilla sat askew upon her red hair, and she greeted her niece with the utmost drama.

'My lamb! To think that you might have been made a sacrifice! Sit here upon the couch beside me and listen to news the most surprising, received by me this very morning from Abbé Rizzini, our Agent in Paris. The brother of the King of England seeks a second wife.'

'Where is this place called England?' inquired Mary Beatrice, whose world was limited to the little Duchy of Modena, shut in by the tremendous walls of the Alps and the Apennines, and bounded on two sides by sea.

'Somewhere there,' replied Leonora, gesturing vaguely towards the north, 'a small kingdom resembling Geneva when St Francis went to convert that terrible place; all our holy rites are most strictly forbidden. Moreover the sun never shines upon it; they have either fog or rain. But to my news. King Charles of England has a barren wife, and therefore is his brother Heir Presumptive; but since he has only daughters, he would marry again to beget a son, though he is old—so old! I do not know how his name is pronounced; it is spelt Y-O-R-K, and so I suppose it is Ork.'

'What a curious name.'

'A curious country! One of their kings had six wives and beheaded them all, and another of their kings was himself put to death in the public street. Do not ask me why; it appears that these English are more savage than the Turk. And now a lord with a very long name, the beginning of which is Peter, so we will call him Lord Peter, is sent by King Charles to fetch the Most Serene Archduchess, Claudia Felicitas, heiress of Innspruck, as the wife of this Ork.'

'The poor Archduchess!'

'She has escaped. A few days after Lord Peter came to Paris, he received an express from the Emperor, telling him that the Empress had just died, and his Imperial Majesty had chosen the Archduchess as her successor. So!' Leonora lowered her voice to a thrilling whisper. 'Lord Peter receives from his master a list of nine other ladies whom he is ordered to inspect, and up and down Europe he must go until the choice is made, burdened with jewels worth £20,000 in English money to be presented at the proxy marriage. And in that list is included your name.'

'Oh, *no*!'

'Courage, my child! Rizzini told Lord Peter, who got a sight of your picture at the palace of the late Princesse de Conti, your aunt, and was enraptured, that you were resolved to enter Religion.'

In her relief at escaping such a fate, Mary Beatrice became curious about the other victims. She knew it was the time-honoured custom for royal brides to be chosen without regard to their feelings, yet there was something both ludicrous and nauseating in the idea of this Lord Peter, travelling about Europe encumbered by a fortune in jewels while he inspected brides for an old, old man. Aunt Leonora consulted her letter.

'The choice of France was his Most Christian Majesty's first cousin, the widowed Duchesse de Guise; but on inspection she was found to be ill shaped. And having seen the picture of the next one on his list, Mlle de Retz, heiress of that duchy, Lord Peter decided he need not travel a hundred miles to view her in person. There is the Princess Marie Anne of Wurtemberg, whose father died fighting for France and so she is lodged in a French convent at his Most Christian Majesty's expense. An Infanta of Spain (but that would offend France, at present King Charles's ally); two nieces of Marshal Turenne, the eldest but thirteen and childish at that; and Princess Eleonore Madeleine, eldest daughter of the Elector of Neuberg.'

'You said there were nine on the list, dear aunt. You have named but eight.'

Leonora simpered.

'I was not going to distress you by mentioning that I too am upon that list. It may be that God demands this sacrifice of me. I have never been able to make up my mind whether my vocation is for the cloister or the married state. It is true that I have a repugnance for marriage; but widowhood certainly attracts me. In this I resemble the Venerable Mère Favre, who was heard to say in youth that if she were assured that he whom she wedded would be dead two hours later, she would consent to the match. And as I have mentioned, this Ork is a very old man.'

The first stroke of the Angelus bell startled Mary Beatrice, who had forgotten the passing of time in so bizarre a tale. And tomorrow she would be going to Sassuolo until September.

'I shall write to you constantly,' promised Leonora, 'and I will not fail to let you know which sacrificial lamb has been chosen.'

Sassuolo was the one place Mary Beatrice knew she would miss when she entered Religion. The ducal palace at Modena was too vast and formal ever to have felt like home; and she was always frightened of hearing on the gates the ghostly knock of St Beatrice, patron saint of the Estes, who thus warned of a death in the family. But Sassuolo was a paradise of orchards and vineyards, with views of little mouldering castles perched on crags. Francesco the Great, her grandfather, had designed everything in the summer palace for coolness and repose, and here even her Serenity became less of a Roman matron. Though not to the extent of excusing her delicate little son from his studies.

'Better that I should have no son, than one without wit or merit,' was her constant refrain.

In previous summers, Mary Beatrice had spent much of her time in the belvedere in the park, chattering with her two favourite friends, Anna Molza and Vittoria Montecuccoli, about that great day when she would receive the habit of the Visitandines from the hands of the Bishop of Modena. They were to be her bridesmaids, and sometimes they would rehearse the ceremony up to the point when, her wedding garland exchanged for a white veil and wimple, she would disappear for ever into the mysterious realm of the enclosure.

But during this summer she was more often alone on her balcony, reading Aunt Leonora's chatty letters. The subject of these letters was not one which should concern her; but on the other hand, she had had a very miraculous escape, and was it not natural to feel some interest in the fate of the other victims?

'This Lord Peter,' wrote Leonora, 'is said to be a very good judge of horseflesh, and upon my soul, he inspects brides as he might mares for his stable. Since you are not to be had, he inclines to Mlle de Wurtemberg, with whom his Most Christian Majesty is ready to give a handsome dowry, and through her confessor has obtained an interview at the parlour of the convent where she lodges. I learn that he was quite smitten, and described her thus to Rizzini: "She is of middle stature, fair complexion, with brown hair; the shape of her face agreeable, her looks grave but sweet, her eyes grey." I understand that he is renewing his visits, and has begun to drop some hints that soon he will be authorized to demand her hand for this Ork.'

Mary Beatrice would dearly have liked to ask Aunt Leonora exactly what Lord Peter had said when he was 'enraptured' by her own portrait. A middle stature, grey eyes, brown hair and fair complexion did not sound as though they would compare with the reflection she saw when she looked in her mirror. That, of course, was vain, and dutifully she mentioned it at Confession on Saturday. She returned to find another letter from her aunt.

'A sudden and mysterious change of policy in England has caused orders to be sent to Lord Peter to leave Paris at once, and proceed incognito to Dusseldorf, where he is to get a sight of the Princess Eleonore Madeleine. The poor man says his head spins round under such a variety of contradictory instructions, and he has gone so far in his wooing of Mlle de Wurtemberg that he was fain to leave without seeing her again.' There was a postscript. 'I would not close this letter until I had further news, and I have just this moment heard that on viewing her, he found the Princess Eleonore to be inclining to fat, and therefore not likely to bear strong children. So he has made a precipitate retreat.'

In her next letter, Leonora described Lord Peter as hurrying back to Paris, where he was to marry Mlle de Wurtemberg by proxy and take her over to England. So that was the end of the story. It had been fascinating while it lasted; and perhaps one day when she was old, Sister Mary Beatrice might relate to the Community at Recreation how she had narrowly escaped being married to an old, old man, and living in a heretic country where it was always winter. She might even have been beheaded, since that appeared to be the usual fate of English queens.

Even here at Sassuolo the heat in August was so great that the ducal family spent most of their time in the Gallery of the Fountains or on the flat roof garden on to which it opened. Thus it was that Mary Beatrice overheard one day the voice of her uncle, Prince Rinaldo, upraised sharply in conversation with her mother.

'It is monstrous! This English lord leaves a trail of affronted

14

brides-to-be in various parts of Europe, and now he is breaking off negotiations with Mlle de Wurtemberg whom he has as good as married.'

Mary Beatrice tiptoed away; it was talk not intended for her ears. But the interest of Aunt Leonora's story had revived; and soon it was plain that something was in the wind which necessitated family conferences, at which Fr Galimberti, the Duchess's confessor, was present. The Duchess herself looked positively grim; the name of Aunt Leonora crept increasingly into conversations; and there was an open discussion one evening at supper on the proper ceremonies with which to receive an Ambassador Extraordinary.

'I do believe,' Mary Beatrice whispered to her brother, 'that poor Aunt Leonora is going to be made to marry an old heretic.'

Francesco was not interested. A delicate child of twelve, he was tossed like a shuttlecock between his dominating mother and his cousin, Prince Cesare, who was at odds with the Duchess.

Mary Beatrice was in the midst of a music lesson, absorbed in an intricate passage on her harpsichord, when Signor Nardi, her mother's secretary, summoned her to the Duchess's private apartments. As soon as she entered, she perceived that this was some formal and momentous occasion. The Duchess sat in her chair of state beneath a canopy painted with the gold lilies and crowned eagle of the Estes. Signor Nardi's brother, the Chancellor of Modena, stood at her right hand in his robes of office. Prince Rinaldo and Fr Galimberti were together on the steps of the dais, giving the impression of allies in a dispute; and in an armchair facing the Duchess was a stranger, a handsome, youngish man, who rose and bowed with great courtliness to Mary Beatrice.

'M. le Marquis de Dangeau,' began the Duchess, speaking in French, 'is appointed special envoy by his Most Christian Majesty to explain to me, as Regent, the situation in regard to his wishes and those of his Majesty of England in the proposed marriage of the Duke of York. M. le Marquis is in a manner of speaking a herald of the Earl of Peterborough, who is at present at Lyons on his way to Modena.'

To ask for the hand of poor Aunt Leonora, thought Mary

Beatrice, tears enhancing the brilliance of her eyes, while she greeted the stranger. He was enchanted by the perfection of her French, he murmured; it was, of course, the language of all civilized courts, but he was sure that any tongue would come naturally to one with so musical a voice. Did she speak any other? Yes, she spoke Latin and Greek, and a little Spanish. But not English? Why, no. She just stopped herself from blurting out that she had never known there was such a place as England until quite recently.

In honour of the Marquis, the quiet life at Sassuolo changed to a round of festivities. On each of these occasions he treated Mary Beatrice as though she were the person he had travelled so far to see, begging her to display her skill on various musical instruments, to show him the translation she was making of Aesop's *Fables*, to recite to him from the works of her great countrymen, Dante and Tasso, to be his partner in saraband and courante. In all these accomplishments she had not her peer in Europe, he assured her; as for her beauty, she was the *beau idéal* of feminine loveliness. It was all very flattering, but incomprehensible. When she asked him whether he had called on Aunt Leonora, he answered evasively that there was plenty of time. Her Serenity, whom he had known in France before her marriage, had invited him to accompany the ducal family to the capital when they moved back in mid-September.

One Sunday after Compline, the Duchess signed to her daughter to accompany her into her cabinet. Seating herself, with Mary Beatrice standing before her, she began at once with the air of one determined to perform an unpleasant duty:

'It is time, daughter, to inform you of a situation which I have been watching closely for several months. His Royal Highness, the Duke of York, Heir Presumptive to the throne of England, seeks a second wife, and both his brother, King Charles, and his Most Christian Majesty, have decided that a princess of our house would be the most suitable choice.'

'Yes, your Serenity, I know. But I thought——'

'What do you mean, you know?' interrupted the Duchess very sharply.

16

'Her Highness, my aunt, did mention to me that her name was on the list—I mean, had been put forward. But I understood that Mlle de Wurtemberg was now affianced to this—this Ork.'

'The Duke of York,' corrected her mother glacially. 'It is most unbecoming that you should concern yourself with such high matters until they were disclosed to you by me. The match with Mlle de Wurtemberg is broken off, and the Earl of Peterborough, his Majesty of England's Ambassador Extraordinary, is now on his way to Modena, to open to me, in his master's name, the earnest desire of the Duke of York to espouse you as his wife.'

The shock held Mary Beatrice rigid for a moment; then she flung herself at her mother's feet.

'Oh no, no, pray no!'

'Stand up this instant, daughter, and behave yourself as becomes Royalty. Now I must tell you that Prince Rinaldo, your State Guardian, is strongly of the opinion that Princess Leonora would be more suitable; and moreover Fr Galimberti has expressed himself as appalled that I should contemplate denying you your vocation to Religion.'

'And her Highness has confided to me, your Serenity,' gabbled Mary Beatrice, torn between relief and terror, 'that she is willing to make this great sacrifice.'

'At her age, I have no doubt she is,' drily observed the Duchess. 'I have not yet reached a decision in the matter; I merely warn you that you may be prepared when Lord Peterborough arrives.'

'But I do not wish to marry *anyone*!' She began to hiccough with hysteria. 'Your Serenity has always encouraged my desire to enter Religion, and to think of this old, old man as my husband, to live in a land where the sun never shines and they are all heretics, and where it is the custom to behead their queens!'

The Duchess slapped her hard across the face.

'Unless you control yourself, daughter, I shall send you straight to your room.' After a pause she continued: 'The Duke of York is in his fortieth year, extremely handsome, a most tender father to his two daughters, the idol of the English when he was Lord High Admiral, and so brave a soldier in his exiled youth that

17

he excited the admiration even of his enemies. Perhaps you would rather wed King Charles of Spain, who is Prince Rinaldo's choice for you. He was wet-nursed until he was five, and even now, at eleven, is only just learning to walk. However, what you wish is neither here nor there; I am not accustomed to stomach independence in my children.'

'Oh your Serenity, pray pardon me, but Aunt Leonora is much nearer in age to the Duke of—of York, and she doubts her vocation to Religion.'

'The fancied objection of too great juvenility in a girl of your age will very soon be obviated by time, while every day will render a lady of thirty less agreeable to a prince whose object is to have strong children. I would wish to know what right you have to make difficulties, since the Duke of York does not. You are not his choice but, for reasons of State, that of the King his brother.'

Mary Beatrice took an instant aversion to the Duke of York.

'However,' went on the Duchess, very slightly softening, 'I am impressed by the arguments of Fr Galimberti, and I will do you the favour to inform you that I have sent Signor Nardi to Lord Peterborough with a message. He is instructed to say that however honourable and advantageous to my daughter such a match would be, she is perfectly settled in her resolve to receive the habit of the Visitandines. Yet since there are other princesses in my family, to one of whom, if the Duke of York thought fit, it was possible that Lord Peterborough might be permitted to address himself, my lord would be welcome at the Court of Modena, and I would esteem it an honour to receive him.'

Only the iron discipline imposed upon her since babyhood prevented Mary Beatrice from flinging herself into her mother's arms to thank her. But at least she could write her passionate gratitude to Aunt Leonora, who was ready to wear the garland of the sacrificial lamb. Leonora replied petulantly. Lord Peter had insisted to Signor Nardi that he was merely a private gentleman travelling to see the beauties of Italy. He was now hanging about in sweltering heat at Piacenza, feigning illness while he awaited further instructions from this outrageously shilly-shallying King Charles of

England. She, Leonora, guessed that these would be for him to return to Paris and marry the long-suffering Mlle de Wurtemberg after all.

4

But on the very day when the ducal family moved back to Modena, Lord Peter arrived there, and was lodged in the Bishop's palace at her Serenity's expense. Mary Beatrice heard the news from Contessa Molza, the Bishop's niece, a fervent young person devoted to obscure saints, who added that she was making a novena to St Rita, patroness of desperate causes, to protect her dear princess in this crisis. Mary Beatrice's hope that Lord Peter had come for the purpose of wooing Aunt Leonora was immediately dashed by a message from her mother. She was to present herself in the Duchess's apartments after Mass next morning to receive the Ambassador Extraordinary of England.

She saw a stout, slightly bow-legged gentleman, who greeted her in bad Italian, scrutinizing her in such a manner that for one wild moment she feared he might ask to inspect her mouth as he would a horse's. Chairs were set, and all three sat down.

'I have already explained to M. de Peterborough,' began the Duchess, speaking in French, 'your aversion to marriage, daughter. And moreover I have warned him that there would be a difficulty in obtaining from His Holiness a dispensation for an alliance with a prince who has not yet made public his conversion to our Catholic faith, let his private opinions be what they will. Yet I have consented that M. de Peterborough plead his cause to you in person.'

The Ambassador, given tacit leave to speak in the universal language of courts, became voluble.

'As soon as I saw your Serene Highness's picture in Paris, I was convinced that I had found my mistress and the fortune of England! Such a light of beauty, such characters of ingenuity and goodness, such dazzling fairness of complexion, and such eyes! Even in the canvas there seemed given unto them by nature power to kill, and power to save. Yet how little justice that portrait did to the original!'

Then, plainly doing violence to his Protestant conscience, he

19

drew a pathetic picture of the Duke of York, who had sacrificed all his offices, with their vast income, rather than subscribe to something called the Test Act. He had made plain his conversion by refusing to receive the Sacrament of the Church of England last Christmas, and he had rejected with contempt a huge sum offered him by her bishops if he would wed a Protestant. Mary Beatrice sat unmoved; she did not in the least understand this talk of Test Acts; while in all simplicity she was aware of her own loveliness, flattery nauseated her; and she had noticed that Lord Peterborough did not present her with a portrait of the Duke of York. Even though princesses must marry complete strangers, a picture of those strangers was *de rigueur*, and its absence on this occasion could only mean that the Duke of York was hideous. With a natural impulsiveness no beatings could eradicate, she spoke.

'I am obliged to the King of England and the Duke of York for their good opinion of me. Yet I cannot but wonder they should persist in endeavouring to force the inclination of one who has vowed herself, as much as is in her power, to the life of the cloister, out of which she never could think she would be happy.'

She heard the Duchess draw a sharp breath; she saw Lord Peterborough gazing at her in mingled enchantment and dismay; but she was past caring.

'I entreat your Excellency, if you have any influence with your master, to avert further persecution of a maid who has an invincible aversion to matrimony. Princesses there are enough in Italy, and even in this house, who would not be unworthy of so great an honour, and who deserve it much better than I could do.'

Lord Peterborough gulped, bowed, and tried again.

'I beg your Serene Highness's pardon if I am made the instrument to cross your inclinations, but first from your picture, and now still more from a view of yourself, I am convinced that you are the only means of making happy a prince who is so deeply enamoured of you, and whose merits, when you come to know him, will make ample amends for anything you may now regard as a grievance.'

Tears of sheer anger stood in her eyes. How dared he! Enamoured indeed, when she was not even the choice of this Duke of York, but only, for cold reasons of State, of his brother. She was struggling to find words in which to remind Lord Peterborough of all those other princesses he had been ticking off on his list, when the Duchess rose to close the interview. Directly Lord Peterborough had complimented himself out of the room, she turned upon her daughter.

'I am profoundly ashamed of you. A child of your age should have no will of her own; a fine Religious you would make, who know not how to obey! As for your suggesting other brides for the Duke of York, I have never heard such gross impertinence.'

Taking this for dismissal, Mary Beatrice, blind with tears, was groping her way across the room, when she heard the stern admonition:

'Daughter!'

She had forgotten to curtsy. She had reached the door when she was again recalled.

'Daughter! I had not yet finished what I have to say to you. I have made up my mind to consent to this match, and I have already dispatched Abbé Dangeau to obtain a dispensation from His Holiness. Despite what I said to Lord Peterborough, there can be little doubt it will be granted, for this morning a Brief arrived for you, which naturally I have read. I believe it is the first time in history when such has been addressed by a Sovereign Pontiff to a maid not yet fifteen. His Holiness undertakes that you shall enjoy the same liberty in the exercise of your religion as the queen of King Charles, and positively orders you to overcome your repugnance to marriage, for in that state you will open to yourself a field of merit wider than that of the virginal cloister.'

She lifted and set down again a document with a great, splendid dangling seal. Her voice when she continued had slightly thawed.

'You are very young and innocent, and your future husband is five and twenty years your senior. Do not inquire into his past life, which is not your business. Amours are the plague of courts, but I am sure that a young and lovely wife will give the Duke of York a distaste for such sins of the flesh, especially since his conversion to our holy religion. As for public matters, you would be wise to let them alone; you have no head for such things. It is my duty to warn you that the English are the most fanatical of heretics, and very much averse to foreigners. For the first, you must strive by your virtuous life to wean them from their prejudice; but in deference to the second, you are to be permitted in your future Household only a very small number of Italians. Lastly, because of the situation in England, which would be beyond your comprehension, there is need for haste; and therefore I shall consent to Lord Peterborough's plea that he marries you by proxy on the last day of this month.'

Mary Beatrice was bereft of speech. The Pope had issued a personal command; her Serenity also had decided. Only twelve days and she would be wife to a complete stranger, and be rushed over to a country of fanatical heretics, very much averse to foreigners. She looked so white and stricken that the Duchess softened.

'I shall myself accompany you upon your journey, daughter, and see you settled in your new home. Though this is against my better judgment, for I dread the influence of Prince Cesare upon my young son while I am absent.'

5

The time between that interview in which her fate was sealed, and her fifteenth birthday when she set out from Modena, was so hectic that only scattered details imprinted themselves upon her memory. Lord Peter (as he still remained to her) presenting her with the glittering hoard of jewels he had been lugging about Europe, and her complete indifference to them; the tiny thrill, whether of repugnance or excitement she could not say, when he placed on her third finger a diamond ring of espousal. The dramatic exclamation of Aunt Leonora at the sight of her in her wedding finery:

'My poor little lamb, decked for the sacrifice!'

A round of farewells merged into each other; but she would never forget those few poignant moments when, for the last time, she was held in Reverend Mother's warm embrace.

'I shall never cross the bridge of sighs to come to you, dear mother! The door into the enclosure will never be opened for me!'

22

'My little one, be tranquil. God has spoken by the voice of your superiors, and no soul was ever lost through obedience. You have such a wealth of ardent affection to bestow on your husband and, if it please God, on your children. Yet be on your guard against excessive attachment. You are inclined to be a little *exaltée* where persons are concerned, and you must preserve the inner chamber of your heart for your Creator. Here is my parting gift for you, a card for your prayer-book with a picture of the statue of Our Lady of the Visitation. Life is a bridge of sighs for all of us, my darling, but when you have crossed that, you will see her in person, and then indeed she will smile at my dear child.'

She seemed to herself to be two distinct persons, Mary Beatrice d'Este, who would be left behind for ever in this familiar beeswaxed parlour and in Reverend Mother's arms; and Mary Beatrice, Duchessa d'York, a stranger going to live with a stranger, whose features were unknown to her, who had not yet written her one personal letter. Her new status sat heavily; to take precedence of her mother at banquets and receptions, to travel day after day through a strange countryside where towns were decorated in her honour and great personages came to kiss her hand, to have presents showered upon her from his Most Christian Majesty as soon as she entered his dominions, these marks of her new greatness only confused and frightened her.

At night in the arms of Pellegrina Turini, who had been her nurse and was one of the very few Italians allowed to remain with her, she wept with home-sickness and a fear of the future, a fear increased by Aunt Leonora's letters, which awaited her at every halt. What kind of man could this be, demanded Leonora, to whom her little lamb was being sacrificed? She had it from an English correspondent that when M. de Croissy, the French Ambassador in London, apprised the Duke of York that the proxy wedding was accomplished, all the Duke said was, 'Then I am a married man.' And he had sent for his two daughters to tell them that he had provided them with a playfellow. A playfellow indeed! Then there was this dreadful English Parliament. King Charles had planned to rush the bride over while Parliament was in recess; but it had refused to be prorogued, and had gone the length of demanding that he stop her in Paris, meanwhile appointing a solemn fast for the purpose of imploring God to avert the dangers with which the nation was threatened if the Heir Presumptive married a papist.

News of this kind, so wounding and inexplicable, made her stay in France a nightmare, in spite of the wonderful kindness of King Louis. Looking back, she saw him always at her side, this tall young man with his tremendous personality. He was in the thick of war, and had only just returned from the front, but he seemed to have all the time in the world to devote to the little bride, insisting on showing her everything himself. Except the old chateau of St Germain-en-laye, where he still held his Court; it was too melancholy for a bride, he said, with its view of St Denis, the burial place of the French kings, and he hoped soon to leave it for his new Versailles. In his private gilt chariot he drove her expertly on a tour of what was still a palace and gardens in embryo, scaffolding everywhere, good-sized forest trees being planted, marble statues lying about for him to say where he wished them erected, moats being filled in around his father's old hunting-lodge, and new marble walls rising upon them.

Though neither her mother nor Lord Peter said anything to her, she noticed that they seemed anxious when the English posts came in. But then one day a letter arrived addressed to herself in an unfamiliar, very firm handwriting. With a catch of her breath, she saw the signature, 'James'.

'Madam my wife, I have charged the bearer, Fr Sheldon, to inform you of what has happened here, in order that you may not be alarmed by it. He will at the same time assure you that I have all imaginable impatience to have the happiness to see you, and to be able to assure you myself that as long as I live, I shall have all the love and true friendship that you can expect from me.'

She was chilled. It was scarcely a love-letter, and it was written on October 30th, a whole month after their proxy wedding. Her mother's hurting rebuke recurred to her, 'You are not his choice'. And what a way to end—'that you can expect from me'! She repeated the words out loud, and Fr Sheldon hastened to explain that

this was the Duke's habitual ending of his letters to his closest relations and friends. He then launched into a diatribe against certain
republicans who used religion merely as a cloak for their treason-
able plotting against the Monarchy. Through their majority in
Parliament, they were blackmailing King Charles by withholding
supplies unless he legitimized his bastard, the Duke of Monmouth,
thus excluding his brother from the Succession. She gazed at him,
bemused. She did not understand what this Parliament was; there
was no such thing in Modena. Carried away by his own indignation,
Fr Sheldon blurted out that 'they' had egged on the common people
to celebrate something called Guy Fawkes Night with such savagery
that if she had arrived then, undoubtedly she would have been
murdered.

It was too much. Her husband's cold letter, and this renewed
evidence that the English hated foreigners and papists, made her ill,
and she was kept in bed for a week. Perhaps it was her fever which
made the personages who came to call seem so bizarre: Queen
Marie Therese, with black teeth and the mentality of a child; the
timid young Dauphin whose tiny feet made him so unsteady that he
clung to the furniture; and that fantastic couple, Monsieur and
Madame. It had been impressed on Mary Beatrice that during the
minority of the Dauphin, Monsieur, the King's brother, was the
First Gentleman in France, but he appeared to her a mere clown, a
manikin with black-currant eyes, teetering on such high heels that
he seemed to walk on stilts, steeped in perfume, covered in ribbons,
his pockets stuffed with comfit-boxes.

His wife, to be addressed simply as 'Madame', was even more
grotesque. She romped into the sick-chamber in a riding-habit
plastered with mud, a man's cravat, a crop under her arm, and her
hair on end. She was the most startlingly plain girl, and drew
attention to her ugliness, which she made worse by pulling faces,
in a German accent so pronounced that it was hard to understand
her.

'My father called me badger-nose; a face more hideous than
mine is not to be found in the whole globe. It was as well that
Monsieur did not see me before our wedding. The Duc de Cour-
lande was sent to woo me; he took one look, and requested to join

25

the army. Not that I wished for a husband, but marriage is like death; the day and hour of it are marked. Did you weep when they told you you must marry? On my wedding journey I howled all the way from Strasbourg to Chalons. The only good thing I have found in this detestable France is hunting the wolf with the Great Man, my pet name for his Most Christian Majesty.'

Struggling to turn the conversation to more pleasant things, Mary Beatrice inquired after the health of the little Duc de Valois.

'My son will die shortly, I think, and I trust I shall have no more. Maternity is an abomination, from first to last an ugly business and most dangerous. I am hoping that Monsieur will suggest separate bedchambers; he is far happier with his male seraglio. Your husband's sister, Monsieur's first wife, is well out of it, even if he did poison her. Oh there is the bell ringing for *Salut*. I detest such devotions. I read my German bible and say my prayers, though I am convinced they are useless.'

Her head spinning, Mary Beatrice tentatively inquired whether Madame was not a Catholic.

'Call me Catholic or Protestant, the label is of small importance since there is nothing in the jar. My conversion was a matter of business.' She rose, knocking over an ornament with her riding-crop. 'Why your husband has chosen to turn papist is a mystery to me, since it has not brought him a penny and undoubtedly will exclude him from the throne. Far better if the entire world was libertine like me, what you call free-thinking.'

Suddenly the news from England was better, though still incomprehensible to Mary Beatrice. It seemed that the Earl of Shaftesbury, leader of something called the Faction, had been deprived of the Great Seal, and his fellow republicans temporarily defeated. A troop of Life Guards was being sent to Dover to await the bride, and yachts to Calais to fetch her. She left Paris on November 23rd, and the crowning touch was set on her bewilderment when she was told that in England, where the reckoning was still in the Old Style, it was only the 12th.

King Louis, kind and attentive to the last, insisted on accompanying her as far as Abbeville. Taking elaborate farewells of his Court, she reflected that though she was going to a strange husband, at least she would never have to see any of these extraordinary people again. Madame's parting words rang in her ears:

'Do not, for God's sake, fall in love with your husband. It always leads to hatred.'

3

A State of Innocence

1

In the gardens of Chaillot, Queen Mary Beatrice paused beside the sundial.

'My memory of the first five years of marriage,' she remarked to Mère Priolo, 'resembles this motto; it tells only the sunny hours, though I was always bearing and losing children, so judge what happiness was that. Yet looking back, it is all bathed in the sunshine of love. I did not like my lord at first, but soon I was writing to Reverend Mother at Modena that I thought more of pleasing my husband than of serving God.'

On the grass lay drying a multitude of flowers made from isinglass, a special skill of the Community at Chaillot. But her eyes saw in their place the rose-without-a-thorn, the varieties of cowslip with their curious names, the double white violets and the clove gillyflowers, all those true English blooms she had planted in the gardens of dear St James's Palace.

She had not liked him at first, because she had taken a silly aversion to him before they met, and their few days spent at Dover merely added to the picture she had formed of him in her mind. Oh, he was handsome enough, consistently kind, at the same time gentle and ardent. It was not, of course, his fault that her real wedding had so little in common with her splendid proxy one; Lord Peter had warned her that she must not expect joyful crowds or a Catholic ceremony. Nor was it his fault that there was a dense fog.

But he might have paid her some pretty compliments; he might have kissed her lips instead of her finger when, during a mere hurried rereading of the contract in the presence of the minimum of witnesses, he placed upon it a gold ring with a small ruby. And during supper, he really need not have harped so much on what appeared to be a passion with him, the sea and ships. Was she a good sailor? Had she remarked the fineness of the frigates which had escorted her? And when she answered in monosyllables, he turned to Lord Peter to inquire how the yacht *Catherine* had behaved in a swell. To be interested in such things on his wedding-day! And not once had he asked her about her dear Modena. He seemed to take for granted she must share his view that this dank, foggy England was the only country in the world of any consequence.

King Charles, who greeted her at Greenwich, made up for his brother's lack of compliments. He looked ten instead of three years older than James, his face deeply lined, his melancholy eyes at variance with his smiling mouth, and his thin curve of moustache giving him an air of cynicism. But he had a vivid charm, a whimsical deep-throated chuckle, and he immediately christened her 'Belle' because, he said, she was the most beautiful girl in the world. Pet names were all the rage in England, she learned; but her husband, when he did not address her formally as 'madam', used her second name to avoid confusion, since she shared 'Mary' with his elder daughter.

'Tomorrow you must dine in state at Guildhall, Belle,' the King informed her, doing his best to steer her through the ordeal of public appearances. 'With your strong sense of the ridiculous, you will enjoy it; all those pompous Aldermen sweating in their robes and getting drunk.'

But she had not enjoyed it; there were such thin cheers for herself along the route, only a sort of grieved silence for James. She caught his disapproving eye during the banquet, when she had such very hard work to keep from laughing. A small jewel came unfastened from the Lady Mayoress's ample bosom and dropped into her soup, and she spent the whole of the first course searching for it with her spoon. James did not think this at all amusing; he explained to her in an undertone that the London citizens were very thrifty, a virtue he admired.

On the drive back, Lady Peterborough, an excitable Irish lady with corkscrew curls, tried to explain to her the lack of cheers.

'The Duke was the darling of the nation for his having so often and so freely ventured his life for the honour of his King and country in our war against the Dutch. There are no qualifications wanting in him which Englishmen could wish for, were it not for what they deem his foul apostacy, which he refuses to conceal. Except he becomes a Protestant again, his friends will be obliged to leave him, like a garrison one can no longer defend.'

This was unpleasant enough; it was worse when King Charles, who had seemed so easy-going, refused to let her use the beautiful chapel at St James's, built for his mother.

'You must have Mass said with the greatest discretion in an oratory, Belle, like all our other papists.'

She could not get used to the silence of the London bells when Angelus should be rung; she was surrounded by a Protestant atmosphere, alien and hostile. When eating in public, her chaplain must not say grace, and if she made the sign of the cross it must be surreptitiously. Most inexplicable of all was her husband's lack of emotion for the religion he had embraced at such tremendous cost. When the Protestants in her Household attended Matins and Evensong, she sensed his wistfulness as he heard the singing.

'Will you not accompany me to *Salut*, sir, in my oratory?'

'What is this *Salut*?' he inquired, pronouncing it wrong. He seemed deliberately to speak bad French; Royalty everywhere was cosmopolitan; he remained fanatically insular.

'It is—I think you would call it in English, Benediction.'

'The Queen my mother took me to that at the Visitation convent she founded at Chaillot when we were in exile. I do not care for that kind of devotion, which is suitable only for pious women.'

She had been so sure that religion would form a common bond between them, but more and more it was borne in upon her that only intellectual conviction had brought him into the Church; she was too young to realize what a special kind of heroism this entailed. He had embraced the Faith as a duty, and it did not colour his life.

The objects of his devotion remained those of his boyhood, England, Monarchy, the sea.

She was beginning to settle down in her small but elegant Court at St James's, and dreaded the occasions when she must appear at Whitehall. It was a town rather than a house, with a constant coming and going of processions, and a hateful undercurrent of intrigue. Everyone was so frighteningly witty; she had learned English with the greatest of ease, but she failed to smile at the *bon mots* of courtiers who were acclaimed the greatest wits of their day. They were either cleverly malicious or obscene; she felt they mocked her chastity; to be chaste was to be out of the mode, and to be out of the mode was the only sin. She tried her best not to be censorious, but she was secretly shocked by King Charles's public acknowledgement of his mistresses, and his neglect of his plain little wife.

There was that evening when she found herself seated on a couch beside the Duchess of Portsmouth, the reigning concubine, and desperately searching for something to say, confided to this baby-faced woman her pride in having an opera, *The State of Innocence,* dedicated to her by John Dryden, Poet Laureate. It had not yet been produced, but perhaps her Grace had read it.

'We have all read it, your Royal Highness,' lisped Portsmouth, regarding her through the peep-holes contrived in a fan, 'and not without some chagrin.' She quoted, raising her voice for the benefit of the bystanders: ' "The prize of beauty was disputed only till you were seen; but now all pretenders have withdrawn their claim, even the fairest in the land not daring to commit their cause against you to the suffrage of those who most partially adore them." Lord, madam, it appears you have rendered mankind insensible to other beauties, and have destroyed the empire of love in a court which was the seat of his dominion.'

Flushed with the most intense embarrassment, Mary Beatrice stammered that of course it was the mere hyperbole of poets, and that what had pleased her in the dedication was the praise Mr Dryden bestowed upon her husband.

'He speaks of the Duke's fidelity to his royal brother, his love for his country, and constancy to his friends.'

'All of which virtues are amply rewarded, it seems, by the gift of your Royal Highness's person. I am sure, madam, such a paragon as Mr Dryden deems you, must amply compensate any gentleman for the loss of all his offices.'

But the most formidable ordeal of those early days was the introduction to her stepdaughters. She had taken it for granted they would be waiting for her at St James's, but it seemed that in consequence of their father's conversion they had been taken away from him, and were being brought up at Richmond. Her impulsive indignation was met by a phrase constantly on James's lips:

'It is by command of his Majesty, whose subject I am.'

Yet that first visit to Richmond opened her eyes to a new side of James. She had deemed him attached to ideals rather than to persons, but on the drive he looked almost like a schoolboy going home for the holidays, his whole face softened with affection as he described the cleverness of Mary, the adorableness of little Anne, relating small anecdotes of their childhood, the romps and games he had played with them.

In the Great Hall, a carefully arranged tableau greeted the Duke and Duchess of York. Lady Frances Villiers, Lady Governess, formed the centrepiece, with her six daughters ranged behind her chair, and her husband, Sir Edward, ready at the door as a kind of usher. The princesses sat upon stools beside her ladyship, rising to make their obeisance to their father and new stepmother. Mary, tall for her age and very affected, managed her long skirts gracefully; Anne tripped, and was assisted by a masterful young lady with startlingly blue eyes who stood behind her like a guardian angel. Embracing the child, Mary Beatrice had the sensation of clasping a pillow, for Anne, small-boned, was plump and round as a ball.

Dinner was rather trying. A vigorous man who looked like a soldier, but turned out to be Bishop Compton of London and the princesses' Preceptor, said grace, contriving to make it belligerently Protestant. Each time Mary Beatrice encountered the eyes of one or other of the Villiers girls, she sensed a veiled hostility. Nervous laughter had to be suppressed at the sight of Anne, stuffing down each course and eagerly watching to see what came next. Mary, on the other hand, picked daintily at her food, talked like a character in some romantic poem, and made gestures which told of long practice before a mirror.

I must make friends with them, thought Mary Beatrice; and after dinner suggested a romp in the garden.

'Mary won't come,' said Anne. 'She always goes to her bower at this time to write her daily letter to her husband.'

'But she is not married!'

'That's what she calls Mrs Apsley, her special friend, and she pretends they live in somewhere called Arcadia, and she has rivals, and Mr Gibson, our dwarf drawing-master, is their go-between. *I* think it's all very silly. Oh leminy!' whined Anne, screwing up her short-sighted eyes as she peered into the box of sugar-plums brought her by her stepmother, 'I've eaten them all, and Sarah will scold me for being greedy.'

'My darling sweet-toothed dumpling, you will be sick! But who is Sarah?'

'Sarah Jennings, *my* special friend. Let's play at grandmother's steps, and you can be grandmother first.'

It should be easy to make friends with this confiding little creature, who at parting said with the utmost innocence:

'You are not at all like the Pope from his pictures. But *everyone* is sure you are his eldest daughter.'

2

Looking back on those days, she found it impossible to say just when her budding love for James expanded into flower. It must have been quite early, for she remembered that the parting with her mother cost her scarcely a tear. She did cry a little, but with remorse, when she heard how the Duchess had returned to Modena to find that in her absence, Prince Cesare had persuaded the young Duke to take the reins of government from his mother. She would never, she vowed, cease to reproach herself for the childish fuss she had made, which had resulted in the Duchess's accompanying her to England.

Her cup of happiness brimmed when she found she was with child, and her physicians advised a quiet domestic life at St James's. It had attracted her from the first, this old red-brick mansion, with its deep-set mullioned windows and its warren of rooms; it was so quiet it might be miles from London. She was told it had not changed since James's boyhood here; she could imagine him playing Crusaders or Robin Hood in the park. In time her own sons would learn to ride the great-horse in the tiltyard, and shoot at the archery-butts.

She was full of little plans. The gardens were rather neglected, and she pored over Parkinson's *Terrestrial Paradise*, dedicated to her late mother-in-law, which showed in text and plate those flowers most suitable for an English garden. The old royal cradle, in which James and nearly all his brothers and sisters had lain, was brought down from the attics, and she spent long happy evenings stitching new lace-edged pillow-cases for it, while one of her bedchamber women, Mrs Dawson, fed the wool into her spinning-wheel and accompanied their work with reminiscences.

Mrs Dawson had been in the service of the late Duchess of York, and enjoyed the privilege of an old nurse who was one of the family. Since it was an axiom with her that all foreigners had difficulty in understanding English, she addressed Mary Beatrice in a loud slow voice as though she were deaf.

'Lord! what a passion did her father, my Lord Clarendon, fall into when he heard that the Duke and Mrs Anne Hyde were secretly wed. Says he, "I will advise his Majesty to cast her into the Tower, and I myself will propose an Act of Parliament for the cutting off of her head." As for the Queen Mother, she swore that whenever that lawyer's daughter entered Whitehall by one door, she would go out by another and never set foot in it again.'

A while ago, the mention of beheading would have revived the horror caused by Aunt Leonora's stories. When first she came to St James's, Mary Beatrice felt nervous each time she passed along the Silver Stick Gallery, for it was whispered that the ghost of Queen Anne Boleyn had been encountered there, carrying her severed head beneath her arm. But falling in love had dispelled all such childish terrors. She said wistfully:

'The Duke must have been deeply enamoured of Mrs Hyde to have defied such opposition.'

'H'm,' mused Mrs Dawson, her foot pausing on the treadle of her spinning-wheel, 'I would say rather that he was caught, if you understand me, madam dear. She was a lady of such spirit and determination that she never failed to gain any end to which she had set her mind. A shrewd knowledge of men, had she, and a keen wit, which much pleased the Duke, who was never one to be captured by mere prettiness, as might be seen in the mistresses he chose.'

'Did not the late Duchess mind his infidelity?'

'By no means. Like a sensible dame, she gave him tit for tat. Let me see; there was Mr Henry Sidney, whose brother Robert, some say, sired the Duke of Monmouth, though his Majesty was pleased to acknowledge him; there was Mr Savile, Vice-Chamberlain, my Lord Dover (Mr Jermyn as he then was), and Sir Charles Berkeley. It was Sir Charles, some insist, who fathered upon her the Duke of Cambridge. Then there was——'

'Please, Mrs Dawson, I don't wish to hear any more,' interrupted Mary Beatrice, ashamed of having pried. 'It is all in the long-forgotten past.'

'Just as you wish, madam dear. Though you must not run away with the notion that my late mistress spent all her time in bed. His Royal Highness applied himself as soon as he returned from exile to the encouragement of trade, which, says he, is the greatest interest of this nation, in all which the late Duchess was a great help to him, she having the head of a business woman. She was far too occupied with public matters to go and plant a dial of living flowers in the gardens here, as you wish to do; and to learn how to take slips of carnations she would have considered a sad waste of time. And as for what I have mentioned about the Duke, I will do him the justice to remark that he never flaunted his mistresses, as does his Majesty, but went to visit them under the rose, and sent them abroad to have their children.'

Mary Beatrice had experienced a sharp struggle at first when she must be courteous to James's bastards; but she tried to put in practice her Serenity's advice. His past life was not her business, and she must not judge him for sins long repented. His first wife was another matter; she might be dead, but St James's was full of reminders of her, and it was very hard to get used to the fact that she had played on this spinet ornamented with gold medallions of the Caesars, had worked the tapestry hangings for the door of the withdrawing-room, had had her bed aired with the same silver warming-pan. Even some of her dresses were still in the wardrobes which Mrs Dawson called 'fripperies'. And in several rooms her frog-eyes regarded her successor from a canvas; cold, shrewd eyes, seeming to appraise. If you could speak, thought Mary Beatrice, what a lot you could tell me about the James who lived for twenty-five years before I was born.

She was beginning to love him, not with her senses only, but with her heart, and she yearned to know what he had been like as boy and youth. He was a man who never spoke about himself; it was quite casually that one day he mentioned that this was the stair-case down which he had crept when he made his escape from St James's as a lad of thirteen. She pounced on him, avid for details, but the only memories which had stuck in his mind were those of his hazardous voyage to France. She must worm out of others the picturesque particulars, the game of hide-and-seek arranged with his gallant little sister, the dressing him up in a woman's gown, his arousing the suspicion of the barge-master by laying his leg upon the table in a most unladylike manner to hoist up his stocking.

And his adventures had begun long before that. At nine, he had witnessed the battle of Edgehill. At an age when boys play with wooden swords, he had seen real ones blooded; their merry games of hide-and-seek had been played by him with his very life at stake. Perhaps, she thought, his being forced into manhood too soon accounted for his gravity, his lack of a sense of fun.

Again there was the occasion when, searching through an inlaid trunk for something, he paused to glance at some plain note-books, their covers not clasped but tied together with common string. They were the journals he had kept, he told her, of his military service in exile. He was enormously surprised when she begged to be allowed to read them, but indulgently left them with her when he went to Whitehall. She found them dreadfully dull, full of military terms she did not understand, with very neatly drawn maps of battles and sieges. They were completely imper-sonal; he recorded the brave actions of others; there was scarcely a word about his own, and characteristically he wrote in the third person.

Yet terse though they were, these journals gave her a new insight into his character. From chance remarks she heard from those who had shared the royal brothers' long exile, she gathered that Charles had been more than ready to accept gifts and to borrow from all and sundry. James, it seemed, would be under obligation to no man; he had obtained from a common money-lender just enough to pay for his field-bed and an equipage so modest that it could be carried on the backs of two mules, and repaid the loan promptly from his wages as a soldier. Charles had lied and flattered, had gone the length of slandering his own parents; James had stuck to his principles, remained constant to his friends, through thick and thin.

'Duty' appeared over and over again in the journals like a watchword. Lack of discipline drew forth his severe censure, courage in an enemy his keen admiration. She could not have said why, but the portrait she built up from his journals aroused her maternal instinct, made her sure that the writer was vulnerable.

3

The little world of St James's narrowed still further during the next few years to the realm of the nursery. She suffered a miscarriage a few months after her marriage, and through her own fault. James had a prejudice against women on horseback, but because it was one of her chief pleasures, indulged her, and this was the result. He said no word of reproach; nor did he betray any disappointment when, in the following January, after a labour so rapid and sudden that there was no time to summon her physicians, she gave birth to a frail little daughter.

She knew by this time that the children of Catholics of any status were taken away from them and handed over to the nearest Protestant kin, and she sensed that the removal from him of Mary and Anne had hurt James far more deeply than the loss of his offices and his seat on the Privy Council. So she had hatched a small conspiracy with Contessa Molza and Fr Ruga, her Modenese chaplain. He was to be fetched immediately her child was born and baptize it. Pathetically she argued that if her babe were baptized a Catholic, it could not be taken away to be bred in heresy.

King Charles arrived in the afternoon, merrily chided her on the sex of the infant, and launched into a discussion of the christening which, said he, must take place in the Chapel Royal at Whitehall.

'My daughter is already baptized, Sir,' she told him defiantly.

He completely ignored this statement, and continued with his plans. Her stepdaughters should be godmothers, the Duke of Monmouth godfather, and Bishop Compton of London should officiate. Exhausted by the ordeal of childbirth, she lost her temper. It was intolerable that the child of Catholic parents, already admitted to the Sacrament of Baptism, be subjected to a Protestant christening. He patted her hand; but she was suddenly aware of the ruthlessness that underlay his surface charm.

'Your children, Belle, are the property of the nation. If you insist on bringing them up papists, I shall be obliged to take them away from you.'

'But why, *why*?'

'Because, sweet heart, I have no intention of going on my travels again. You must try to get it into that lovely head of yours that what they call popery is a bogey with the common folk, and that this gives a handle to certain great rogues who are still busy plotting underground for a republic.'

'The Duke will never agree to our children being reared as heretics!'

'So long as he is my subject, James will do as I bid him, and to give him his due, he has always proved himself most loyal and obedient. When I'm dead, he may do as he pleases, and no doubt will lose his throne in the process. He is like the strong oak which will not yield to a storm and so is shattered; I resemble the supple reed which bends and recovers. God knows how often I have pleaded with him to conceal his conversion, to make a mere appearance at my side in the Chapel Royal; but no, it would be a mean, base thing, says he, to dissemble. He is too good for this world, my dear Belle.'

Under his lightness, there was a sneer. It dawned on her that despite his own popularity, he was secretly jealous of his brother. As for the upbringing of her daughter, all too soon it ceased to be a problem; the child died of convulsions in October.

'You ought to take more trouble, madam dear,' chided Mrs Dawson. 'A short labour never yet produced a healthy child. I attended the late Duchess in all her lyings-in and should know. Ten hours she was in labour with the Princess Mary, and see what a fine young lady she's turned out to be. It says in the Scriptures that we must bring forth children in sorrow; not that you, madam dear, are allowed to read the Bible, being a papist and a foreigner.'

'I was taught from infancy to read a portion of the Scriptures night and morning,' said Mary Beatrice, fretful with grief.

'That would be the Pope's Bible, full of lies. Now cheer up, madam dear, and make up your mind to go more slowly about it next time. Though I must say, it's a very strange thing how healthy bastards always are. That Madam Churchill now; never a convulsion in her sons by the Duke; but then of course she's a very good Protestant.'

Another baby soon filled the vacant cradle, and though it was again a daughter, James so completely concealed his disappointment that she was unaware of it. Nor did he make any demur when she asked that the child be named Isabella, a virgin martyr of whom plainly he had never heard.

'Now don't you get too fond of that babe, madam dear,' warned Mrs Dawson, 'for the coffin is always near the cradle. Eight babes of the late Duchess I laid in that cradle, and six of them died in it. It was a marvel the Princess Anne survived, for her mother let her eat anything she had a mind to, and dose her as I would with Turkey-rhubarb, she was always costive.'

Their education completed, Mary and Anne were now allowed to come to St James's for long visits, and their stepmother's passionate love for her husband overflowed on to them. It was true that Mary still puzzled her, with her attitudinizing and her living in a dream world of sacred friendships and hopeless loves, but she would soon grow out of that. She tried for a while to interest both girls in the lovely little Italian orchestra she had imported, but found that they cared for nothing but cards or, in the case of Anne, cards and the pleasures of the table.

'The late Duchess, my mother,' Anne solemnly explained, 'had an extraordinary stomach. I heard her physicians say so. I have inherited it, and require more food than other people.'

'But if my darling dumpling eats so many sweetmeats, she will turn into a big bag-pudding.'

'That's what Sarah says.'

Whatever Sarah Jennings said was an oracle to the child, and privately Mary Beatrice wondered whether the ascendancy of this thrusting young nobody might not prove bad for Anne if it endured.

It was during the summer of 1677 that the shadow of William, Prince of Orange, intruded into the domestic sanctuary of St James's. He had been but a name to Mary Beatrice, her husband's nephew, son of his favourite sister, now dead. She had seen his weekly letters to James, and had marvelled at that extraordinary handwriting, so large that a few words filled a page. She gathered that James cherished him only for the sake of his dead mother; gossip described him as a young man devoured by ambition, fretted by his lack of power in Holland where, for all his title of Stadt-holder, he was but a figure-head. There was an ugly tale that he had instigated the murder of the brothers de Witt, leaders of the Dutch oligarchy, but it was the kind of scandal Mary Beatrice particularly detested, and to which she turned a deaf ear.

What did concern her was the discovery that this stranger had inquired of the English Ambassador at The Hague the disposition of Princess Mary with a view to seeking her hand. Beauty, it seemed, was of no importance to him; obedience was all he re-quired in a wife. Pursuing his favourite policy of playing off one Power against another, King Charles was encouraging the Dutch-man's suit; and meanwhile Mary was being kept in complete ignor-ance of the fate in store for her.

In her withdrawing-room at St James's, Mary Beatrice watched the rehearsal of a masque to be staged at Whitehall, in which Mary had the principal part. As the chaste heroine, she declaimed her lines with relish, addressing them to Frances Apsley whom she called her 'husband'.

'Is it wise to keep her in ignorance?' whispered Mary Beatrice to the Duke, who sat beside her.

He winced. He had just broken his collar-bone out hunting, but the pain she saw on his face was not physical.

'I shall break the news to her myself,' he said, 'but not until this masque has been performed. She is so happy in it.'

'But you are not happy in the proposed marriage.'

He withdrew at once behind the armour of his reserve.

'It is a match decided upon by his Majesty, and the King shall be obeyed. I would be glad if all his subjects would learn of me how to obey him.'

Oh if only, she thought, you would share the burden of your grief with me, who desire to share everything with you. Mary was his darling, his favourite child; once he had remarked that he considered only the Dauphin of France worthy of her hand. And Mary was to be sacrificed to this Dutch princeling with his unsavoury reputation, simply because it happened at this moment to suit King Charles's statecraft to play off Holland against France. Meanwhile Mary herself, living in her little tinsel world, declaimed the refinement of her love for an imaginary husband.

Though far gone in another pregnancy, Mary Beatrice must be present at Whitehall when William of Orange was formally received. Her first sight of him increased the aching of her heart for her stepdaughter; at twenty-seven he looked middle-aged, a narrow-chested, undersized and wizened person, breathing asthmatically, his eyes as cold as a fish.

'Brought his he-whores with him, I see,' remarked Mrs Dawson, assisting her mistress to undress.

'Hee-haws? Do you mean asses?'

'No, madam dear, I do *not* mean asses. I was referring to the things I saw looking out of a window in the Prince's apartments, with their painted faces and their preening of their perukes. What they were doing inside of a pair of breeches is more than I can say, for at first sight you would have sworn they were women. Not that the Prince is averse to our sex; I hear he's lost no time in seducing the eldest Villiers girl, squint-eyed though she be. Still, he's a good Protestant, and that's the main thing.'

The news that she was to be married in a week's time was broken to Mary by her father, and she spent the ensuing days weeping in her stepmother's arms. Mary Beatrice tried in vain to console her; she too, she confessed, had felt a repugnance for marriage.

'But my darling, I am so very happy now, and so will you be. I hope you will find Holland grow as dear to you as England has become to me. I shall write to you every week, and in future I shall give you the pet name of Lemon,' she added, in an attempt to make the girl laugh.

Mary did not laugh. All unprepared, she had been banished from Arcadia and its rarefied air of romance; bowers and go-betweens and interesting declines had vanished, and the stark reality was William of Orange, twelve years her senior, who did not pretend to be enamoured of her, cared nothing for her beauty, but merely hoped she would prove docile, telling her frankly that he was not an easy man to live with unless he was acknowledged master.

'It was *cruel* of my father to permit it!' snarled Mary.

She is just hysterical and must find a scapegoat for her wretchedness, decided Mary Beatrice. Nevertheless she was disquieted by the shrill bitterness of those words. She tried to explain what indeed Mary very well knew, that it was not her father but the King who had arranged this marriage. It was useless; and suddenly it occurred to her that both this girl and her sister must have been prejudiced against their father all through their formative years. Yet James was so devoted to them, and they seemed to return his affection; surely she must have imagined a frightening venom in Mary's outburst just now.

It was a dismal wedding. Tears rolled unchecked down the bride's cheeks, her father's face was mask-like, the bridegroom's morose, and Anne was too unwell to be present. At the betrothal banquet she had gobbled up a whole 'subtlety', one of those sugar and paste erections intended only for ornament, and had vomited at intervals ever since. The King, perhaps in an attempt to lighten the proceedings, made slightly repulsive jests, interrupting Bishop Compton's homily with, 'Hurry up, lest my sister-in-law is delivered of a son, and the marriage be disappointed!'

Overtired and depressed, Mary Beatrice sat by the fire in her bedchamber, waiting for her husband to come from his own side of the palace by the private stair. Her heart quickened as always when she heard his step approach the small door by the bedhead; she thought that tonight it lacked its firmness. Without his peruke he looked much older; there was a glint of grey in his cropped hair, and a nervous tic lifted one corner of his mouth. Her impulse was to fly to him, hug him, beg him to let her share the grief she knew he must be feeling for his daughter; but she had learned by now that he shrank from emotional scenes. Always he withdrew into himself when deeply hurt, like an animal seeking its lair. She asked, trying to keep her voice steady and neutral:

'What did his Majesty mean by the marriage being disappointed if I bore a son?'

For a moment he did not answer, making rather a to-do about snuffing a candle. Then he said, carefully matter-of-fact:

'His Majesty was rallying the Prince of Orange on his well-known ambition to succeed to this throne through the claim of my daughter Mary when I am dead, if I have no male heir.'

4

Guy Fawkes Night was particularly riotous, and the frightening echoes of it penetrated even to St James's, where Mary Beatrice nervously awaited her confinement. Mrs Dawson sought to cheer her by a description of the show.

'I never did see in any other year so many dummies, all in honour of his Highness of Orange, the Protestant champion of Europe. Besides the Pope and the Gunpowder plotters, there were half a dozen Jesuits, what the common folk call Geometers, and even a nun or two. And not one without a live cat sewn up inside to make it seem to squeal when it was flung on the bonfire.'

The acrid reek of these fires still hung in the air when, two days later, she received the answer to so many prayers; after her usual rapid labour, a living son was laid in her arms. Next day he was christened Charles, with the title of Duke of Cambridge, a very glum Prince of Orange standing sponsor, and little Isabella carried in the arms of her Governess, Lady Villiers, to play the part of godmother. Lady Villiers looked ill, and Anne's absence was excused on the usual score of overeating.

Obsessed with her baby, Mary Beatrice did not notice at first how anxiously her ladies whispered, though once she caught the dreaded word 'smallpox'. She woke on November 9th to hear bells tolling, and was told that Dr Sheldon, Archbishop of Canterbury, had died of the disease. There was an epidemic in the City, spread by the crowds who had flocked to Westminster for Guy Fawkes Night, and the passing-bell became monotonous.

'My Mam has caught it,' wailed Mary, referring to Lady Villiers. 'And though the doctors won't admit it, I'm sure Anne has too.'

Outside her door, Mary Beatrice could hear Orange's voice scolding his bride for not removing to Whitehall, and Mary's choked reply; she would not leave her father and sister a moment before she must. She seemed to have rediscovered her childhood love for James, clinging to him while she stared at the weather-vane on the Tennis Court across the Park. While the wind remained in the east, she could not sail to that dreadful, unknown Holland. Lady Powis, acting Governess for the baby prince since the illness of Lady Villiers, chattered to her mistress about the conduct of Orange.

'At Whitehall they call him either Caliban or the Dutch Monster, for I do declare, madam, no one ever saw his like for rudeness. He spoke not a single word to his wife during their bridal ball, except once to snarl out, "This damnable east wind!", and he has refused to allow her chaplains to accompany her to Holland, being himself such a hot Calvinist.'

Each time she closed her eyes, Mary Beatrice seemed to see the hurtful green and orange of the bridegroom's livery, and to hear the squeak of the weather-vane still pointing east. Anne's smallpox was confirmed, and James spent most of his time at her bedside; in his anxiety for her, and the pain of his imminent parting with his other daughter, he seemed almost indifferent to his wife.

On November 19th the wind veered into the west, and Mary, still weeping, came to take farewell. But not of Anne; their father had insisted that Anne must not be told of her sister's departure until the crisis of her smallpox was past. At least, sobbed Mary, she would have a few friends with her, three of the Villiers girls, including Elizabeth. Apparently she had not heard the gossip about her bridegroom and this squint-eyed damsel. She had scarcely left when Lady Villiers died; but a few days later a recovered Anne paid her first visit to her infant half-brother in the lying-in chamber. She seemed actually to have put on weight, and betrayed no distress at her sister's departure.

'I am to have her apartments here, and all the talk is of who will succeed my Mam as Lady Governess,' said she, peering myopically into a bowl of fruit to find the largest grapes. 'Sarah says his Majesty will appoint my aunt, Lady Clarendon, but I hope he won't. She scolds me because I play cards on Sunday.'

'I had the most strangely vivid dream last night,' Mary Beatrice said, half to herself. 'My Lady Villiers appeared to me and said she was damned and in the flames of hell. "How can that be?" I asked her. "I cannot believe it." "Madam," said she, "to convince you, feel my hand", which was so fiery hot that it woke me in fright. It was only a dream, but I shall say some prayers for her ladyship's soul.'

The silence grew so marked that she realized she had said the wrong thing. Her religion was as natural to her as breathing, and she had never grown used to her new country's hatred of it.

'My Mam's soul is in heaven, madam, and does not require your popish prayers,' snapped Anne, waddling out of the room in deep offence.

On the morning of December 10th, no little procession emerged from the nursery to place her baby in her arms. She waited, fighting a sudden, intolerable dread; presently a physician

44

entered in his black velvet gown. He was sorry to inform her Royal Highness that a rash had appeared on the infant's chest. He had been bled, and other remedies administered, but smallpox in so young an infant . . . He left the sentence unfinished.

For two days and nights she sat by the cradle, her eyes fixed on the tiny figure twisting restlessly in its swaddling-bands. A torrent of broken prayers raged in her mind, her fingers, slippery with sweat, tried to tell her beads, her eyes burned with tears a long training would not permit to fall in public. At intervals the face of her husband appeared among the anxious ones round the cradle; he did not look at her, he seemed unconscious of her presence; he too gazed steadily at the precious heir.

She did not know whether it was day or night in that darkened room when someone whispered that she must leave the nursery. A physician straightened from bending over the cradle with its royal coats-of-arms, and significantly shook his head. She had one glimpse of a waxen-faced doll lying motionless, before a sheet was drawn over its face.

That night, for the first time since their marriage, her husband did not come to her bed. She lay listening tensely for his step, aching to give and to receive comfort, cheating herself that in the firelight she saw the small door open from the private stair. She tried to be reasonable. Though Mrs Dawson had assured her that the death of infants was too common to merit more than a passing sigh, she had heard someone else whisper that the Duke had never been known to grieve so much at the loss of any of his other children. And the blow had fallen just after the serious illness of Anne, the ordeal of his parting with Mary. His iron self-control must have broken under the strain; if that were so, he would be too proud to let his wife see it.

Such was still her state of innocence, that it did not for one moment occur to her that he might be seeking solace in someone else's arms.

4

Farewell Content

1

'We arrive at a period,' said Mère Priolo, upright on her stool, 'when Our Lord was pleased to lay many heavy crosses on your Majesty. Yet how blessed was the late King, your husband, in the conjugal devotion which made you choose to share his several banishments.'

'If he was to be sent a vagabond about the world, I would be a vagabond also, *ma mère*. Exile, whether in Brussels or in Scotland, cost me little, since we were together. Except that I was obliged to leave my frail little Isabella in London, and she died in her fifth year. During all that period I might have said with Eve in the opera Mr Dryden dedicated to me, "With thee to live is paradise alone".'

She shivered, and Mère Priolo rose at once. They must move out from the shade of the walnut tree into the sun; M. Fagon was so anxious that her Majesty avoid a chill. Perhaps, even, they should go indoors.

'No, *ma mère*, I shuddered at a painful memory. But I see that you have brought many old Gazettes and other papers, and for the period between the death of my first-born son and that of my royal brother-in-law, I must beg you to refer to these, for my recollection is strangely blurred.'

'*Eh bien*, we go straight to your Majesty's coronation. The Duke of Powis, that great sufferer for our holy faith, was good enough to send us a copy of the illustrated record. Oh how much we would have loved to see such splendid ceremonies . . .'

The gentle voice flowed on beside her, accompanying such bitter thoughts. Not even to 'my angel', as she called Mère Priolo, could she speak one word about the serpent who, unknown to her, had been lurking for years in her paradise. How blind she had been! How readily she had agreed when, a Maid of Honour having left her service to be married, James suggested Madam Sedley, who was about her own age, to fill the vacant place. Mrs Dawson's voice spoke from the long past.

'I only hope she won't bring her latest bastard to St James's, madam dear. Had it abroad discreetly by the wish of its father, though who he is is a matter of much speculation below-stairs. She'll bed with anyone, that huzzy, and they do say—but there, madam dear, I know how you do detest gossip.'

Silly gossip into the bargain. Catherine Sedley had no charms to attract a lover; her greatest defect was a mouthful of sharp white teeth; her only attribute a coarse wit.

A flying visit to Mary in Holland, from whom every post brought fresh wails of distress, and who by this time was all too well aware of her husband's liaison with Elizabeth Villiers.

'I am sure you must be mistaken,' her stepmother soothed her. 'How could any man prefer such a fright to my lovely Lemon?'

'All cats look grey in the dark, madam,' giggled the Princess.

'Even Madam Sedley,' chimed in Anne, exchanging a sly glance with her sister.

It was a side of both these girls that Mary Beatrice had decided long ago to ignore, a rather nasty side, tale-bearing and lewd.

She became aware of silence beside her, and met Mère Priolo's anxious glance.

'I am sure the pain is worse this afternoon, dear madame. Let me fetch you something.'

'No, *ma mère*, it is—I am a little *distrait*. I will fill in a few details about my coronation to make you laugh. Such a searching into precedents! And when I asked why, dear Mr Strickland, my Vice-Chamberlain, grew red to the ears while he explained that the last Queen Consort publicly crowned was Queen Anne Boleyn, who very shortly afterwards lost her head. Oh I wish you could have seen the banquet! Each course was preceded by a great Court official on horseback, and the horses being so restive because of the bursts of applause, it was a marvel to see how expertly their riders made their exit backwards, since they must keep their faces turned to the King and me. And then there was a rustic Lord of the Manor who claimed that ever since the Norman Conquest his ancestors had presented a delicate white soup called diligrout; but when he came bearing it up to the King, the poor man was so excited that he spilled it all!'

So she chattered on with nervous gaiety, reliving in her mind so much that must never appear in the Annals of Chaillot.

That cold February morning of 1685, when she received both the condolences and the congratulations of the Court in her mourning-bed, ushered in a new era, and she must adjust herself to it. Henceforth Whitehall, and not quiet St James's, was to be her home; she must live in public; wherever she went, eyes watched her; domestic evenings with her husband were a thing of the past. For days at a time she scarcely saw him; he was occupied with a thousand public matters, not least by the threat of invasion; by Monmouth in England, by Argyll in Scotland. Meanwhile there was the Coronation to arrange, and she must be coached in her part.

A room in her apartments was set aside for the splendid robes she would wear, and she must inspect them daily, try them on, watch her women sew diamonds in every seam, and line with ermine a velvet train seven yards in length. She had never cared for jewels, and was secretly dismayed when told that the cost of those for her regalia came to more than £112,000. When she was asked if she had some personal suggestion to mark the great day, she could think of nothing except that she would like to take upon her the liabilities of all debtors in the kingdom imprisoned for sums under £5. She was suddenly so very rich, and longed to share her affluence; otherwise it was James's day, not hers.

After hours spent learning responses and intricate ceremonies, it was pleasant to be carried in her chair to Anne's lodging in the Cockpit, for a domestic evening with her dumpling. Without any reference to Anne's father, the late King had tried to obtain a husband for her as long ago as 1680, selecting Duke George of Hanover. Far from being smitten by her plump charms, the German had turned tail for home with indecent haste, where he married his cousin, heiress of the Duchy of Zell.

'I shall never forgive him for such an insult, never!' Anne had raged. 'Not that I wished to marry a German princeling, who was almost as rude to me as the Dutch Monster was to Mary.'

A year or two later she had fallen so madly in love with Lord Mulgrave that she even went off her food. A particularly amorous letter from her falling into the hands of her uncle, King Charles had packed Mulgrave off to Tangier and married Anne to another George, this time of Denmark, a blond, stout, silent person, fifteen years her senior, who shared her vice of gluttony. Deeply concerned about his other daughter, whose marriage seemed so unhappy, James had obtained his brother's permission for Anne and George to reside in England, on condition that he settled a handsome income on them from his own purse.

Anne's interest in the coming Coronation appeared to be confined to the banquet, of which she demanded a written description beforehand in case she was unable actually to partake of it. Since her marriage she had been in a practically uninterrupted state of pregnancy, which so far had resulted only in miscarriages and still-born infants, and this served as a perfect excuse for 'cravings'.

'A whole porpoise swimming in orange broth,' read Anne. 'A calf's head stuffed with oysters, a pasty-royal garnished with fried cocks-combs—oh leminy! it makes one's mouth water even to read of such dishes.'

'*Est-il possible?*' muttered George, studying the menu over her shoulder. It was one of the few remarks he ever uttered, and it had been bestowed upon him by the Court as a nickname.

'Bless me, madam dear,' said Mrs Dawson later in her mistress's apartments, 'one would think that his Royal Highness was in the same condition as his wife. I never did see in all my life so big a belly in a gentleman.'

'Your Majesty on the other hand is so very slender,' observed Lady Sunderland, whose husband James had inherited as a member of the Privy Council, 'and looks so fragile, that I much fear you will be unable to stand the strain of these long ceremonies.'

'It is the greatest day in the life of his Majesty, and assuredly I shall not fail him.'

'St George's Day, according to our English calendar; but I understand that in the Romish Church it is what you call the Finding of the True Cross. Alas, madam, we all have our crosses. Your Majesty will have heard of Madam Sedley's loss? No? Her infant son, James Darnley, died this evening. It was in tune with her brazenness to choose for him a king's name.'

Mary Beatrice expressed conventional sympathy. She had been only too glad to give Madam Sedley a long leave of absence from her Household, simply because that coarse tongue, and that great mouthful of sharp white teeth, had always been distasteful to her.

She stepped delicately in her gold-embroidered slippers over the carpet laid all the way from Westminster Hall to the Abbey; it seemed a shame to crush these bushels of violets, cowslips and sweetbriar sprigs, strewn before her by Mrs Dowle, hereditary Herbswoman, and her six maidens. Lattices rattled and the ancient buildings seemed to quiver at the roar of saluting cannon, the brazening of trumpets, and the sustained cheers of the crowds kept back by ranks of Life Guards. Her heart warmed to those cheers. It was these very same folk who, egged on by the Faction, had either execrated or ignored James for more than a decade; now every voice in the kingdom was loud in clamorous applause.

She was unaware of fatigue during the long ceremonial, concentrating on when to sit, when to rise, when to make the responses from the little book given her by Bishop Compton. There was just one moment when the bright day was clouded for her; 'His seed will I make to endure for ever,' sang the choir, and she thought of all those short-lived children she had given James. She had a woundingly clear picture of Mrs Dawson, enshrouding the doll-like corpse of her last little girl, Charlotte Mary, as though wrapping up a parcel, heard the brisk, tactless voice telling her there was not much doubt that the good Lord intended no papist child to inherit the throne of England. That was three years ago, and since then everyone seemed to take for granted that she could never bear the son her husband yearned for, though she was still only twenty-seven.

The atmosphere grew tense when Sir Charles Dymoke, King's Champion, rode into the Hall on a fully barded horse, and proclaimed his challenge, for Monmouth, gathering troops in Holland, was allowing his adherents to term him the rightful King.

'If any person, of what degree soever,' shouted Dymoke, 'shall deny or gainsay our Sovereign Lord, King James II, to be rightful heir to the Imperial Crown of Britain, here is his champion, who saith that person lieth sore and is a false traitor, being ready to do combat with him.'

But no one picked up the gauntlet; and listening to the heralds recite her husband's titles in Latin, French and English, Mary Beatrice thrilled with pride for him. For the past seven years he had been banished, persecuted, defamed, and for ever on the point of being disinherited by a Bill of Exclusion. Yet he had given an example of the most consistent loyalty to the brother who had failed him. He had upheld the cause of Monarchy almost single-handed; and here at last was his reward.

2

'We dance once more down the room,' begged Willem Wissing, a Dutch artist, 'and then assuredly we bring some colour into your Majesty's cheeks. Your Majesty lacks only ambitious feet to be perfect mistress of the minuet.'

It would be hard for any feet to be ambitious, she thought, when they had to dance impeded by heavy robes and a seven-yard train. The portrait Wissing was painting of her in her Coronation robes was designed as a present for the widowed Duchess of Monmouth, whose husband had just paid the price of a lifetime of treasons. On the day he suffered, James had called upon his duchess, presenting her with the inheritance legally forfeited to the Crown; and Mary Beatrice was showering marks of friendship on a lady whose husband had been as consistently faithless to her as to his King and country.

When today's sitting was finished, Lady Sunderland rustled in, followed by a waiting-woman who bore on a salver a silver coffee-pot, a filigree cup with a cover, and a fringed napkin. Dismissing her attendant, Lady Sunderland inspected the portrait through a quizzing-glass. She was an extremely aggressive woman; she used strong scents, wore bright colours, appropriated any room into which she came by throwing down her gloves on one table, her fan on another, altering by the fraction of a degree some ornament or clock. She was like a teasing wind, making unnecessary movements and uttering exclamations as she viewed the portrait from various angles, at length pronouncing, with the air of a connoisseur, that not even Wissing's habit of dancing his pale-complexioned sitters about the room had given her Majesty a colour.

'I have asked the King if he objects to rouge,' said Mary Beatrice, sipping her coffee. 'He does not, but one of my Capuchins, Fr Seraphin, was so shocked that he cried, "I would rather see your Majesty green or yellow than rouged!" I laugh whenever I think of it.'

'I am enchanted that your Majesty can laugh. True, the kingdom is peaceful and prosperous again, and the Court reminds me of what I heard from my father who held office under King Charles I, when drunkenness, duels and swearing were absolutely banned. But in other matters, both your Majesties are so extremely tolerant.'

Mary Beatrice had been trained to be on her guard against an animus which might not be disinterested in its origins, and thus she had struggled against an instinctive dislike of this woman and her over-effusive husband who, from being a violent Exclusionist, had trimmed at precisely the right moment and thus had kept his post of Secretary of State. But apart from dislike, the Queen shrank from Lady Sunderland's ceaseless innuendo which, while incomprehensible, smelt of malice.

'If by toleration, your ladyship is referring to his Majesty's encouragement of the Huguenot refugees to settle in England, I must confess I am not so tolerant as the King, seeing that they are rebels against the Sovereign of another country. But it is not a matter in which I have any right to meddle.'

Lady Sunderland spread her fan, and regarded her mistress over the top of it. Her eyelashes, artificially darkened, were like little sharp iron spikes.

'Dear madam, I was not referring to the Huguenots. Is it possible you are still unaware of what is the common gossip of the Court?'

'It is quite possible. I close my ears to gossip.'

'Even when it concerns his Majesty—and Madam Sedley?'

A coffee cup rattled as it was clumsily set down.

'Now I speak as your Majesty's true servant and well-wisher. The scandal has become so open! My husband supped with Lord

Treasurer Rochester last night, and was shocked to hear that he positively encouraged the intrigue because, if you please, Madam Sedley is a Protestant. If she attains her ambition to be recognized as official mistress, as was the Duchess of Portsmouth in the last reign, Lord Treasurer believes it will increase his Majesty's popularity, she pretending so much zeal for the Church of England——'

'Be quiet this instant!'

Mary Beatrice had risen in such disorder that she knocked over the coffee-pot. Unaware of the hot liquid burning her hands, she said in quick, breathless gasps:

'How could you dare—I will not hear another word—pray leave the room directly.'

'Sweet madam!' groaned her tormentress, sinking to her knees and mopping up coffee with the napkin. 'I would not for one moment have touched on this matter had I not been convinced it was for your Majesty's good. It is a cruel kindness in your other ladies to pretend to you it does not exist, when the very pages snigger over it. That so strict a Catholic as the King should indulge in amours, is bound to give rise in his ill-wishers to a suspicion of hypocrisy, and for you to ignore it will be interpreted as condoning——'

She broke off in some alarm. The Queen's pallor had spread to her lips; she was shaking so uncontrollably that the plain gold circlet over a cap of purple velvet rocked upon her head. The contrast between the royal robes she wore and the look on her face as of a hurt child, touched even Lady Sunderland. As the Queen was struggling to speak, there came the sound of persons entering the ante-chamber, and the discreet scratch of a key upon the door.

'Bless me,' shrilled Lady Sunderland, 'here is your Majesty's Chamberlain come to warn us that the reception of the new Spanish Ambassador is due in the Presence in half an hour. We must make haste to change your Majesty's dress, if we are not to be late.'

It is just venomous gossip, she told herself, sitting in her chair of state beside James, mechanically uttering compliments, bowing at the right moments, giving her hand to be kissed by Don Ronquello's entourage. The ceremony, and dinner afterwards in the

Banqueting House, forced her to preserve an outward calm, though a curious constriction in her throat made it impossible to do more than pretend to eat. James talked with animation to the Spaniard on the topic uppermost in his mind, the Revocation of the Edict of Nantes, and the resulting persecution of French Protestants.

'The Ambassador of his Most Christian Majesty, M. Barillon, assured me at the time that those of the *Religion Prétendue Reformée* would not be molested if their consciences forbade them to conform. But the situation has been made all too plain to me since then by my own subjects domiciled in France. I abhor the employment of jack-booted missionaries, and while I wish to see my own religion embraced, I think it contrary to Holy Writ to force any man's conscience.'

He went on to describe the efforts he was making to succour the Huguenot refugees, ordering a collection for them in all churches, to which he himself had subscribed £1,500, and insisting that they be denizened without paying the usual fees. He could not use that word conscience with such patent sincerity, she thought, if he were outraging his own. She had so much admired his unwavering reply to all the pleas of his late brother that he dissemble his religion, like many another papist:

'My principles do not allow me to dissemble my beliefs after the fashion your Majesty urges, and by God's grace I will never do so damnable a thing.'

That was James, straightforward to a fault, a man on whom one could rely, detesting any sort of prevarication. It was monstrous to suspect that one so attached to honour could be carrying on a base intrigue.

But the seed of suspicion had been planted, and she could not uproot it. When she was free from her public duties, she tried by hard exercise to distract her thoughts, riding recklessly in all weathers. The heart of her torment was lack of understanding; she knew of the existence of lechery, just as she was aware that in remote parts of the globe there were cannibals, but it had never entered familiarly into her experience. Sin for her was a matter of vanity about her looks, slothfulness in prayer, small fibs, uncharitable thoughts, lack of resignation to God's will. Until she was fifteen, her emotions were absorbed in that supernatural love to which she would be dedicated in the cloister; since then, she had been indifferent to any man except her husband. .

Like a swarm of flies which would not be left behind, however hard she galloped, newly born doubt stung her, trivial little memories injected poison. Charles, the merry mask dropped, calling her 'poor child', begging her not to set James on a pedestal, saying, with that familiar twitch of the eyebrow, 'If you think of sins, Belle, to which you have no temptation, let it be only in your prayers for the sinner.' She had taken it for granted that he was referring to his own bevy of mistresses. The meaning glances between her other Maids of Honour when Madam Sedley was mentioned. James, several times lately, making an excuse for not receiving Holy Communion with her; conversations broken off abruptly by her ladies when she came upon them unawares; a stifled titter when she innocently remarked that his Majesty was kept very late at the Council-board tonight.

Yet it was too preposterous to be true. She had accepted the fact that he had been consistently unfaithful to her predecessor, but everyone assured her that a young and lovely wife had given him a distaste for such amours; and besides, all that was before he had embraced, at such stupendous cost, the Catholic religion. Moreover he was fifty-three; Sedley was plain to the point of ugliness (she stifled the new voice of doubt which said, 'So was his late duchess'); she delighted in making fun of the beliefs and ceremonies of his Church. Above all, it was indecent even to suspect that he could be unfaithful while he continued to take his marital rights for granted.

To seek advice in her anguish would be to admit there was cause for it, and to do that would be a betrayal of her own trusting love. To doubt those she loved was utterly alien to her nature; and yet to exorcize the devil raised by Lady Sunderland seemed beyond her capacity. For weeks she struggled against it unaided. She had learnt self-control in a very hard school; the warning word, 'Daughter!', had punctuated her childhood; Royalty did not weep in public, did not laugh out loud, did not show fear. But such command of herself was not always equal now to the strain put upon it; again and again when she dined and supped in Hall, her throat constricted, and she could neither swallow nor speak. It was remarked; she knew it; she heard whispers. 'Her Majesty used to be so extremely pleasant, full of discourse and good humour.'

She sought the guide she had followed all her youth, St Francis de Sales. His *Introduction to the Devout Life* was so practical, written as it was for the benefit of women living in the world. He had advised that when we wish to be delivered from some evil, we must strive above all for tranquillity. 'Birds remain ensnared because they flutter in their wild attempts to escape from the net, and in doing so become the more entangled.' His sovereign remedy was to confide our disquiet to our confessor.

Her own confessor, Fr Ruga, was a good man and had known her from childhood, but somehow she shrank from the pious platitudes she felt sure he would suffer. She, who knew nothing of the world, needed a man of the world in such a crisis, someone more head than heart, experienced in the ways of a court, but without self-interest; such a man, for instance, as Fr Edward Petre. An English baronet, he had renounced his rank and estates to enter the Society of Jesus. James had summoned him to a seat on the Privy Council, and was now trying to persuade the Jesuit-hating Innocent XI to give him a cardinal's hat. A man totally without ambition, Fr Petre had not wanted the seat, nor did he covet the hat; the former would give grave scandal, he said, not only to Protestants but to Catholics, for it was contrary to the Rule of St Ignatius. But on the Privy Council he was; and James had told her, rather testily, that the only piece of advice Fr Petre had contributed so far was not to allow the Religious Orders to wear their habits publicly in England. A strange confidant, and she scarcely knew why she chose him.

He awaited her by appointment in a chair set just within the rail of her little chapel; she could see him in profile in the half-light, with a purple stole over his shoulders. He did not rise as she approached, for she was now no more than any other penitent. She knelt and asked for a blessing; his hand moved in the sign of the cross, then shielded his face in a traditional attitude. She went through her little list of venial sins, paused, licked dry lips, and said:

'There is more, Father. I wish to seek your advice on a matter which necessitates my mentioning persons by name.'

'You know that as far as possible you must never disclose in Confession the identity of anyone who has shared your sin.'

'I know that, Father. What I have to say concerns the sin of others of which I may be the victim. I have struggled against rash judgment, but I have to know, for otherwise I think I shall go mad.' Again she had to moisten her lips before she could articulate the words: 'It concerns the infidelity of my husband with Madam Sedley.'

He answered at once, simple and grave:

'It is permitted, my child, to speak freely of infamous and notorious sinners, so long as we do so in a spirit of charity. What you have asked me in intent is too public for there to be the slightest doubt that it exists. I am not the King's confessor, and therefore am not bound by the seal of secrecy in this matter.'

He had put in the knife without hesitation, and waited till her storm of tears subsided, offering no comfort. When she was quieter, he continued in the same businesslike tone:

'No sin can be grievous if committed in such a condition of violent excitement as obstructs completely the use of reason. In this case it is impossible for you to know whether or not such a condition exists; therefore you must beware of rash judgment.'

'Do you mean that I should condone this outrage to my marriage-bed?'

'I mean, my dear child, that you should do your duty lovingly, and then mind your own business. Have the goodness to remember the great penitents, St Augustine and St Mary Magdalen. There are sins to which you yourself are not tempted; you must learn to place the most charitable complexion on the sins of others.'

'But it is a public scandal! You yourself, Father, have admitted that. I am made one of a seraglio!'

'For the first,' he said, disregarding her passion, 'do you not imagine that his Majesty is well aware of it? Should you not compassionate a man who, having given up so much to embrace a faith for which he felt no sensible attraction, succumbs to fleshly vices which give heretics the excuse to sneer at him? For the second, you are too innocent, my child, to understand the difference between a mere sensual appetite and true affection.'

'Affection! When he breaks my heart! He did not even choose me for his wife; I was selected only that I might breed children to inherit a throne. If he has even respect for me, at least he might beg my pardon!'

'I have no doubt he begs pardon of God. He is old enough to be your father; his pride forbids him to confess to you. The Faith does not make men perfect, my dear child; you know that well enough. What perhaps you do not know is the agony of shame your husband suffers under the armour of his reserve. He has good reason to be devoted to you; Madam Sedley would not have shared exile with him, stood by him in persecution, as you have done. And does he not, in all things save one, show his devotion? Is he not kind and affectionate to you, does he not put himself out to accommodate himself to your tastes and wishes, does he ever betray irritation at little faults (for we are none of us perfect) which may be uncongenial to him?'

'He is everything to me, everything! I desire to be the same to him; is that so wrong?'

'It is unwise. It is a grave mistake to regard anyone simply as our husband, our mother, our child. They have an individual life apart from us which we must not seek to invade, much less to possess. Nor must we give any creature the adoration due to God alone.'

For the first time he lowered the hand which had shielded his face, and in the dimness she saw him smile at her, very kindly.

'You were reared, I understand, in the spirituality of St Francis de Sales. Though you have at present much excuse for being angry, remember how he warns his Philothea not to let our wrath stay the night, since it may well awake as hatred, and there will be little we can do to free ourselves from it. Your husband is the King of England, surrounded by perils and enemies. He needs your loyalty, which hitherto you have always given him, whether you agreed with his opinions, or not.' He paused. 'Is there anything more?'

'There is no more, Father.'

'Then you will say for your penance the Act of Charity.'

Pondering on Fr Petre's advice, ashamed by his hint that she was self-righteous, she struggled to accept a husband who had become a stranger all over again. Then, like the paroxysms of an illness, storms of jealousy would buffet her, made worse by resentment against Fr Petre, who had been so singularly unsympathetic and had made her feel a Pharisee. She resumed her reckless riding, with the result that her horse threw her; she was dragged and kicked, taken up unconscious, her face masked with blood and her body so bruised that she was confined to her room for weary weeks.

'That lovely riding-habit is ruined,' sighed Lady Sophia Bulkeley. 'I have examined it, and it is past repair. But the accident has not marred your beauty, madam, God be thanked.'

'I wish it had broken my neck!' burst out Mary Beatrice; then clapped a hand across her mouth in horror at what she had said.

Lady Sophia took one quick glance over her shoulder to see whether the other ladies on duty had overheard, but they were immersed in a game of cards. She said with apparent irrelevance:

'My dear Rogue is on the prowl again. Sunderland's girl is his latest fancy, I hear.'

Rogue, Puss, Mischief; all other married couples had pet names for each other. And no doubt James had one for Catherine Sedley.

'Your ladyship says it so lightly.'

'Bless me, madam, I am well accustomed to it. It means no more to them than a dish they fancy, and of which they very soon tire. If my dear Rogue asked the Sunderland chit to make his shirts for him, then I *would* be worried.'

The Queen tried to smile, but her sense of humour appeared to be moribund. She murmured:

'You have children to console you.'

'And so will you, dear madam, if you are patient. You yourself were such a child when you married, and saplings do not bear strong fruit.' She lowered her voice. 'From certain remarks you have let fall, I believe you suppose the cause of his Majesty's infidelity to be his despair of having further children by you. I do not know whether it will add salt or be balm to your wound, but the amour with Madam Sedley is not new. I would say it began about the year 1678.'

This disclosure certainly added salt. For it confirmed her suspicion that he despaired of having a son by her; the intrigue must have begun just after the death of her baby Charles, and immediately before her flying visit to her stepdaughter in Holland. That was why he was so willing to let me go! her heart raged. And whatever Lady Sophia says, he has not very soon tired.

The ladies of her Household were devoted to her, and now that the secret was out, they inundated her with well-meaning advice. Contessa Molza advised a novena to St Monica, who by many years of prayer had obtained the conversion of her son, St Augustine; Lady Peterborough made no bones about suggesting a tit for tat. Everyone knew that Lord Godolphin, her Majesty's Chamberlain, cherished such an ardent love for her that he outraged his Protestant conscience by leading her into her chapel for Mass, just for the sake of touching her hand. Lady Strickland, a practical woman, chided her on her indifference to public affairs. One of the chief attractions of the late Duchess of York was her shrewdness; James had turned to her for advice in all political problems.

But her Serenity had impressed on the child Mary Beatrice that she should not concern herself with matters for which she had no head. As for trying to arouse James's jealousy, it appeared to her utterly cheap and base. To add to her misery was the double measure of paternal affection James now bestowed on Anne. Mary had grieved him by her rudeness to his friend, William Penn, the Quaker, sent to The Hague to explain to Orange the King's reasons for wishing to repeal the savage penal laws against dissenters, both Catholic and Protestant.

'I have not seen the Princess of Denmark once today,' was his constant refrain. 'I must step across to the Cockpit to see how she does.'

He was never at ease unless Anne was with him, anticipating her every wish, paying without reproach her endless gambling debts, giving orders that she be allowed the same honours in the Chapel Royal as would have been paid to himself. Watching her waddle across the Stone Gallery, thrusting her stomach before her like an offering, chaplains preceding her, the Master of the King's Music and his choristers following, and a bishop making a congie at the door, Mary Beatrice thought it all unwise. Since Mary remained childless, her sister was being encouraged to look upon herself as ultimate heiress to the throne, and was full of an absurd self-importance.

The King, meanwhile, was completely absorbed in his plans for religious toleration, and his wife, nauseated by the contrast between this lofty ideal and his marital infidelity, listened with a new cynicism while he went on and on. Such toleration, it seemed, had been promised in the Treaty of Breda at the Restoration, but the late King's attempts to implement the pledge were consistently foiled by Parliament.

'It is my constant opinion that conscience ought not to be constrained, nor people forced in matters of religion. Nor can I be persuaded to depart from this opinion, and I am sure my subjects, both here and in Scotland, will thank me when I have attained my aim to give Catholic, Quaker, Baptist and Jew the right quietly to enjoy the exercise of their religion, so long as they behave themselves as obedient subjects.'

Stop talking about your subjects, she longed to cry at him, and think what lacerations you are inflicting on your wife. There were frightful moments when she realized how wise St Francis de Sales had been in his warning that to admit resentment is to risk it turning into hate. She felt as one poisoned, and she could find no antidote to the venom.

Her health was suffering; she overheard her ladies whisper that only her youth was keeping her alive. That keen sense of humour, which had been to her such a good friend when she was tempted to melancholy, awoke for a moment when she learned in a roundabout way that Terriesi, the Tuscan Envoy, was actually talking of a marriage between James and the Grand Duke of Tuscany's daughter in view of her own rapid decline. What made it so specially funny was that Mary Beatrice, ignorant of this, had approached Terriesi for his aid in furthering a match between her brother Francesco and this same princess.

But her laughter was quenched abruptly when Whitehall buzzed with a tit-bit of news. Hitherto James had done his best to keep his intrigue with Madam Sedley to the region of the back-stairs. Now he created her Countess of Dorchester, and there was a strong rumour that she was to be given the apartments of the Duchess of Portsmouth, thus attaining her ambition to be recognized as official mistress. And ennobled to the rank of countess, she had the privilege of being kissed by the Queen.

On the day when she received this further shock, Mary Beatrice was unable to keep up even a façade of self-control during supper. She was past caring that the eyes of everyone, down to the humblest page, were fixed upon her, savouring her open distress. She could not articulate a single word throughout the meal. But she would speak to her husband later; either she must have it out with him, once and for all, or lose her reason.

Directly supper was finished she retired to her bedchamber on the excuse of indisposition. Dismissing her ladies when they had assisted her to undress, she made the only preparations of which she was capable for the coming scene, doggedly saying her prayers, imploring guidance, invoking the aid of favourite saints and calm from a God who seemed deaf, rehearsing little sentences torn away next moment from her memory. It was a bitter cold winter night; she sat down by the fire after a while, waiting for James to come. He had been occupied all day receiving addresses in connection with his grand scheme for religious toleration; either he was still so engaged, or he was with Catherine Sedley at her house in St James's Square.

The clocks had struck eleven before she heard the approach of the procession which escorted his Majesty from his own apartments to the door of the bedchamber. There were murmured good nights, and soft footsteps retreating. She returned to her prie-dieu in the alcove, and there she remained for another five minutes, shivering with cold and nerves, frantically bracing herself for the ordeal. Her lips framing the opening sentence of what she intended to say, she approached the bed.

James lay there, breathing evenly, fast asleep.

Something seemed to snap inside her brain. The voice of

reason told her that he was worn out after a hard day's business. In sleep he looked curiously defenceless. Reason and love were as if they had never been. She screamed with the shrill abandonment of hysteria:

'Give this woman my dower, make her Queen of England, but never let me see her face again!'

'Eh?' he grunted, roused from deep sleep, making a half movement as if to reach for a sword, a gesture from youth when there was the sudden attack, the night alarm.

'I will bear no more. You offer me a public insult by ennobling your concubine. You have deceived me, I am told, throughout many years of marriage; was that not enough without brazening your infidelity abroad?'

'Madam,' he began. Then for the first time since she had met him, she heard him stammer. 'I beg you will—pray remember those who lie in the anteroom—lower your voice—if you please.'

Madam! Such cold formality! It was like offering advice to a drowning man when all he needs is a hand to pull him out of the water. James rose from the bed, knuckled his eyes, threw on his furred night-robe, and came across to the fire. She was aware, fleetingly, that he was half-drunk with fatigue, but with his inflexible devotion to duty, was resolved to hear what she had to say. She stepped away from him; duty, courtesy, fairness, of these alone he was capable when it was a question of his wife. Love was only for his daughters, passion for Catherine Sedley. She gave her latent fury full rein, gasping out reproaches, descending to cheap attempts to inflict wound for wound, even while her whole nature was outraged by the words her lips uttered.

He stood silent under the bombardment, mechanically warming his hands at the fire. When he spoke it was in short sentences to combat that nervous stutter.

'I bestowed this new title on a certain condition. She is to leave at once for either Holland or Flanders. I have instructed my Lord Middleton to provide a yacht. She objects. She is, she says, a freeborn Englishwoman. She can live where she pleases. I cannot use force.'

'You *want* her to go?'

'I do.'

'Then—then why in God's name didn't you tell me so?'

'Madam, this is not a matter I could decently discuss with you. My intention in deceiving you was to spare you pain. I have kept hoping to conquer the temptation before it reached your ears.'

Her silence was one of blank bewilderment. Evidently he mistook it for indignation and, his back turned, for the first time he betrayed how deeply he was moved.

'Do you suppose I am not ashamed? Do you think I am indifferent to being denied the Sacraments? Do you know nothing of masculine pride? What is it you desire? That I kneel at your feet and beg forgiveness? If that will prove to you my remorse, I am ready.'

'I don't understand! If you had only told me that you wanted her to go! And if I hurt someone I love, I find it the easiest thing in the world to ask their forgiveness.'

'Your little sins!'

There was such a confession of self-hatred in his tone that reaction surged up in her. She whispered:

'I'm sorry.'

'*You* are sorry. For what, madam?'

'For being too small to know great temptations. For being cruel and bitter and rude in what I said. For presuming to judge you; for speaking as though I did not love you with my whole heart. For forgetting that as the King you have many enemies, and are entitled to my loyalty.' She gulped back tears, laid a hand softly on his arm, and asked: 'May I, for this one night, lie alone? No, I am not sick and do not need my ladies. What I need is to—to commune with myself.'

But she did not commune with herself. Men might hate emotional scenes; women needed them as a purge, and she slept soundly. Waking in the small hours of the morning, huddled like a child in the great bed, she found herself kissing something she thought to be his hand. But instead it was the cold nailed feet of a favourite little crucifix, taken to bed so often in Modena when she was afraid and insecure and starved of love.

4

Mlle Sedley, as the French Ambassador continued to call the new Countess of Dorchester, went off to Dublin in style, but after a week or two wrote to her friends that she found the multitude of convents distasteful to so good a Protestant, and in any case she needed to take the waters at Tunbridge Wells. Though absolutely forbidden by James to reappear at Court, she caused a sensation by walking into the Queen's apartments and actually offering her cheek to be kissed.

'The minx appears to have gathered a fresh stock of impudence in Ireland,' exclaimed Lady Sophia. 'I hear she has bought a country house at Weybridge, convenient to Windsor.'

The Court was about to transfer to Windsor for hunting. As a result of his hard riding, James often became separated from the rest of the hunt; each time this occurred, Mary Beatrice was tormented by the suspicion that he was visiting Catherine Sedley.

Yet that night when she had made such a scene had taught her much. It must be, she supposed, a kind of illness, or perhaps a bewitchment; he was under a spell from which his better self longed to be released. She marvelled at the crass obtuseness of the male. If only he had told her why he had given Sedley a title, what a lot of pain she herself would have been spared!

Meanwhile he was trying his best to show her he was sorry, not in the way she wanted, but in the only fashion he knew. He took new pains to consider her tastes; on her twenty-eighth birthday, he who had always showered jewels on someone who did not care for them, gave her instead the most beautiful set of silver filigree dishes. Because she was forced to spend most of her time at Whitehall, a place she detested, he entirely redecorated her apartments there, commissioning Verrio to paint the ceilings, Grinling Gibbons to carve mantelpieces with foliage and fruit. Then there was the new chapel at Whitehall; scrupulous in leaving the Chapel Royal for the use of Protestants, he was building a new Catholic one from the ground, and consulted his wife on each detail of it.

But Madam Sedley hovered in the background, and the raw heart of Mary Beatrice was exposed for every hand to touch. She was mortified by the realization that for years the Court had laughed at her naïvety; poor little convent-bred innocent, living in a fool's paradise. All kings kept mistresses, her ladies now reminded her; surely she must have met Mme de Montespan in France? Why should she expect her husband to be the exception to the rule? Of course it ought to have been the other way round; being so very much the younger, and so very beautiful, she could have had as many lovers as she pleased. Chastity was admirable, no doubt, but perhaps a little dull. And though one deplored Madam Sedley, she was so amusing, such a born mimic; even if one were a good Catholic, one had to laugh at her clever imitations of Fr Petre, and her naughty stories about the goings-on in Irish convents.

One May evening, the Queen was walking on the terrace at Windsor with M. Barillon, who was earnestly explaining to her his views on James's newly published Declaration of Indulgence which dispensed with the penal laws. She tried to attend, but the hour approached when James usually returned from the Privy Council meeting, and if he was late she could not conquer a suspicion that he had been with Sedley.

'I fear it is most unwise,' said Barillon, referring to the Declaration. 'The Pope himself disapproves on the accepted principle that it is unlawful for a Catholic prince to encourage or maintain heresy in his dominions; while as for the English, I hear it said on all sides that his Majesty desires toleration only for Catholics.'

'I do not understand how anyone can say that,' she objected, rousing herself, 'when so many thousands of Protestant dissenters have been released from prison by the Indulgence.'

'Madame, the English are hardly sane on the subject of our faith. Even the educated among them believe that no papist can be trusted because he is taught by his priests that it is meritorious to lie in the interests of his religion. Moreover the Declaration threatens the monopoly of the Established Church, whose bishops will resent any rival, Catholic or Calvinist. But I think I have not your Majesty's attention.'

She flushed and murmured an apology. She had been shrinking from the knowledge that James was already late.

'But there is someone else, madame, to whom I fear this

66

Declaration will give a dangerous advantage. I hear from his Majesty that the Prince of Orange, his son-in-law, has refused to approve of a measure which gives English Catholics the same toleration afforded by the States General to the Dutch. His Highness makes no secret of the fact that through his wife he hopes to succeed to this throne, and now he has an excellent excuse for parading as the Protestant champion. There are backstairs whispers that already he is in secret communication with great malcontents here, who would invite him over to mediate between his Majesty and his Protestant subjects. Let the Prince once set foot on English soil, and I fear his ambition will not let him stop short at mediating.'

She was deaf to this ominous talk, for her husband's coach was approaching up the avenue, a full hour after his usual time. He came briskly on to the terrace, and was about to engage Barillon in conversation, when the tears standing in his wife's eyes halted him. Excusing himself to the French Ambassador, he drew her apart.

'I was summoned by the Queen Dowager to Somerset House, on the matter of her quarrel with her former Treasurer over his accounts. This is the truth, madam, upon my honour.'

Yes, she thought, it is the truth this time; but what of to-morrow and the next day? It was one thing to understand that James was under a spell he hated; quite another to stand by without any power to release him from the bewitchment. Prolonged emotional stress was making her so frail, and the summer was so excessively hot, that her physician, Dr Waldegrave, demurred at her attending public functions. Yet a dull sense of duty seemed her only refuge now, and she was present at the reception of Count d'Adda, Papal Nuncio. His mission, she heard, was political; he had come to try to induce James to join the Pope, the Emperor, Spain and the Prince of Orange in the League of Augsburg, directed against the might of France. James refused; he held to his belief that the good of England consisted in peace at home and abroad; and the Papal Nuncio was observed to turn frosty.

'I hear that His Holiness, in his temporal capacity, is very much displeased,' Barillon remarked to the Queen. 'And this may be of dangerous consequence, since he is the ally of the Prince of Orange.'

In the thick of trying to comprehend these public matters, she was stricken by a personal loss. An express brought the news that her mother had died of pneumonia in Rome. Duchess Laura had become a very dim figure to her, and she wept with repentance rather than grief; it was her own fault that all these years her mother had been living in exile. She put on her new mourning, and sat down to write a letter of condolence to her brother, but tears kept blotting the page. Not only her gown but the whole world seemed black; she had failed her mother by that childish fuss she had made over marriage; she had not been able to keep her husband; all her children were dead, and the choice of her by Lord Peter had proved a mistake. Oh why had they denied her the cloistral life to which she had dedicated herself! There at least she might have been useful.

Hastily she dried her eyes at the sound of someone's approach; so completely had she yielded to self-pity that she had not recognized the footstep dearer to her than any other, and turned in surprise to find her husband pacing about the room. He appeared embarrassed, making little clearings of his throat, checking his watch by her chiming-clock, fidgeting with a vase. He said at length, abruptly:

'Dr Waldegrave has appealed to me, madam. He insists that unless you spend some time in the country, you will fall into a consumption. It is our duty to take care of our health.'

Her mood was such that she at once suspected the worst. In other words, she decided, you wish to be free to enjoy the society of your concubine. She said, cold and bitter:

'You order me to go away, Sir. Very well. I will go anywhere you please.'

He sighed sharply, and spoke with his back turned.

'I do not wish you to go away for any other reason but that of your health. I too am leaving London; I intend a Progress through the West and Midlands, that I may discover at first-hand how my subjects like my Declaration of Indulgence before I summon Parliament to approve it. I could, therefore, escort you to Bath, and bring you home again at the end of my Progress.'

She was suddenly attentive. Something in his tone and manner made her certain that he was trying to convey a message he was too shy to put into words. But as she did not speak, he said with a great effort:

'I have not seen Madam Sedley for a month, and by the grace of God I will never see her again. I hear that the late Duchess, your mother, made her last pilgrimage to the shrine of Loreto, to intercede for us that we may have a son. I design a similar pilgrimage to St Winifred's Well in Flintshire. Even the prayers of such a sinner as I am, may——'

He could not complete the sentence. She saw his shoulders shaking, and with a great thrill of compassion she realized that he, so reserved, so self-controlled, had broken down. She rushed to him, and held him, murmuring broken endearments, her heart singing a hymn of gratitude to God. For she knew that the spell of Catherine Sedley was gone for ever.

5

It was like coming out of a dark tunnel. After he left her at Bath she had daily letters from him; they were not love-letters; she knew by now that he was incapable of such. They were filled with accounts of his Progress, and of the daily addresses he received, welcoming his Declaration. One borough, it seemed, had gone so far as to describe liberty of conscience as God's Magna Charta to all His reasonable creatures. But underneath this obsession with his ideal, he conveyed to the sensitive heart of Mary Beatrice his dependence on her sympathy, just as his asking her to go away had been an appeal to her trust.

The black world turned golden, both within and without. In halcyon weather she drove about the countryside; in villages, little groups collected to cheer, the beadle, the waywarden, a strolling rat-catcher, apple-cheeked girls offering posies. Here surely was the real England; walking in the King's Mead, the gentry and their wives approached her with simple, rustic courtesy, chatting to her about the weather and the crops and local affairs. Whitehall and its intrigues, and a curious undercurrent of whispering she had noticed there of late, seemed a thousand miles away.

The mornings she dutifully devoted to taking the waters, and now that she could laugh again, she found it hilarious. Arrayed in a stiff canvas wrapper with great sleeves, she descended into the Cross Bath to the strains of her Italian orchestra; she felt like a Baptist being 'dipped' as she waded chin-high in the queer-tasting water which turned everything yellow. Privileged ladies, vastly inflated by their canvas gowns, clung to rings in the sides, or called for another stone cushion as they sat in alcoves. It was all so solemn a ritual that she could keep a straight face only until she was shut up again in her baize-lined chair, and carried home through streets too narrow for wheeled traffic.

A brief visit from her husband, on his way from Salisbury to Gloucester, underlined her conviction that the Sedley nightmare was past. It was not that he was more demonstrative, rather that he gave the very definite impression that he had no longer secrets of which he was ashamed. He was once more the James with whom she had fallen so deeply in love after her initial aversion.

Before he fetched her from Bath in late October, she received another visitor, Count Zulestein, who came rather belatedly to condole with her on behalf of his master, the Prince of Orange, on her mother's death. She had met him during James's exile in Flanders in 1679, a smooth courtier, Orange's kinsman on the wrong side of the blanket, rather too effusive for her taste. But at the moment she was so happy that she could like anyone, and she was eager for news of her dear 'Lemon'. The Princess Mary, it seemed, now lived in perfect accord with her husband; she so much appreciated her Majesty's always writing to her without the least formality.

'Formality is not to be thought of between such friends as we are. I will reply at once to the Prince's kind letter of condolence, for doubtless you are in haste to return to Holland, M. le Comte.'

She thought it just a trifle curious, nothing more, that her remark should cause Zulestein embarrassment. He had, he said, so many appointments to keep in London that he did not know when he would return. Not, he hastened to add, concerned with any public matters, since he was sent for the sole purpose of conveying his master's sympathy to her Majesty. He enlarged on this to what seemed to her an unnecessary length, giving her an overall impression, unsuspicious though she was by nature, that he had something to hide.

But Zulestein vanished from her mind when she noted half-forgotten symptoms in herself. Metaphorically she held her breath; that she could be pregnant again after all these years was almost too much to hope. But the symptoms continued, and on her return to London she could not resist just hinting at them in her weekly letter to Mary. She was writing it, when her other stepdaughter called.

'I do declare, madam,' said Anne, 'that the King and you are like turtle-doves; one would think you were newly wed. *I* could never forgive an unfaithful husband; not that the dear Prince ever so much as looks at another woman. Of course Madam Sedley was very entertaining; whereas your Majesty is what we call in England a housedove, for ever plying your needle, and disapproving even of a harmless game of cards.'

'I don't disapprove of cards, dumpling, though I don't like to see huge sums won and lost at them, and whole evenings spent at the gaming-table. You and I used to have such fun in the evenings, laughing and romping and telling silly jokes.'

'That was when I was a child. Now I'm the Protestant Heiress Presumptive—after Mary, of course, but she's far away in Holland, and has grown very Dutch. Mrs Freeman says that my heart being entirely English, and devoted to the Church, the nation would rather have me than my sister for Queen, especially as she would have to bring Caliban with her.'

Sarah Jennings, now Lady Churchill, had maintained her ascendancy over Anne. They called each other Mrs Morley and Mrs Freeman, because they had no secrets they did not share. Fraying out the feathers of her quill, Mary Beatrice frowned. It had been, she was sure, a grave mistake to encourage Anne in her ambition to be ultimate Heiress, for she would not be pleased to relinquish this distinction at the possible birth of a brother.

'Dumpling, you speak as though the King and I can have no more children. Yet I am only twenty-nine.'

'Mrs Freeman is positive that your Majesty will never bear a living son.'

'I really fail to understand how Lady Churchill is in a position to know,' exclaimed the Queen, half amused and half irritated. But then, hugging her stepdaughter, she cried: 'Oh dumpling, please God the new year will prove such a joyful one for all of us, this coming year of 1688!'

5
The Night of Judas

1

Deftly and without fussing, Mère Priolo arranged cushions in the wicker chair, placed a footstool, opened the cheap sunshade, saw to it that the Queen had brought her black paper fan.

'This heat fatigues your Majesty, I fear. Sister Philomena reports that you ate no dinner today.'

'Because again there was no letter from the King my son.'

'No news is good news, dear madame.'

'So I tell myself. Yet I think we mothers are anxious about our children from their cradle to our grave.'

It was so hot that even the birds lay flaccid, wings outstretched in the dust as though they were dead. But below the gardens, habits tucked up beneath rough sack aprons, the sisters weeded busily between the vines. From their cradle, she mused; it was just such a scorching June day as this when little James was born. She smiled wryly; a simple fact of the weather had given rise to that monstrously absurd story of the warming-pan.

Late in December of 1687, her pregnancy was announced in the Gazette, and a committee of Anglican bishops composed a special prayer to be read in all the churches. She kept a copy of it, the very one Anne had flung down on the table with such venom.

'I'm sure you cannot believe that our Protestant prayers will be answered, madam. And while it is very kind of the King to add a petition that the whole Royal Family may be increased and multiplied, it really turns one's stomach to see how certain he is that he will have a son, just because he prayed at some popish well.'

'Our child will be son or daughter as God pleases, dear.'

She was carrying badly, dreading another miscarriage, teased by the fact that she had two reckonings, June and July, and hurt by an increasing hostility in Anne. She tried to make allowances; Anne, still childless, was jealous. She herself had been taught a sharp lesson with Sedley, had descended to a cheapness and even to a cruelty of which she would have deemed herself incapable. And Anne was being led into a certain bad habit by her husband, who drank vast quantities of brandy without any visible effects except for the enlargement of his already stout figure.

'A glass of *aqua vitae* is good for my condition,' explained the ever-pregnant Anne, when a whiff of spirits was noticeable on her breath. 'Mrs Freeman says so.'

Jealousy and drink must be held responsible for the spiteful remarks Anne now made constantly.

'I cannot help deeming it very odd that the Bath, which all the *Protestant* doctors thought would do your Majesty a great deal of harm, should have so good effect that you should prove with child from the first moment when the King visited you there. Was Fr Petre with him?'

'No. Why do you ask?'

Anne tittered, and there being nothing in the room to eat, began to bite her fan.

'There are so many things I cannot help deeming very strange, madam. That you should choose, all of a sudden, to go to Confession to this Jesuit a while ago. Mrs Freeman had it from Mrs Dawson that you were *hours* shut up with him alone in your chapel.'

'I think, my dear,' said Mary Beatrice, trying to keep her tone level, 'that you really ought not to listen to backstairs gossip, which should be beneath your notice.'

'It is not just backstairs gossip. Does not your Majesty see all these tracts and lampoons which are scattered about the town?'

'I have seen certain very seditious and hysterical pamphlets which mislead the people into believing that his Majesty is trying to force our religion on his subjects. I could not help laughing when

73

I read in one that not only their lives, estates and liberties, but even their chastity depended upon a maintenance of the penal laws.'

'I don't think it's a laughing matter. And the tracts to which I was referring, madam, are not those concerned with the King's scheme to make us all papists, but with your Majesty's condition.'

'Oh dumpling, what's the matter? We used to be such friends.'

Anne resisted the attempted embrace, excusing herself by saying that she had a painful spot on her tongue.

'That means you have told a fib,' said Mary Beatrice, trying to lighten the atmosphere.

'*I* don't tell fibs. But it has been known this hundred years and more that papists are taught from their cradle to lie. Mrs Freeman says that if the King should make an assault on my religion, I ought to choose rather to live on alms than change.'

'No assault will ever be made on your religion, dear; you know how careful the King was to give you your own chaplains when we were in Flanders, and to make over to you the Chapel Royal here. As for living on alms, do you truly forget that on his accession he increased your allowance to £32,000 a year, and how many times he has paid, without a word of reproach, your gambling debts?'

She began to dread Anne's visits, which almost invariably coincided with her own dressing or undressing. The myopic eyes scrutinized her increasing figure, the slender white hands, Anne's only beauty, offered to paw, grossly intimate questions were for ever on Anne's lips, and several times she surprised her stepdaughter whispering with her own Bedchamber Women.

'Why are you always so afraid that I should touch your belly, madam? And if I, or any of my friends, should happen to be at your *levée*, why do you always go into the next room to change your smock? There being so many jests and stories told about you, I think you should see how important it is to convince *me* that you are really with child.'

The Queen made that familiar gesture of clapping a hand across her mouth, then abruptly changed the subject.

'I am hoping so much that I can lie in at St James's, but my apartments there are undergoing alterations. It has always been my favourite home.'

'And such a fine place for smuggling people out—or in,' sniggered Anne. 'I was referring, of course, to the King's escape from St James's when he was a boy. Madam, surely you used to have another cushion on this couch; I distinctly remember a plump round cushion which seems to have disappeared since it was announced that you were enceinte. I believe I myself am breeding again; perhaps I shall have a daughter to be a playmate to your son. But as I am going to Bath to take the waters, it may turn out to be a man-child; they seem to be quite miraculous.'

Ignoring such childish spite, her stepmother exclaimed:

'But surely you will not leave before I am brought to bed?'

'Since you reckon on June, and the physicians on July, madam, I really cannot be expected to remain in London when I need to take the waters. But I shall leave Mrs Freeman here, who will send me all the news.'

Preoccupied with her coming confinement, the affair of the Seven Bishops with which the whole town rang was remote to Mary Beatrice. It appeared that on the very day when the Declaration of Indulgence was to be read from London pulpits, these seven exploded a mine beneath the King's feet in the shape of a Memorial explaining that they could not read it because it was founded on the dispensing power of the Crown, though this had been declared lawful by the Judges. Studying a list of names from which to choose her future child's Household, Mary Beatrice heard the frenzied cheers of the populace; the Seven Bishops, having refused to give bail, were being rowed to honourable confinement in the Tower, shouting to the crowds to keep their religion.

It must be this bolt from the blue, she supposed, that kept her husband wandering restlessly about their bedchamber that night. She really must make an effort to comprehend this bewildering public affair; but even as she framed a question, he sat down suddenly on the bed beside her, and took her hands in a hard, hurting grip.

'Beatrice, I have tried my best to keep from you a plague of vile rumours that inflame the town, the same as were spread before our last child was born, and ceased abruptly when it proved a daughter. But they increase daily; they are to the tune that I would foist a spurious Prince of Wales upon my kingdoms.' He smote the bed-post with a clenched fist. 'Those base forgers of iniquity must certainly think we do not believe in God, if they imagine we could be such hellish impostors!'

His rare anger braced her; she asked quietly what was to be done.

'It is necessary that our child be born in the greatest possible publicity. I am summoning no less than sixty-seven persons to be present, the majority of them Protestants.'

'But not here at Whitehall! You have told me there is no precedent for any queen being brought to bed in this seat of government. And with the new Treasury Office adjoining my apartments not yet finished, the dust and the noise——'

'It shall be, please God, at St James's.'

She nodded dumbly. The thought of this public ordeal appalled her; and yet, as with all past hazards by land and sea, his presence seemed to give her the power to confront any trial.

2

On the morning of June 10th she was awakened by her husband's rising to dress in his own apartments, and for a moment or two lay wondering where she was. Then she remembered how last evening at Whitehall, certain that her time was at hand, she had vowed she would sleep at St James's though she had to lie on the boards. It was one of those impulsive remarks she had tried very hard to repress of late, for because of the monstrous slanders she noticed how everything she said, however trivial, was twisted by the writers of anonymous tracts.

But here she was at dear St James's; the workmen had left while she was supping at Whitehall, and at eleven o'clock she had been carried in her chair across the Park. There was an offensive smell of paint, but that was nothing compared with peace and quiet. As for lying on the boards, she was in a brand-new bed; her hand stroked the cut-velvet coverlet embroidered with the Royal Arms within the collar of the Garter, and her own gold lilies and eagle of Modena.

Turini, her old nurse, came hobbling in, followed by the

76

necessary-woman. Where were all her ladies? sleepily inquired the Queen. It was Trinity Sunday and they had all gone to church, but would be back soon to assist her Majesty to dress. Meanwhile she must take an astringent draught ordered by the five doctors who were attending her; she grimaced at the potion of black hellebore, tartar and oil of cloves in mulled wine. Then she spilled it all over the new coverlet as pain tore at her vitals.

From that first onset of labour, pain imprisoned her, and only scattered fragments penetrated from the outside world. The voice of Mrs Wilkes, the midwife, talking on and on about a certain Dr Chamberlen whom she hoped would not arrive in time. Dr Chamberlen, it seemed, would insist on using the obstetric forceps invented by his grandfather, and kept such a family secret that the design for them was hidden under his floor boards.

'And he'll tie one end of the sheet to your Majesty's neck and the other to his own, for reasons of modesty, he says, but really that no one shall catch a glimpse of his precious forceps. I don't hold with such tools; Nature designed the hand which will always succeed except in cases of some monstrous birth. Nor don't I hold with he-midwives; let the doctors mind their business and I'll mind mine, pocketing half my fee, the rascals, who have my licence to practise from the Bishop of London himself.'

The voice of Mrs Dawson addressed the necessary-woman.

'Kindle a fire on the hearth, and be quick about it before the doctors come. I know them and their wanting to have the room cool. Go fetch a warming-pan and pass it well between the sheets; now madam dear, I know it's June, but you'll shiver right enough when the proper pains come, for what you have at present are such that Mrs Wilkes can do nothing with at all. Let the doctors say what they will about child-bed fever being caused by overheating, Mrs Wilkes and I know better.'

'Indeed we do, ma'am. And please your Majesty, make up your mind to a good long labour, you that was always in such a hurry before, and look at the result!'

She was writhing under the velvet coverlet. The face of James, still with the shaving lather on one side of it, swam into her vision, and from behind him the whole of London seemed to be jostling

77

to get at her. The voice of Dr Waldegrave vainly scolded; a woman in child-bed ought to be kept as quiet and as free from agitation as possible. She was an animal in a cage; through the bars she could see nothing but eyes, salacious, embarrassed, compassionate, mocking. The aggressive scent of Lady Sunderland poured in upon her. There was no screen; by the King's special order it had been removed; once and for all he would defeat this vile campaign of slander, though he must outrage his wife's womanhood to do so.

She was suffocating; the strong sunlight of June streamed through the tight-closed windows, the fire roared on the hearth, the warming-pan had done its work so thoroughly that the sheets seemed to scorch her; beneath them, Mrs Wilkes's hands were murderous.

'I die! Oh you kill me, you kill me!' she screamed, but with the third shriek she was delivered. Physical anguish at once gave place to mental dread as, remembering all those still-born babies, she whispered : 'I don't hear the child cry.'

The child itself answered this appeal with a lusty wail. There was a kind of stampede, frenzied questions, the King's voice upraised, and then another voice shouting importantly, 'Way for the Prince of Wales!', and a surge towards the anteroom.

It was achieved. She had given him a living son; after nearly sixty years, England had an Heir Apparent. The ordeal of that public birth, ghastly though it was, had been worth while.

But almost at once, joy gave place to worry. Though her son was the largest and finest she had ever borne, on the very day of his appearance the doctors started dosing him, trying in turn some thirty different potions, and keeping a running sore open in his little arm. They would not allow him a wet-nurse; breast-feeding had caused the convulsions which had carried off so many of her Majesty's other babies, they asserted. They ordered a diet of currant-gruel, with syrup of violets. In her lying-in chamber she could hear him mewl like a kitten next door, and the voices of Turini and Mrs Dawson upraised in a quarrel. In Italy, infants were never swaddled, said the old nurse; it was these tight, ten-foot rollers which caused convulsions. No such art was needed to produce a fine shape in animals.

'A brute beast is one thing, Mrs Turini, a Christian infant quite another. And we want none of your popish customs here, which would make our prince break a limb or grow up deformed.'

At rare intervals his own nurse, Mrs Labadie, would bear him in for his mother to see, and each time there seemed less of him, as though he were shrinking away inside his long robe, his stringed cap and lace mittens. There was one ghastly night when she wakened to find herself alone, and called feebly for her women. From the anteroom a young maid entered, saucer-eyed.

'The doctors dosed his Royal Highness a second time by mistake, madam. All your Household is about his cradle.'

James would be among them, James who had looked twenty years younger when the sex of the infant was revealed to him, had shed his reserve and fairly hugged Dr Waldegrave before knighting him on the spot, had given the midwife a purse of five hundred guineas, 'for your breakfast'. But the crisis passed; his Royal Highness, the Prince of Wales, defied both potions and currant-gruel.

Dr Chamberlen of the famous forceps, who had been out of town when summoned to the Queen's confinement, was as much concerned for her as for her baby, hot Whig though he was. Because the child's condition was so often critical, she was neglected, and her women often forgot to give her the concoction ordered when she was restless, of crabs' claws pounded in a mortar with syrup of poppies. Dr Chamberlen was lecturing her on her failure to recover any strength, when the Princess Anne, just returned to town, came waddling in.

'The excessive heat at Bath really turned one's stomach, madam, but here in London it must have been quite chilly, for Mrs Freeman tells me that you ordered a warming-pan when you were brought to bed. It has given rise to the most extraordinary rumours. They were selling a broadsheet in the streets just now in which— well, I scarcely like to tell you, madam, but that you would be sure to hear it from others, the town is so full of it. It says that a child was smuggled into your bed inside this warming-pan.'

Dr Chamberlen burst into a loud guffaw.

'Has your Royal Highness seen your brother? He weighed eight pounds at birth. And where were the coals, pray?'

'It says in this broadsheet,' persisted Anne, nettled, 'that the warming-pan was never opened, which Mrs Freeman thinks most unwise in view of all the rumours there have been.'

Mary Beatrice, who had kept a hand pressed over her mouth to restrain hysterical laughter, cried hotly:

'Even though the King and I could be thought so wicked as to practise such a cheat, how could it have been contrived when there were no less than sixty-seven persons who saw my child born? Yet it seems that to satisfy some, I ought to have been delivered at Charing Cross!'

Ashamed of her outburst, she gave Anne a kiss, and begged her to pay a visit to her half-brother.

'He is not well, so pray do not disturb him if he sleeps, dear. Lady Powis, his Governess, and I are convinced that he should have a wet-nurse, but the doctors will not hear of it.'

Anne's short-sighted eyes had a gleam of malice in them when she returned from the nursery.

'Well, madam, if the Prince of Wales is as sick as he looks, I believe it will not be long before he is an angel in heaven.' The Queen drew a hissing breath of pain. 'But I have often heard your Majesty say, that while other women bear children for this world, you have borne all yours for God.'

What had come over the old affectionate dumpling, who had been like a younger sister? Just plain envy because she herself had suffered another miscarriage? If so, it was taking a very virulent form. Mrs Dawson, when on duty, gossiped.

'The questions her Royal Highness sees fit to ask me, madam dear! Fairly pesters me, morning, noon and night. Did I see live coals in the warming-pan? Yes, I told her, and so did Mrs Wilkes, not to mention the necessary-woman who filled the pan. Wasn't it possible that Fr Petre smuggled in a babe after your own died? No, said I, for Fr Petre resigned from the Council after his Majesty wouldn't heed his advice not to prosecute the Seven Bishops, and went out of town (which was some Jesuit trick on his part, I have no doubt). Well, says she, it was most vexatious I should happen to be at Bath, and therefore I did not see the Queen and her child parted. Madam, says I, I do swear to you upon my Bible oath that

I myself, standing behind Mrs Wilkes in her Dutch chair, handed her the receiver and saw her cut the navel-string.'

Mrs Dawson paused for breath.

'But now I will tell you what I think, madam dear, and no disrespect intended. The Princess Anne is like a jelly; pour her into any mould and she'll come out that shape. And the hand that pours is Lady Churchill's, you mark my words, she whose mother was a witch, and her father of the underling gentry that never had two groats to rub together.'

'But Lord Churchill is the King's dearest friend!'

'That's as may be, madam dear, but his wife wears the breeches. Set about ruling others in her cradle, and whatever she says is gospel truth to the Princess Anne. Over and above which, as I've mentioned before, the Princess is costive, and constipation always breeds spite.'

Besides Anne, there was a change in Mary. The fulsome Zulestein had come over from Holland once more, charged with formal congratulations from the Prince and Princess of Orange; but Mary Beatrice was hurt and bewildered by the fact that in her weekly letters, dear Lemon never once mentioned the Prince of Wales.

'Does Mary write to you about my son, dumpling?'

For some reason this question appeared to cause Anne the most acute embarrassment. She bit her fan, mumbled no, Mary scarcely ever wrote to her at all now, not since they had quarrelled years ago when Anne would not dismiss her Mrs Freeman, to whom Mary had taken the most unreasonable dislike. As for herself, it was always a labour to write letters, especially when she was with child, as she was again at present. Mrs Dawson told a different story.

'Bless me, madam dear, I never did know the Princess Anne to write so often to her sister, as Jane Danvers tells me, who is her Bedchamber Woman. And pumping me harder than ever on the subject of your lying-in. I have to answer a whole list of questions, says she, sent me by my sister, and how may I do it when I was persuaded into going to Bath at the time? Then off she goes as though reciting from a book. Was the treating of your breasts for drawing back the milk, madam dear, managed openly or mysteriously? Were you given what she calls restringing draughts? (That Bishop Compton never had much learning himself, and allowed the princesses to study or no as they pleased, which the Princess Anne did not, except it were cookery-books.) Did your face, madam dear, look like that of a woman in labour? Were there only popish doctors present? Is everybody permitted to see the child, both dressed and undressed——'

Mary Beatrice covered her ears. That not only Anne but Mary could be so grossly inquisitive, could be on the side of faceless slanderers who, regardless of consistency, found that each convulsion fit had killed a real but never before acknowledged Prince of Wales, and had occasioned the substituting of yet another child. She must write frankly to Mary, James's favourite daughter, who had seemed so fond of her short-lived brother and sisters when she was still in England.

'My dearest Lemon,' she began, 'I know you will rejoice to hear that your brother has begun to thrive since Lady Powis and I defied the doctors and insisted on a wet-nurse, one Mrs Smith, the wife of a tile-maker at Richmond, whither he has been removed for the pure country air.'

She paused, wondering how to express her hurt without giving offence.

'I fear you are not so kind to me as you used to be, and the reason I have to think so (for since I have begun I must tell you all the truth) is that since I was brought to bed, you have never once in your letters to me taken the least notice of my son, no more than if he had never been born. Only in that which M. Zulestein brought, which I look upon as a compliment you could not avoid, though I should not have taken it so, if ever you had named him afterwards. And now I learn from Mr Skelton, his Majesty's Ambassador at The Hague, that neither you nor the Prince attended the grand fête given by the States General to celebrate my son's birth, and that he is no longer prayed for in your chapel there.'

Mary replied stiffly.

'I am sure that long ere this your Majesty will have heard from others that it was only sometimes forgot to pray for the Prince of

Wales in my chapel. All the King's children shall ever find as much affection and kindness from me as can be expected from children of the same father.'

Of the same father. Was that a sneer? The anonymous lampoons were now informing London that the father of the Prince of Wales was either Fr Petre or the Papal Nuncio. Alternatively that his mother was Mrs Smith, styled by them 'the brick-bat woman'. But no, Mary could not stoop to crediting such vulgar libels; it was just natural jealousy because she herself was barren. Her stepmother wrote again, appealing to her filial love.

'Pray, my dear Lemon, be very kind to your father now. For he receives warnings both from Mr Skelton and M. Barillon, that the Prince your husband is gathering a great armament with intent to invade us. I believe this will be as grievous a shock to you as it is to me, for it is not in your nature to approve so unjust an undertaking.'

Of the warnings to which she referred, she herself could make nothing. Why should Orange wish to invade the dominions of an uncle and father-in-law to whom he still wrote the most dutiful letters? Barillon tried to explain.

'Your Majesty seems unaware of the vast difference the birth of your son has made to the calculations of so ambitious a gentleman as the Prince of Orange. The King your husband came to the throne in middle age; while he had no son, the succession of the Princess Mary seemed assured, which would have meant, in effect, that of her husband.'

It still made no sense to her, and in any case she was absorbed in the joys of motherhood. Her baby throve; he was with her now at Windsor; she watched the dawning of intelligence, his efforts to sit up; this was the real world, all else but vexing rumour. James was absent, inspecting the batteries on the Medway and his fleet anchored at the Nore, when in mid-September a M. Bonrepaux, special envoy of France, urgently requested to see her. Reluctantly she left her occupation of teaching little James the names of his toes by singing him a nursery rhyme.

'Madame,' began Bonrepaux abruptly, 'I have things to communicate to his Majesty of no less concern than the crown he wears; but I find myself referred always to Lord Sunderland. It pleases my lord to scoff at the warnings I bring from his Most Christian Majesty, he insisting they are but a trick to embroil his master in our war against the League of Augsburg.'

She began to say as usual that she never meddled in these public affairs, but the Frenchman swept this aside.

'It is an open secret throughout Europe, madame, that the Prince of Orange intends, as soon as the wind veers east, to come in a hostile manner against these shores—did your Majesty speak?'

She blushed and said no. A foolish little memory had stirred in her: Mary, clinging to her father and watching the weather-vane on the Tennis Court, while her bridegroom cursed 'this damnable east wind'.

'To do so, he must deceive his Catholic allies, the Pope and the Emperor, and very willing are both to be deceived. The Holy Father was much displeased by his Majesty's cold reception of the proposals brought him by Count d'Adda; as for the Emperor, his third wife is that same Princess of Neuburg who was rejected by Lord Peterborough as a bride for his Majesty when he was Duke of York. She has not forgiven the insult, madame. But there is worse. Certain letters have been intercepted in France, which prove that the Prince of Orange has undermined the loyalty of many great men here, in the Army, the Navy, the nobility and even in the Privy Council.'

She stared at him in incredulous horror.

'You do not know what you say, monsieur! Because it was so short and simple, I remember well the Oath of Allegiance given by the Lords Spiritual and Temporal at the Coronation. "I do become your liegeman of life and limb and earthly worship; and faith and truth I will bear unto you, to live and die against all manner of folks. So help me God." Do you ask me to believe that men who have so solemnly sworn could betray their King to a foreign invader?'

He sighed sharply, and raised his shoulders.

'Nowadays, madame, there is often in my mind a remark made by one of your Dukes of Norfolk when he found himself betrayed by his closest friends: "I die because I have not known how to suspect".'

The first fortnight in October was a time of great festivity at Whitehall, for the Queen's birthday fell on the 5th, the King's on the 14th. But this year the balls and receptions were poorly attended; on one excuse or another, a large number of courtiers had retired to their country seats. Those who remained tended to congregate in little groups, sibilantly whispering, heads close together; even in their open conversation they gave the impression of men speaking in code. The drawling voice of Lord Sunderland ridiculed all these rumours of invasion; as Secretary for Foreign Affairs, he was in the best position to know. The armament gathered by the Prince of Orange was designed solely against France.

At supper on his fifty-fifth birthday, James seemed ill at ease, and afterwards, watching a display of fireworks from the leads of the palace, confided to his wife that for the first time he had received no letter from Mary. Then he hastened to excuse his darling.

'Doubtless she is embarrassed how to write in the present situation, torn as she must be between filial and conjugal love. She is a very good wife, but I must believe she will be still as good a daughter to me who have loved her so tenderly, and have never done the least thing to make her doubt it.'

But after they retired that night, he confessed it was not only Mary's silence which had made his birthday such a sad one.

'There is a Declaration scattered about the town, purporting to be published by the authority of my nephew, wherein he says that one of the reasons why he is coming to England is to inquire into the birth of my son. I deem this Declaration an impudent forgery; nevertheless, because the common folk here are easy to be gulled into believing the most monstrous lies, I find it necessary to summon an Extraordinary Council, before which all those who were present at the birth of my son will give their testimony.'

Her heart bled for him. That such a man, nicknamed on his accession James the Just, should be driven to proving in public that he had not imposed a spurious child upon his subjects!

In so miserably anxious a time, she could find peace only in the realm of the nursery. Little James lay naked in her arms while his night-gown was warmed at the fire; the homely voice of Mrs Smith sang a lullaby, and Lady Powis, his Governess, described a novelty just come over from France, a go-cart in which babies could learn to walk without the risk of growing bow-legged.

'It is a wooden frame with wheels, madam, and the baby——'

A knock on the door interrupted her. The King requested the presence of his wife. He was walking up and down the ante-chamber; her heart missed a beat, then raced sickeningly, as she saw that he was wearing armour.

'I have been sitting for the portrait I promised old Pepys, and have not had time to change. An express has brought the news that the Prince of Orange has been sighted in the Downs. Though he assured both the Pope and the Emperor that he was coming peace-fully, he has in fact fifty-six ships-of-war and five hundred trans-ports. Within the next few days, therefore, I must put on armour in earnest.'

He seemed inspired rather than dismayed, and she tried to share his confidence as he told her that his preparations were com-plete; the navy he had created lay in wait to intercept; he had an army of forty thousand men; he was convinced that his people would stand by him to resist a foreign invader; and the bishops, forgetting their late quarrel with him, had composed a special prayer for his safety.

'A campaign of filthy libels I knew not how to fight; the sword I well understand.'

But her blurred vision saw an old man wearing armour, his hand fidgeting with a weapon he had not used for forty years. She pinned her hopes on Lord Dartmouth and the fleet; if they inter-cepted, there would be no land fighting. They failed; and by clever timing, Orange landed at Torbay on the anniversary of the Gun-powder Plot.

She concealed her dismay when James told her that he had appointed her head of a Council of Regency to manage affairs when he went to his troops, rendezvoused at Salisbury. She dreaded lest she should prove quite useless in such a role. But meanwhile she would need all her courage for the moment when she must say good-bye to James; hitherto she had shared all his perils. Whitehall was noisy with the clatter of steel and tramp of martial feet; even the Gentlemen Pensioners had exchanged their gilded poleaxes for sword and pistol; she was the wife of a soldier king now, and she must not fail him.

He had fixed on November 17th for his departure. It lacked a few days of that date when he who hitherto had maintained as far as possible the ordinary routine of Whitehall, failed to appear at dinner. There was news from his army, she was told, which had necessitated a meeting of his general officers here. She forced herself to eat, to talk, to smile; whatever this new crisis was, she must keep her nerve for his sake.

She saw at once, when at last she was alone with him that evening, that he was badly shaken. It appeared that Lord Cornbury, Clarendon's son, and a Colonel Langton had attempted to take their regiments over to the invader, and though the inferior officers and common troopers had refused to follow them, such treachery on the part of commanders was ominous on the eve of battle.

'I summoned the rest, giving them leave to surrender their commissions if they doubted the justice of my cause. With loyal officers at my back I am content to leave the issue to God and my arms, but no general can fight with would-be deserters in his ranks. One and all swore they would serve me to the last drop of their blood, and it did not surprise me that my dearest friend, John Churchill, was the first to take this voluntary oath.'

But that night he was restless, tossing in the bed beside her, muttering to himself. This threat of internal treachery had hit him hard, and it was not the first. Already Sunderland had been denounced in full Council of having, through his wife, sent copies of secret documents to his uncle and her lover, Henry Sidney, at The Hague, and the Seals had been taken from him. Then there was Lord Dartmouth; James had accepted his excuse that weather had prevented him from intercepting the invader, but there were whispers that he was in Orange's pay.

'The safety of my son,' she heard him mutter. 'How to secure the safety of my son.'

87

She put her arms about him and begged for his full confidence, steeling herself to listen quietly while he confessed the fear that gnawed at him. Should he himself fall in battle, or be made prisoner, how would Orange deal with a rival five months old? The child must be taken down to Portsmouth whence he could be transported swiftly into France. She rose to the occasion; very well, she said, she was ready to part with her precious baby if that were for his good.

Winter descended with a hard frost on the day when she watched her two loved ones set out from Whitehall, the King on horseback, the Prince of Wales carried in the arms of Mrs Labadie into a coach. She waved with forced cheerfulness to his wet-nurse, good, simple Mrs Smith, and she managed her farewell to her husband dry-eyed. Only something made her say to him:

'I beg you to be cautious what steps you take in such suspected company, not knowing but the ground you think to stand upon with most security may sink beneath your feet.'

She, like James, was by nature unsuspicious, yet of late treachery was in the very atmosphere, as elusive but as positive as a smell. She found herself glancing at those who composed the Council of Regency, wondering what went on behind those grave faces, whether what they said in their nervous and futile debating was only a smokescreen concealing an intention to betray in their turn. She pulled herself up; James depended on her; she must set herself to understand public business at last, to give orders and study petitions, to keep her head when the Council lost theirs, to confer with Mr Caryll, her secretary, about selling the Monti lands left her by her mother, so that the proceeds might add to James's war-chest.

Then she would write a tactful letter to His Holiness. It was hard to believe that he would wink at the invasion of a Catholic king's dominions, but she remembered that one of his predecessors had made no bones about annexing Ferrara from the Estes.

'With most humble thanks, I acknowledge the paternal goodness of Your Holiness in willing that my son should be admitted to the sacred font of Baptism under Your holy auspices. And I place him once more at the feet of Your Holiness, that he may be protected by the Apostolic Benediction against the incursions of so many and so cruel enemies who at this very moment, sword in hand, are making public manifestation of destroying the Catholic religion and wresting the Succession from this our heir.'

Such practical affairs sustained her during the day; at night there was the empty nursery, the lonely bed, the visions of an old man in armour and a helpless infant. And in those dark hours when her vitality was at its lowest, she could not quite control a suspicion so hideous that it drove her to wandering up and down, up and down. Why did Anne so studiously avoid her? The King might make all the excuses he could invent for Mary's part in this tragedy; she was her husband's victim, or else his unwilling tool. He judged others, she knew, by his own high standards, he who had never forgotten a friend or a service rendered, and was a man of such strong family ties. Often he had related to her how he and his brothers and sisters had stood together in exile. What if Anne . . .

He had not the very faintest doubt of Anne's loyalty. Before he left he had commissioned her favourite bishop to break the news gently if he were killed. He had been so concerned for the grief she must feel when her own cousin and First Gentleman of the Bed-chamber, Lord Cornbury, deserted. Almost his last words had been to beg his wife to have a care of Anne, who had announced herself as pregnant once again. But Anne kept close to her lodging in the Cockpit, and always had some excuse not to see her stepmother.

When daylight came, Mary Beatrice resolutely put away this nightmare doubt. The real world was frightening enough without giving way to imaginations. One of those fits of mass hysteria had seized London, such as she had witnessed during the 'revelations' of Titus Oates. Rumours bred like maggots on a rotten carcase; bells rang 'awkward' to warn of an Irish army pledged to cut all Protestant throats, shops were shut, the Embassy chapels looted, and a priest attempting to save the Blessed Sacrament had his hand severed. The situation was so ugly that she was warned not to leave the precarious safety of Whitehall. The very same folk who had cheered themselves hoarse when at the Coronation she had taken upon herself the liabilities of thousands of small debtors, now shouted threats and obscene epithets outside her windows. She was bewildered by these mobs; the homely, good-humoured Londoners seemed turned into wild beasts, reminding her of a masquerade when the dancers wore animal masks.

The humiliation to which the King had subjected both himself and his wife by calling that Extraordinary Council had not quashed the slanders. A tract assured London that the real mother of the pretended Prince of Wales had been brought over in Orange's invasion fleet. Drawing on her gloves one morning for a walk in the Privy Garden, Mary Beatrice recoiled as though stung by a snake. In the finger of one of them was a devilishly clever caricature of herself and Fr Petre; a glance at it made her retch. Whoever had inserted this obscenity must be someone in her own Household.

On Sunday, November 25th, a letter arrived from her husband. She took it into her closet to read; summoned the messenger and questioned him narrowly; then astounded her ladies by ordering her chair to be brought without delay. The priest was ready to say Mass, they demurred; Mass must be postponed, she told them, her voice unsteady, her lips trembling. She must see the Princess of Denmark at once.

Anne was playing a game of ombre with her Mrs Freeman and two of the Villiers sisters, Lady Berkeley and Lady Fitzharding, when a flustered Gentleman Usher announced her Majesty. Wasting no time in compliments, Mary Beatrice took the Princess by the hand, led her into her bedchamber, and closed the door.

'Anne, I have just received the most alarming news. The King has suffered a seizure; he—he fell down in a fit, and only the most violent bleeding from the nose averted apoplexy. It was occasioned by shock; his Majesty was warned that an intended visit to his out-posts at Warminster was being used by Lord Churchill to betray his person into the hands of the Prince of Orange.'

'Oh what a wicked libel! My dearest Mrs Freeman's husband, who has served him from a boy!'

'I don't think you can have understood what I said, dear. The King in his letter to me makes light of his haemorrhage, but the messenger who brought it tells me that only an immoderate nose-bleed saved him from death.'

'Of course I'm sorry his nose bled,' mumbled Anne, looking

wildly round for her Mrs Freeman, 'but as for being in danger of death, he is a soldier at present.'

Mary Beatrice walked to the fire and back, fighting for calm. She had come with the determination to discover whether the spectre that haunted her was real or imaginary. She tried an oblique attack.

'Why have you had a new backstair constructed between your closet here and the Park?'

It was impossible to tell when Anne blushed; over-indulgence in food and drink had made her face permanently red. But she was a poor actress; she bit her fan, shuffled her feet, and would not meet her stepmother's eyes.

'It is for my convenience. I wish to be able to receive letters from the dear Prince my husband as soon as they arrive. I am so anxious about him, now that he is with the King's army, for he was always easily catched by fevers.'

You are lying, decided Mary Beatrice, horrified by the success of her shot in the dark. You are meditating flight.

'Your uncle, my Lord Clarendon, has confided to me that many times of late he has seen messengers coming and going by means of this new backstair, all in the livery of Bishop Compton, who was suspended for seditious preaching, and recently left London, no man knows whither.'

'*I* know—that is, I know he was suspended, but it is natural that this good Bishop, who was my Preceptor in childhood, should send to ask me how I do.'

'There are other things I have learnt from Lord Clarendon. He tells me that several times he has surprised you making unseemly jests with your women about the birth of my son. And now you express no concern for the news I have given you about your father, who has always been so kind and tender to you, and has never troubled you about religion, as you have owned to me.'

'I've told your Majesty I'm sorry his nose bled. But as for my jesting, it is only what the whole town is doing, for everyone says this child is suppo—sup—well, one foisted on the nation in a cheating way,' said Anne, unable to pronounce 'supposititious'.

91

'When the members of the Extraordinary Council waited on you,' said the Queen, resisting a strong impulse to shake her, 'with the depositions of the witnesses to the birth of my son, you said these were unnecessary, for you had so much duty to the King that his word must be more to you than any depositions. Yet you continue to make these gross jests with your women.'

Anne wriggled, looked at her watch, and mumbled that her Majesty must excuse her, for it was time for dinner. But as she made to rise, Mary Beatrice seized her.

'Dearest dumpling, let us forget your new backstair and Bishop Compton and your jesting. Only think how the rumour about Lord Churchill must have affected the King to have brought on this fit! Churchill owes everything to his Majesty, his fortune, his posts, even his life, which the King saved at the risk of his own when the *Gloucester* was wrecked in '82. Think, think, my dear, what this must mean to a man so trusting as your father!'

She might have clasped a bolster for all the response Anne made.

'He is so sick in mind and body that, so the messenger tells me, he can no longer command his armies. When he returns to London, let him at least find the comfort his wife and daughter can give him. Move over into the royal apartments with me, that you may be at my side to welcome him.'

'I would sooner jump out of the window!'

They stared at each other, speaker and listener alike appalled. 'But dumpling——'

'Don't call me by that insulting name!' screamed Anne. 'I was always mortified by it. You just mock me, madam, because I am well-fleshed. You please to treat me as a child, but I am the Protestant Heiress, as this nation will proclaim me, which you will find out very soon.' She rang her hand-bell wildly. 'To bait me as you have done in my condition! I vow it will be your fault, madam, if I miscarry again!'

A brisk tap on the door, and in bustled Lady Churchill, all anxiety and tenderness, with a flicker of her blue eyes towards the Queen. Her Royal Highness must be got to bed immediately; her Majesty, being herself a mother, would understand the danger of such agitation in a breeding woman. And the blue eyes could not quite conceal their malice, as their owner assisted Anne away.

Mary Beatrice sat flaccid for a long time before she could summon her own attendants. Through her empty mind there echoed words, the most shudderingly horrible in all the Scriptures: Judas went out immediately, and it was night.

4

She was at Mass next morning when a flurry of footsteps, rapidly approaching, distracted her. They were at the Last Gospel; she stood rigid, bracing herself for an expected blow. Just as she genuflected at *Verbum caro factum est*, a woman's voice came screaming along the gallery, accompanied by others attempting to quiet her. The Queen waited in her place until the celebrant had left the altar; as she herself reached the door, the wildly distraught figure of Mrs Buss, Anne's old nurse, flung itself upon her.

'What has your Majesty done with our Princess? She's gone, murdered by papists, and Lady Churchill with her!'

Without waiting for a reply, Mrs Buss scuttered away again, shrieking to everyone she encountered that her mistress had been made away with by order of the Queen. From outside the palace a muffled roar proclaimed the mob; guards at the gates reported that these ruffians were threatening to lynch her Majesty unless she produced their Protestant Princess safe and sound. Mary Beatrice was surprised to find herself quite calm; she sent a message across to the Cockpit, summoning such of Anne's ladies who were on duty. But only Mrs Danvers, a Bedchamber Woman, appeared, who, interrupting her tale by sobs, related what little she knew.

'It was my turn of duty to lie in the anteroom last night, and my sweet mistress says to me, Jane, she says, I am so distressed by what the Queen has said to me that I'm sure I shall not sleep till morning, so don't disturb me till I ring. And even when two hours had passed beyond her usual time for rising, enter the bedchamber I could not, seeing that the door was locked upon the inside.'

Here Mrs Danvers broke down again, and it was some while before she could answer the Queen's question: Who were the Bedchamber Ladies on duty?

'My Lady Churchill and my Lady Berkeley, murdered along with her, I have no doubt, seeing they chose to lie in the closet at the head of the new backstair. I said to my mistress, often and often I said, don't you have no backstair built, madam, up which papists may creep with their consecrated knives. And when at last I summoned her gentlemen to break down the door, what did we find? My sweet mistress's bed open but cold, and her precious self vanished along with her ladies, and a note stuck on the pin-cushion addressed to your Majesty, which I make no doubt was a last appeal to spare her life.'

No, she did not know what had become of this note; she was in such a state about her mistress that she had no time to trouble about such trifles. Perhaps one of her Highness's gentlemen took possession of it. She was beginning to rave again, when the Queen interrupted in an even tone:

'You will find, Mrs Danvers, that the Princess has gone away of her own accord, and will send word of her whereabouts when she thinks fit.'

During the day, fragments of a story were gleaned. One of the sentries on duty by the garden door of the Park had seen a hackney coach drawn up under the shelter of some trees. A roisterer, weaving his way homeward, had nearly cannoned into four shadowy figures, one of them male, ploughing through the mud towards this vehicle, and swore that he had recognized the Princess's voice, choked with laughter, complain that she had lost a shoe. From the City came another detail; just before daybreak Bishop Compton had been seen, booted and spurred, to emerge from his house near St Paul's and usher into his coach a group of masked persons, before he himself mounted the box. And lastly it was found that the lodging of Lord Dorset, Anne's Vice-Chamberlain, was empty and showed signs of a hurried departure.

The mysterious letter on the pin-cushion, though addressed to the Queen, evidently had been left for one of Anne's gentlemen who was in the secret. Next morning the whole town was devouring it in the Gazette. Mary Beatrice forced herself to read it in that organ; Anne's hand might have written it, but if so it was under dictation by someone who knew just how to appeal to popular sympathy.

Prince George, it seemed, had joined the trail of high-born rats who were sneaking off to the invader, and Anne expressed herself as so affected by this surprising news that she had gone away to avoid the King's displeasure. She pulled out all the stops in her conflict of loyalties between husband and father; 'I know not what to do but to follow the one to preserve the other, for I am confident that my husband did not leave the King for any other design than to use all possible means for his Majesty's preservation.' According to the writer, the Prince of Orange had come over for this identical purpose; and after some pious strictures on what she termed 'the violent counsels of the priests, who care not to what dangers they expose the King, so they may promote their own religion', Anne concluded:

'God grant the King a happy end to these troubles, and that his reign may be prosperous, and that I may shortly meet you in perfect peace and safety. Till when, let me beg you to continue the same favourable opinion that you have hitherto had of your most obedient daughter and servant.'

She had a vision of Anne, inky-fingered, whimpering with fatigue, writing the original in her strange spelling, to be corrected by her Mrs Freeman before it was rushed into print. Had she suffered even one pang of remorse? It did not signify; the only thing that mattered was the effect of Anne's treachery upon her father.

He was on his way back with his army for the defence of London; a short note, giving her this news, warned her by its handwriting of his physical state. She heard from others of his recurrent haemorrhages when the Dukes of Grafton and Ormond followed Lord Churchill on his mean flight. In case he had not yet heard of Anne's defection, the Queen gave strict orders that no one was to mention it until she herself had seen his Majesty in private. Then she made what little preparations she could for his return, consulting the doctors on what should be done in cases of haemorrhage, praying for inspiration as to how to break the news, asking for a list of the Household on duty, and choosing from it those gentlemen most congenial to James, selecting for his supper the dishes he liked best. It was pathetically feeble, and she knew it, but it was all she could do.

She had prepared herself to see a change in him; but not this change. His upright back was stooped, his face putty-coloured and freckled with broken veins. He breathed loud and rapid, and in greeting her he stuttered. Slipping to her knees beside his chair, holding his gaunt body in her arms, she stumbled out her tale, labouring to put the very best construction on it, insisting that Anne was wholly under the influence of Lady Churchill, had merely done as she was told.

His face remained vacant, his once firm mouth hung slack. With a thrill of horror she realized that he was temporarily deranged. For a long while he sat there with his lips moving silently. Then he said, like a man talking in his sleep:

'These strokes had been less sensible had they come from hands less dear to me. Pray God my daughter will not miscarry, fleeing by night in her condition.'

5

His own condition was alarming. Suddenly he would fall as if pole-axed, while twin fountains of blood gushed from his nose. The doctors, as usual, disagreed; one school insisted that these haemorrhages prevented a phrensy and should on no account be stanched; the other used lancets on the principle that blood drawn away purposely from one part would stop that which was bleeding naturally. But neither school could be sure whether the blood came from his nose or his brain, and whether, having arrested it, he would continue to bleed inwardly.

The aftermath of his attacks terrified Mary Beatrice even more than the attacks themselves, his extreme pallor of lip, the coldness of his extremities, his double vision and not knowing where he was, often addressing persons not present. These were the very symptoms his brother had suffered immediately before his death. Yet more crucifying was her realization of his mental state; what had happened to him was comparable to the loss of sight or hearing. The least suspicious of men, he now was incapable of trust; he looked askance at the most loyal; he could no more rely on any man than the blind can see.

Except on his wife. That was the one gleam of comfort in this pitch-darkness. He was suddenly more her own than throughout all their years of marriage. No longer did he withdraw behind an armour of reserve. He who had always hated to be fussed, was as obedient as a small child when she bathed his feet in warm water and lemon juice, brought him the twelve grains of nitre his doctors had prescribed, gently inserted lint soaked in blue vitriol up his nostrils before he slept. When he started awake, her name was on his lips; his hand groped for hers even in public; he wept unashamedly in her arms at the news of Anne.

Far from being surprised by Prince George's defection, it now leaked out that Anne herself had written to the invader as early as November 18th, wishing him success, and hoping that by this time George had joined him. Mrs Dawson had it from Mrs Danvers that Anne was not in fact pregnant; she had given out that she was in order to appeal to popular sympathy during her flight. She was now at Nottingham, where Bishop Compton had raised the militia for the protection of the Protestant Princess, and she was allowing her adherents to revive the Association of Queen Elizabeth's day, to destroy all papists (who would include her father) in case Orange was killed in the course of his invasion.

But the spectre that haunted the sick King's mind was the peril of his heir. Orange, already using the royal 'We' in proclamations, was putting out tentacles all over southern England; the Prince of Wales was not safe at Portsmouth, and the fleet being riddled with high-ranking traitors, he might be captured at sea if he were taken thence to France. He must be brought back to London, in spite of the threat of hostile forces lying in between.

For an appalling twenty-four hours there was no news of him; then, at three o'clock of a December morning, Mary Beatrice saw weary coach-horses stumble into the courtyard below the window where she had kept watch. Lady Powis laid her son in her arms, while Mrs Smith triumphantly described how the best baby in the world had slept through all the alarms upon the road. His mother lingered while he was changed and fed, only half understanding the tale of their getting lost in the Forest of Bere, their narrow escape from an ambush of Orange's troops.

James was hunched over the fire when she rejoined him. He had that look of deathly exhaustion which often preceded a haemorrhage, and she was about to summon the physicians when she heard him mutter to himself:

'All is lost. All is lost.'

'But our son is safe!'

He looked at her, but his eyes were unfocused.

'Wildman,' he said. 'Major Wildman; an ancient desperado. He boasts publicly that I shall go to the block like my father, and that my son will be hung in his swaddling-bands.'

The room spun round for a moment, and she had to dig her nails into her palms lest she should faint. The mumbling voice went on beside her:

'It is my son they aim at. He must be got over secretly to France. I care not what they do to me. I have spoken with the Comte de Lauzun and his friend St Victor. They came over on purpose to contrive it. I will trust no Englishman now. Terriesi will lend his coach; there must be two yachts in case either Dover or Gravesend declares for the invader. We must have a conference . . .'

His voice trailed away in a heavy sigh. She took one of his ice-cold hands and began to chafe it, unable to speak, cut to the heart by that sentence, 'I will trust no Englishman now'. That, more than anything, showed her on what a sea of doubt he drifted. The destruction of his capacity to trust extended even to his beloved England; to everyone, except his wife.

'There must be costumes provided. The Queen's Keeper of the Wardrobe can manage it as if for some stage-play. I saved the life of St Victor's father at the battle of Dunkirk; Lauzun served with me in Flanders—was it thirty years ago? I think they will keep faith with me. But the Queen must——'

She could bear no more. Almost roughly she took his grey face between her hands, and forced him to look at her.

'My dearest love, I am here. Talk to *me*; tell *me* what plans these are you are making. I understand that I must be parted from my son again; I am willing, if that is for his safety.'

He blinked once or twice; recognition returned, and he said:

'No, no. It is you who must take the Prince of Wales to France.'

She rose clumsily, everything, even his sick condition, swept clean from her mind by the instinct to fight. She gabbled:

'I cannot obey you. I chose to share your exiles in Flanders and Scotland; I have proved my readiness to stand by you in every misfortune, preferring this to the greatest security. I will try to endure the parting from my son with the same patience as I bore the separation from my Isabella. But from you I cannot be separated, nor have you the right to ask it.'

He did not speak. He moved a little, like a man in pain, and his dull eyes implored her. She refused the appeal; the blood hammered in her veins, and she was reckless.

'You spoke just now of some ruffian who had sworn that you would meet your father's fate. My place is beside you, let it be in the Tower or on the scaffold. I care nothing for crowns and king-doms; only for you. I cannot live without you; if you force me to go I shall die.'

She heard him mutter, 'The safety of my heir', and resorted to a kind of loving blackmail.

'I will take charge of our son's escape on one condition: that you follow us to France. If you refuse this, I swear I will not go.'

'My duty as King . . . if I desert my subjects . . .'

'Of what use would you be to them in the Tower? From over-seas you could regain your throne by the aid of his Most Christian Majesty, whose former offers you so unwisely refused.' (She had not known that she possessed such cunning; she would snatch at any weapon if only she could win.) 'You cannot fight the invader with an army riddled with traitors, nor in your sick state. You have told me that as a soldier you recognize that you have lost a battle; from France you could win the campaign. Only promise me that you will follow, and I will brave every hazard, I will use all my woman's wits to carry our son to safety.'

She had beaten him. He gave her his promise, he who had never been known to break his word. She was the one creature in the world he trusted now, and that to her was bliss.

But, lying sleepless, she had a qualm of conscience. Instead of strengthening, she had weakened him. Treachery had deranged him; had her very love for him completed the collapse of his morale? She crushed down the doubt. When she was a child, she had often heard the story of how the Venerable Jane Chantal, later foundress of the first Visitation convent, had prayed, 'Lord, take all else I have in the world, but leave me my dear husband'.

The moral of that story, so the child Mary Beatrice had been taught, was that we must learn detachment from all creatures. But the wife Mary Beatrice chose to disregard the moral.

6

Holding on to James's promise as to a life-line, she learned her part in the adventure ahead as carefully as she had that for her coronation. She must appear perfectly natural, dine and sup in public, play cards, avoid giving any impression of having secrets. In her closet at dead of night, she received the two gentlemen who were managing the escape and listened to the details they had arranged. The Comte de Lauzun, pugnacious and self-important, did most of the talking, but his much younger friend, St Victor, was the practical planner. He it was who had hired a yacht at Gravesend, ostensibly to carry Lauzun back to France; he kept a rowboat at the Horseferry on the excuse of night fishing; he had obtained from the King a master-key which would enable the little party to pass through Whitehall; he had a coach waiting at the Swan in Lambeth.

On the evening of Sunday, December 9th, the Queen ate well at supper, warned that she would need her strength. In her with-drawing-room afterwards, she played a game of basset, asked for some music, mentioned that she hoped to spend Christmas at Windsor, regretted that the Comte de Lauzun would not be with them for that feast. At ten o'clock, the Bedchamber Gentleman and the pages on duty came to escort the King to his undressing; Lady Strickland and old Turini performed the same office for the Queen.

Instead of her night-gown, she put on with their assistance the costume provided by Francesco Riva, her Italian Master of the Wardrobe, a coarse gown and petticoat, a hooded cloak and sabots.

Both these attendants were to follow her; at intervals during the day, and as inconspicuously as possible, others of her party had gone ahead to Gravesend by water, Sir William Waldegrave, Lord and Lady Powis, Fr Ruga and Fr Galliard, and the Queen's childhood friend, Donna Vittoria, over here on a visit with her brother, Comte Raimonde. So far there had been no hitch, but the real peril was to come.

'*Dio!*' muttered the old nurse fearfully, as rain bit at the windows like grape-shot, 'hark to the storm!'

'It is our friend,' said her mistress. 'It will keep the mob indoors.'

She felt perfectly cool; the only thing she dreaded was the moment of saying good-bye to James, and she had nerved herself for that by his promise to follow. With Lauzun, who scorned any disguise, and St Victor, dressed in canvas slops and a sea-cap, she hurried along the private way to her son's nursery. There were no lights here, and Lauzun carried a muffled lantern to guide them. As he lifted it to warn of a great court-cupboard which intruded into their path, its rays illumined a portrait of Anne Hyde upon the wall. It was only for an instant, but Mary Beatrice caught the shrewd, protuberant eyes of her predecessor; in her wrought-up state she fancied they were saying, *I* would never have extorted a promise which may cost him his throne. But *you* never loved him, riposted Mary Beatrice defiantly.

From this point, memory played her its usual strange tricks. Little trifles were etched; the rest was a blur. Sentries taking shelter in doorways against torrential rain, easily satisfied when St Victor showed them his master-key. The clumsiness of her feet in the wooden sabots. A wildly rocking boat; old Turini huddled beside her, moaning as each wave hit them that they would be drowned; her own concentration on shielding her baby, swathed to pass as a bundle of linen, from the drenching spray. Lauzun cursing because the coach had been taken inside the Swan courtyard out of the weather; a scuffle between St Victor and a watchman who came across to see who these belated travellers were; apologies, grumbles changing into thanks at the chink of money, the watchman's lantern receding towards the inn.

She stood with the two nurses behind a buttress of St Mary's church, a poor shelter from the storm, hugging her baby, staring across the water at a light, fancying that it came from a window in Whitehall, imagining James there, making his preparations to follow.

Extreme physical discomfort, squashed in a coach; the rattle of stones against its panels, a drunken voice shouting that here were escaping papists, and the crisp tones of St Victor from the box, warning that he was armed. Now she was ploughing ankle-deep through marsh to reach another rowboat, and was plagued by a memory of Anne, squealing with laughter on her mean flight through the mud of the Park.

A timeless nightmare, shut up in a cabin, vomiting into an enormous earthenware basin, procured from somewhere by Turini, and distracted by the howls of her son. Even the best baby in the world, who so far had slept soundly, must protest when his wet-nurse was too sick to feed him. Lauzun putting his head round the door at intervals; the cannon shot they heard were from an English squadron in the Downs, to whom they had not dared give the usual salute. Now they were anchored and wallowing in darkness; the gale was too high to risk running on the French coast. It was all part of an incubus she suffered in her old nurse's arms. Light-headed, she fancied she was the reluctant bride, making her first sea-voyage to marry a stranger called Ork.

It was dawn on the second day, she was told, when they reached Calais. The stink of her own clothes and those of her scare-crow ladies made her sick all over again, and she reeled giddily as she was assisted on to the quay. Lauzun, an excellent sailor, offered comfort; she was safe under the protection of his Most Christian Majesty; the Governor of Calais had a lodging prepared for her. There was a chorus of congratulations; how undaunted she had remained in the extremest danger; now she could rest and refresh herself before travelling on to Paris.

'I stay here,' she said hoarsely, 'until the King my husband comes.'

Lauzun fairly goggled at her.

'But madame, I have a letter from his Most Christian Majesty commanding me to bring you and the Prince your son to the Chateau of Vincennes. It is an order, I am his subject, we are now in his dominions, your Majesty is his guest.'

'I will not stir one step until my husband joins me.'

Lauzun's dismay turned to exasperation. He blurted out the real reason why he had undertaken the management of her escape. For years he had been banished from Versailles and had tried one scheme after another to get back into favour. Now not only was he invited to Court, but was given the supreme privilege of assisting at the *Petit Lever* on his return. He saw that she was indifferent to his troubles, and attempted to reason with her. If King James fled, it would be given out that he had abdicated and that the throne was vacant.

'I have his solemn promise,' she said obstinately. 'He never breaks his word.'

'But his Majesty may not be able to keep this promise, madame. We do not know what the situation is in England since we left.'

Her hand sprang to her mouth. She had achieved her mission on borrowed courage, unreasoningly she had taken it for granted that because James had promised he could perform. The hint that he might be under some restraint made her demented; she spoke wildly of recrossing the sea in a fishing-boat to get back to her husband. The only argument that could move her was that this must increase James's difficulties; if she were captured his enemies would hold her as a hostage. A second, more urgent, letter from Louis positively ordered her escort to bring her to Paris without delay, and it was with something approaching force that they took her to Boulogne.

She shut herself up in her lodging, waiting for news. There was none; the English ports were closed and no letters could get through. But there were rumours. The ship in which James had embarked had foundered with all hands; he had been captured by Orange and lay in the Tower; London had risen for him and he was back at Whitehall. Training and a natural dignity enabled her to control her panic when she must receive French personages; in private she could not be still a moment, could neither eat nor sleep.

Here in France where the New Style was observed, it was

Christmas. She forced herself to assist at the three Masses, to receive Holy Communion, to listen while Fr Ruga gently rallied her. His Majesty was in the best of hands, for they were those of God; where was her faith? She had none; it had disappeared as completely as had James's trust in men.

The feast of St Thomas of Canterbury, eighteen days since she had landed. She stared unseeingly out of the window upon a glittering white world of snow. Suddenly she tensed; down there in the courtyard Fr Ruga and Fr Galliard were deep in talk with a man whose boots were splashed to the thigh and his spurs reddened. He turned as she stared; he was Ralph Sheldon, one of her husband's equerries. She flung open the casement, frantically beckoning; the fact that the two priests accompanied Sheldon to her apartments increased her dread of news to be broken gently. The three of them exchanged embarrassed glances; then Fr Ruga took her hand and said:

'*Sacrée Majesté, le Roi est arresté.*'

She turned so pale that they made an instinctive movement to catch her, but she did not feel faint, only numb. She drew long shuddering breaths, trying to understand Sheldon's tale. Something about the King's attempted escape from the Kent coast in a hoy, his being mistaken for Fr Petre by a party of ruffians, his imprisonment in the nearest town, his return to London amid the acclamations of the fickle populace. What had happened since then, Sheldon did not know, but blurted out that when he left, Orange was advancing steadily upon the capital. Fr Galliard broke in with a practical suggestion; the only person to advise and help her in this crisis was his Most Christian Majesty, who had sent word that he would meet her at Chatou.

Her heart was as cold as the snow, banked shoulder-high along the route. At Abbeville a wagon-load of complete Court costumes met her; his Most Christian Majesty was horrified to learn that she was still dressed *en petite bourgeoise*. With the costumes came a maitre d'hotel, valets de chambre, clerks of the chapel, and M. de Saint Viance, Lieutenant of the Bodyguard, at the head of three royal coaches and fifty footmen for her use. Lauzun was enchanted; what marks of honour! Doubtless she would wish to send a note of thanks to the Most Christian King, in which perhaps she would be good enough to describe his own care of her throughout her flight.

Dutifully she wrote, but her nerves were so shattered that it was in bad French, and beginning in the third person, she concluded in the first.

At Beaumont on January 5th, she was trying to swallow some breakfast when two great personages were announced, the Comte d'Armagnac, Grand Ecuyer, and the Duc de St Simon, representing King Louis and the Dauphin respectively. She knew by their expression that they had news to give her, and waited like a prisoner expecting sentence of death. They had to repeat themselves several times before she understood. James had landed at Ambleteuse and was on his way to join her.

'Oh how happy I am! I am the happiest woman in the world!'

They looked at her, amazed. She was as flushed and bright-eyed as a child; she did not ask them one single word about the state of her husband's kingdom; all she wished was to know if he was well, had he suffered any more of his nose-bleeds, how long would it be before he could reach her?

Her happiness had an element of hysteria. She had to bite her lips to keep from laughing when Lauzun lectured her on Etiquette. On her bridal visit to France, Versailles was only in the making; now it was the most splendid Court in the world, and it was Etiquette, no less than its material magnificence, that made it so. He did not know precisely which planets which revolved about the Sun King would be at Chatou; certainly not Mme de Maintenon who, though privately married to the King after the death of Queen Marie Therese, never appeared on public occasions; and of course not Mme de Montespan. She was part of his Most Christian Majesty's past to which one must never refer since he had returned to the duties of his religion. Possibly Monsieur and Madame; if so, she must kiss them both, but Monsieur first. Then there might be . . .

She could not attend. The shock of joy had made her delirious.

Driving along the icy roads next day, she heard what sounded like the approach of an army, trumpets brazening, kettle-drums rat-tatting, a confusion of hooves and wheels. Her own little cavalcade halted, and Lauzun appeared at her window, wreathed in smiles.

'Madame, the moment has arrived! And what a royal welcome! I have counted more than a hundred coaches, at least three detachments of the Maison Militaire; the livery of both Monseigneur and Monsieur proclaims their presence.'

He bustled away to give orders; all must alight; his Most Christian Majesty was indifferent to cold, and even the Prince of Wales must be carried out of the coach to hear an address of welcome. She stood in the snow and waited, fearing that old temptation to laugh in the wrong place. But what she saw was as beautiful as a ballet, as impressive as a military parade. The snowbound world made a perfect background to those uniforms of blue, white and red, the Cent-Suisses in their parti-coloured doublets and ruffs, the Negro cymbal-player as gorgeous as a sultan, the spotted horses from Poland, all with white bridles tied up with crimson, every livery ablaze with Louis's device of the sun. Smooth as a well-oiled machine, each courtier fell into his appointed place behind a tall figure, distinguished by a hat in that bare-headed company. The hat was swept right off, as Louis addressed the infant Prince of Wales in an elegant oration.

She was touched by his magnanimity. Not only had her husband harboured rebellious Huguenots, but had refused with hauteur repeated offers of French aid. The pomp of her reception was designed to make her feel that far from being a poor fugitive, she was a specially honoured guest. Exquisitely polite but never fulsome, he listened attentively to everything she said; and when she told him how touched she had been by the marks of affection shown her by the French people on her journey from Calais, he made the perfect reply.

'I am indeed glad to learn from your Majesty that my people have entered into my feelings. They could not find a better means of paying court to me.'

The Dauphin and Monsieur were presented, the former now a tall, round-shouldered man, still walking uncertainly on his tiny feet, Monsieur as highly scented and beribboned as ever, and becoming pot-bellied. She had a sudden memory of comforting herself the last time she was in France that though she was going to marry a stranger, at least she would never have to see these extraordinary people again. When at last she was ushered into the royal coach, a hamper of exquisite food and wine was presented to her by footmen.

'His Most Christian Majesty will expect you to make a hearty repast, madame,' Lauzun hissed into her ear, 'though he himself never eats between meals.'

The transition from acute anxiety to joy had combined with the cold to bring on an attack of neuralgia, but she did her best to eat, and to listen while Louis explained that he had decided to prepare the chateau of St Germain-en-laye, his own birthplace, instead of Vincennes, for her residence. Unfortunately St Germains had been neglected since the Court moved to Versailles eight years previously, but he had done his best to make it worthy of her, and she must be sure to tell him if there was anything he had overlooked. He described in his inimitable way, never making a meaningless or unnecessary gesture, the furnishings he had ordered, the toys he had provided for the Prince of Wales, the number of orange-trees he had transported from Versailles, the choosing of her Majesty's apartments to give her the matchless view over the Seine.

But then suddenly he took her hand, and kissed it, and said with endearing playfulness:

'Soon, madame, I shall be bringing to St Germains a gentleman of your acquaintance whom you will be very glad to see.'

6

St Martin's Summer

1

'*C'est bon*,' approved Mère Priolo, surveying the papers and the souvenirs the Queen had taken from her special cabinet. 'From this point in our history we have much material to aid us.'

The Queen smiled, and continued to cut off the gold buttons, each with a pearl in the centre, from several pairs of gloves; she had been told they might fetch as much as 1,000 livres if she sold them. The contents of that special cabinet had released a flood of bittersweet memories. Letters in a large childish handwriting between ruled lines; travel-stained dispatches, full of cant names, dashed off on a drum-head in the midst of a campaign. Old news-sheets and tracts, abusing or defending persons long dead. The programme of an opera, blotched with a drop of wine from the gay party afterwards; a fan, a silver-bound hornbook, some pressed flowers.

She said, to test the steadiness of her voice:

'How quickly this summer is passing. Already there is a glint of bronze on the chestnuts, and it is no longer warm enough for us to compose these memoirs in the garden. Soon I must be returning to that dreadful St Germains.'

She had not thought it dreadful when first she lived there. It was just a temporary lodging, such as she had known in former exiles, a halt on their return voyage to dear England. And any place was home so long as James was with her. Certainly St Germains was cold, even in summer, with a continual wash of air from the hills, and despite Louis's lavish gifts of tapestries, carpets and fine furniture, it retained an air of melancholy neglect. Yet with James at her side she could truly admire that breath-taking view over the Seine to distant Paris, as they took their daily promenade upon the long, wide terrace designed by Le Notre.

'I shall work at my memoirs here,' decided James, inspecting the top storey of the chateau, glassed all round by Francis I so that he could watch his hounds in the forest.

The old King had been to extraordinary pains to preserve these memoirs, sending nine tomes of them to Terriesi, who had undertaken their transport to Paris by way of Tuscany. His near obsession with them was one of the few indications he gave of how he had suffered from incessant vilifying, both as Duke of York and King. To those who did not know him, he appeared almost indifferent to his misfortunes. He spoke as though they had happened to someone else, relating trifling details of his rough voyage in a fishing-smack from Rochester, of bacon fried in a pan with a hole in it, which had to be plugged with a tarry rag, of ale drunk from a cracked can, and so on. When questioned about the reasons for his flight, he withdrew instantly into his shell, explaining them in a sort of formula, as though writing his memoirs.

'Things were come to that extremity, by the general defection of my Peers, officers and clergy, as gave little reason to trust those who remained. I have ventured my life very frankly on several occasions for the good and honour of England, and am ready to do so again, old as I am. Yet I thought it not convenient to be made a prisoner of the Prince of Orange.'

Uneasily Mary Beatrice wondered whether he was shielding her; the promise she had extorted during the collapse of his morale was a secret between them. His bastard son, the vigorous young Duke of Berwick, raged against whoever it was had persuaded him to flee; it had played straight into the hands of the invader, and had forfeited the nation's respect. But she could not regret her loving blackmail; he was safe; and in comparison with that his throne was as nothing.

Safe but permanently scarred. His strong constitution had enabled him to defy the threat of apoplexy; his spirit was wounded beyond all healing. Under his deep and sincere gratitude to Louis, she sensed the lacerations his pride suffered in being under an obligation. A shutter came down over his face when either of his daughters was mentioned. He turned the conversation when anyone inveighed against the scandalous treachery of Churchill. She guessed that those wounds were deepest which were most carefully concealed.

She set herself to make St Germains as home-like as possible, to create a background of repose. But her hope that they could live here as private persons was quickly dispelled. They were the guests of le Roi Soleil; formal visits must be made to Versailles. Unless they took their appointed place in this new Olympus, they would risk being regarded as having fallen not only from regal power but from royal rank. And there could be no question of such visits until they had mastered the mysteries of Etiquette.

Monsieur, a mine of information on these mysteries, took upon himself Mary Beatrice's instruction. She dreaded these lessons, for it appeared to her that personages at Versailles were hardly sane upon the subject, and she had constantly to stifle her mirth. Enveloping her in a cloud of strong perfume from the musk-apple he wore on a chain, he illustrated his lectures with little sketches he had drawn of Versailles, beginning at the Place d'Armes. Further to guide her, he had made a list of the principal honours, the Door, the Coach and the Hat.

'Only a very few are privileged to be greeted at the Door or the Coach; if your Majesty is ignorant of the rank of those you encounter, observe the management of the Hat. If the King merely puts his hand to it, those he thus greets are but of the nobility. For Princes of the Blood he will take it half off, holding it either against his ear or in his hand according to their degree. But what chiefly concerns us is the question of sitting.'

He very neatly sketched an armchair, an unarmed chair and a stool.

'The first of these, the *fauteuil*, is for those of the Blood, the *pliant* is for duchesses, and below that rank come *les dames à tabouret*. After exhaustive discussion, it has been decided that while Monseigneur may have only a *pliant* in the presence of King James, he may occupy a *fauteuil* in your own, but only on condition that the Prince of Wales has a *pliant* in the presence of his Most Christian Majesty. Then there is the Fan. It must not be opened in the presence of the Dauphine, except for use as a tray to hand things on . . .'

It was a full fortnight before such questions, as serious as if the fate of nations depended on them, were decided, and their Majesties of England received a formal invitation to Versailles. A very different Versailles from the palace in embryo the bride Mary Beatrice had been shown. Her feet were frozen from contact with marble floors by the time she ascended the Grande Escalier, over the railings of which the Court, in strict order of precedence, watched her slow ascent like spectators in a playhouse. The Galerie des Glaces dazzled her with its seventeen enormous windows reflected in the same number of giant mirrors, its solid silver consoles and vases, and its glittering candelabra. There appeared to be no means of heating it, and even now, in the depths of winter, several of the

110

windows were open in accordance with Louis's passion for fresh air. No one must wear gloves in his presence, and everywhere she looked she saw hands blue with cold. She was not surprised to see a chip of ice floating in her glass when waiters in blue livery handed a tray of liqueurs.

Moving with incomparable grace towards a window, Louis invited her to view the gardens. She had the impression of a world of water, jets shooting an immense height into the air, cascades rushing down steps of rosy marble. Only on such a very special occasion as this, he told her, did all his fifteen hundred fountains play at once, for they were capable of using up a river. She was touched by so many delicate indications of how he had laid himself out to honour the exiles. He had placed *fauteuils* for them slightly higher than his own; he watched narrowly to see that the personages who came to be presented made the proper obeisance; and he took his hat right off each time he addressed James.

The great clock above the Cour de Marbre began to strike the hour, and immediately Louis rose. Her Majesty, he said, had been so gracious as to express a wish to call upon the Dauphine; he would escort her thither, but only as far as the door, since it was not etiquette for his daughter-in-law to sit in his presence, and she fancied herself unwell. From the hint of disapproval in his tone, Mary Beatrice gathered that physical needs or disabilities were not supposed to have any place in the solar system of Versailles. Meanwhile, said Louis, he had arranged a private talk between '*mon frère*' of England, himself, and certain French Ministers of State.

The Dauphine, a plain young woman who did indeed look ill, conducted her to the centre one of three armchairs. When she was seated, her hostess sat down upon her right, Madame (untidier than ever, still in riding-dress, and growing stout) on her left; the three Enfants de France, the Dauphine's sons, came to perch upon miniature *fauteuils* opposite. The eldest being but six, their feet did not reach the ground when they were seated. These preliminaries achieved, the duchesses entered and occupied their *pliants*.

'They ought to have kissed the hem of your Majesty's gown,' Madame observed in a loud whisper. 'Monsieur will have something to say to them later.'

Conversation was stilted, and Mary Beatrice was glad when the striking of the clock brought the punctual Louis to the door to escort their Majesties of England to the coach which was one of his many magnificent presents. James was silent on the drive back to St Germains; it was not until they were alone that night that he told his wife what had passed in private talk with Louis and his Ministers.

'His Most Christian Majesty has proposed my regaining England by way of Ireland. According to his civilian envoy on the spot, there should be no difficulty in raising an army of fifty thousand recruits. He was good enough to offer me French troops, but I expressed my desire to recover my dominions with my own subjects. Gratitude, however, will compel me to accept his offer of a hundred noble French volunteers, and money to pay my forces.'

She was stricken. He had only just returned to her arms, and he looked so old and worn.

'But you have told me that your purpose in coming to France was to be within call when your subjects return to their duty and invite you home. Did you not refuse the offer of several loyal lords to rally your army and drive out the usurper, because it would cause a civil war?'

'I owe everything to his Most Christian Majesty, even to the clothes on my back. In his war against the League of Augsburg, he is now upon the defensive, and it is his policy to divert the Prince of Orange by attacking him from Ireland.'

The cold world of politics. Louis had been so generous and unfailingly kind that she had not guessed his underlying ruthlessness. She had never learnt that the king and the man are two different persons, and had been hurt and bewildered when Charles made no scruple about banishing 'the best of friends and brothers' if it suited his statecraft of the moment. And now Louis, solely in the interests of France, was using a broken old man, his pensioner and guest, to make a diversion.

2

James left on February 20th, equipped by his host with everything deemed necessary for a king on campaign. There was a silver table service for formal occasions, another in silver-gilt, a field-bed, a toilette, his Most Christian Majesty's own travelling-chariot, and even his sword, unbuckled and presented at the last moment with the graciously expressed hope that it would prove as fortunate to James as it had to its owner. As for the Queen, she was inundated with invitations to Versailles to cheer her in her husband's absence.

She did her best to respond with gratitude, but the brief letters she received from James made it hard to take part in festivities. The Irish recruits were raw and undisciplined; artillery was practically non-existent, the magazines empty, the muskets so unserviceable that only one in twenty would fire. Veteran troops were desperately needed; so also was money, for a chestful of gold had been lost when the vessel containing it sank at the Pont de Cé, and in Ireland itself there was none. To Mary Beatrice, Ireland was like another planet; she could not envisage the conditions there. All she understood was that James needed money, and that she must try to obtain it for him. It was her first taste of something that was to plague her for the rest of her life: poverty and its attendant humiliations.

She had been warned not to apply to Louis direct, but she had received the impression that his morganatic wife had more influence with him even than his Ministers, and that the real policy of France was worked out in her apartments. Mme de Maintenon had called at St Germains several times already, but so far nothing but compliments had been exchanged. Mary Beatrice determined that she would swallow her pride and make an appeal, though she did not find Mme de Maintenon a sympathetic character. She was the personification of piety and the touchstone of correctness; her marble-dark eyes softened only when she bent over the cradle of the Prince of Wales, and it was known that her excellence as a governess to Louis's bastards had resulted in his marrying her when she was forty-seven. That and her even temper; she was always entirely in command of herself.

'I know your Majesty will excuse me,' said Mme de Maintenon, taking out a netting-needle with which she made a narrow kind of lace. 'I try to model myself upon the Valiant Woman in the Book of Proverbs, whose hands were never idle. I have heard so much of your Majesty's piety that it will be a privilege to welcome you into the little circle I have gathered round me, the Abbé de Fénélon, Père de la Chaise, his Most Christian Majesty's confessor, and Monseigneur de Noailles, Archbishop of Paris. Our conversation is confined to spiritual matters, just as my time is spent in charitable works. Your Majesty must do me the honour of visiting St Cyr, the school for noble young ladies I have established, where I endeavour to teach them the emptiness of the world. Oh, if only the young could realize the boredom which devours the great and the trouble they have in occupying their time! Whole evenings wasted at the card-table!'

Mary Beatrice was ashamed to find herself wondering how much that gold netting-needle, decorated with miniature paintings, had cost. She tried a hint.

'Certainly it gives me pain, Mme la Marquise, to see thousands of francs squandered on games of reversi and lansquenet, when I think how the King my husband could use even a fraction of these sums in his campaign.'

'I hope your Majesty will pardon me, but I do not like being addressed as Mme la Marquise. So far as possible I live as a private person at Versailles. I have tasted the pleasures of this life, I had an incredible favour forced on me as the price of persuading our King to return to his religious duties, but I swear to your Majesty that all these conditions produce in me a fearful emptiness, and only the love of God keeps me from going under. I am grateful to his Most Christian Majesty, but I long only to save my soul.'

She rose.

'Your Majesty must excuse me if I make my visit short. I have been up since six this morning, for I must take time for Mass and my prayers while others sleep. Once they begin to enter my room I have not a moment to myself. The King will come as usual to my bedchamber after his *coucher* to work with his Ministers there, when all my women must be dismissed. Mine is not a glorified body, and it does not enter the King's head that I must lie for hours without relieving myself until the Ministers take their leave. I swoon often with the constraint, but I try to offer it up for the conversion of sinners.'

Desperate now, Mary Beatrice tried a direct appeal.

'Dear Mme de Maintenon, you spoke just now of charitable works. It would be indeed an act of charity if you would mention to the King how much my husband is in need of arms and money.'

'I was born in the precincts of a prison, and my long experience of poverty has taught me its blessings. I have no ambitions, either for myself, my relations, or my friends, and take care to meddle in nothing. Your Majesty must pardon me, but I have made it a rule never to ask the King for any material favours; but you may rest assured that the welfare of your royal husband is a subject of my prayers.'

There was but one thing for it; she must practise economy, and send what she saved to James. He had refused the lavish pension originally offered by Louis, accepting only so much as would enable him to maintain his exiled household in decency. But that household was swollen almost daily by the stream of refugees who preferred exile to taking the Oaths to a usurper; the problem of feeding them was formidable. Then there were the entertainments at Versailles; she must have a new costume for each, and she was expected to return such hospitality. She took counsel with Mr Dicconson, her Comptroller; how much could she save if she retired into a convent while the King was in Ireland? He reckoned it up and named a sum. But she was the guest of his Most Christian Majesty, he reminded her, whose consent she must obtain.

She chose an occasion when she was invited to Marli, the splendid hermitage where Louis played at being a private person surrounded by those with whom he felt most at ease. It was a summer evening, and the privileged guests were conveyed along the canal to Marli in the little fleet of gondolas presented to Louis by the Doge of Venice. Alone with Louis in his gilded boat, she did her best to admire the flowers in the parterres on either side, changed overnight so that none ever withered, Neptune driving his sea-horses through a great basin, the soft music played from the bosquets, and the swans on their artificial mere. Meanwhile she rehearsed to herself how most tactfully to broach her plan.

'Sire, I wish very much to visit the convent at Chaillot which was founded by Queen Henriette Marie, my husband's mother. In my childhood my desire was to enter the convent of the Visitation where I was educated, and it would be like going home if I could stay at Chaillot.'

'But on a short visit only, I trust, madame. It would be most unwise of your Majesty to bury yourself in a convent, for the world would say that you had despaired of your husband's restoration. Pardon, but in misfortune it is most necessary for us to remain in the public eye and preserve a bold front.'

Having gained her point, she dared not mention the real reason why she wished to retire to Chaillot. She sensed his disapproval of even a short visit, but with his unfailing generosity and thoughtfulness he gave her presents which would make her stay cheerful. The good nuns possessed no mirrors, so he gave her one concealed in a book-cover decorated with turquoises. Doubtless she would spend much time with her needle, and so he begged her to accept a work-box of porcelain and ivory, with a handle of carved coral; inside were gold scissors in a sheath, and *etuis* of the same precious metal. He had ordered the best apartments in the convent to be prepared for her, and promised to send her news by express directly it came to him from Ireland.

So for the first time she set out on what was to be so familiar a journey, a two hours' drive with several crossings of the Seine. She saw, pricking up through the trees on a hillside, a small severe spire above a lofty dome, and heard a grave bell ring out its summons to the Divine Office. It was like a return to childhood; the pervading smell of polish, the living silence, the unanxious poverty, the soft footsteps and smiling cheerfulness, the smooth routine which was so like and yet so unlike that of gorgeous Versailles. Dinner and supper in the refectory had something almost sacramental about them; she shared the sisters' plain fare, ate like them at scrubbed wooden tables, listened to the nun in the little wall-pulpit reading from some spiritual book, and joined in that long but well-remembered Latin grace before and afterwards. For the first time since the turmoil of the revolution, she felt soothed and quiet; even her anxiety and longing for James could be kept under control.

It was not only in obedience to Louis's wishes that she made her first visit to Chaillot a short one. Letters from her secretary, John Caryll, told her that there was business at St Germains which required her presence. She was James's factor during his absence; at long last she really must try to understand public affairs. While she had been away, some very unexpected letters had arrived, deciphered by Mr Caryll. One after the other, the very men who had betrayed their lawful King were now ready, it seemed, to betray the usurper. Godolphin, Danby, Pembroke, Shrewsbury, Admiral Russell, and even Churchill, created Earl of Marlborough, wrote to express their penitence and offer their services. Best of all, Churchill hinted that Anne had experienced a change of heart.

'Yet they continue to hold office and accept titles from the usurper, madam,' Caryll warned her. 'I would be cautious in trusting such double traitors.'

'They write that it is only to serve their lawful King more effectively. And did not St Peter deny Our Lord and repent?'

'Your Majesty does not believe in the existence of hypocrisy.'

'It is true I cannot suspect evil, and I have not the spirit of intrigue. But it is my duty to encourage those who would redeem their former treachery. Was not General Monck a rebel, and yet it was he who brought about the return of King Charles.'

This was said with simple pride to show her knowledge of English history, and she set herself to master codes wherein she might establish a correspondence with these great men. She would answer them with frankness and dignity, making no promises of reward. Truly believing in their repentance, she would appeal to their honour; certainly she would not descend to bribes. According to what they wrote, all they desired in return for sending over useful information was a pardon in writing from the King; and knowing James, she was very sure that would be given them.

The double traitors had their own go-betweens; she needed brave men who were willing to risk the extremely dangerous mission of carrying her letters to the consistently loyal. One such volunteer presented himself in the person of young William Fuller, a humble refugee. He had the face of a saint in a stained-glass window, was often to be found praying alone in the chapel, and scarcely opened his mouth without uttering some pious sentiment. He was ready to risk prison or death, he told the Queen, by smuggling her letters over to England.

From one of these trips he did not return, but not because he had suffered either prison or death. Caryll broke the news to her as gently as possible; the saintly Mr Fuller had taken her letters straight to the Prince of Orange, from whom he was now enjoying a pension. Lords Dartmouth and Preston were in the Tower; others under house arrest; and Fuller boasted of his cleverness in the Gazette.

'I shall first set down the true copy of a letter writ by the late Queen to Lord Dartmouth, which being writ obscurely, I had the honour to make the writing appear to his present Majesty, his royal consort, and several noble lords then present at Kensington, by the steam of compound sulphur. Which secret was imparted to me by the late Queen at St Germains, in order to my conveying the same to her correspondents in England enclosed in a mutton-bone.'

Caryll was shocked to find her Majesty convulsed with laughter.

'He credits me with such ingenuity, I who find it a labour to learn even the simplest code! And a mutton-bone; oh, I wish I *had* thought of that!'

'Fuller has published a tract, madam,' said Caryll soberly, 'in which he sets forth a new and marvellous variation of the slanders on the Prince of Wales's birth. He swears that a certain Mrs Gray, being with child by the Earl of Tyrconnel, was most obligingly escorted by Lady Tyrconnel from Dublin to St James's to be brought to bed of a pretended prince.'

Well, she must try to be more careful in her choice of agents, though suspicion was something left out of her character. Meanwhile there were rumours of a major engagement in Ireland; she was wakened one morning by the peal of church bells and crowds cheering; King James had won a great victory on the banks of the River Boyne. For twenty-four hours the rejoicings continued; bonfires had scarcely burnt themselves out when the news was contradicted. With a force less than half his enemy's, James had fought a defensive action, lingering on the stricken field long after all hopes of retrieving the disaster were at an end. Someone let out in her hearing that on his return to Dublin he had suffered so violent a return of his haemorrhages that the doorpost of the house was stained crimson.

But he was safe, and he was coming back to her. That, now and always, was all she could desire.

He hurried back to France because, before the news of the Boyne, Louis had written promising him forces for a descent on England, where there was massive discontent against the usurper. But Louis, still the most kind and generous of hosts, was first and foremost King of France, and a realist. The Boyne had altered everything. Advised by his most astute War Minister, Louvois, this was the reply made by his Most Christian Majesty to all James's pleadings.

'My life has been a chain of disappointments and misfortunes,' James remarked to his wife, after a visit to Versailles when Louis had feigned illness as an excuse not to see him. 'But this, I must confess, is the greatest trial of patience I have yet endured.'

She for her part thanked God that in this bitter hour she had comfort to offer him; she was again with child. She was hurt to find that both he and his advisers regarded her condition almost entirely from the political angle; it disproved definitely that old slander that she was incapable of bearing any more children at the time of her son's birth. Invitations were sent to the English Privy Council, the Lord Mayor and Sheriffs, and the hot Whig, Dr Chamberlen, to be present at her lying-in; was she to be subjected a second time to the nightmare of a public delivery? Ashamed of her relief when none of these invitations was accepted, she struggled to share James's joy when a change of French policy made it convenient for Louis to finance a descent on England. Far gone in pregnancy, and always subject to depression at such times, she forced herself to take a cheerful farewell of her gaunt old warrior of sixty, setting out on yet another expedition with the eagerness of a boy.

It was a period she strove to forget; she was attacked by an emotion she had experienced only once before in her marriage: resentment against James. The French fleet which was to have taken him over was almost destroyed in the bay of La Hogue, and there was nothing to keep him from returning to her side. Yet he lingered, scandalizing his allies by an outburst of national pride;

none but his brave English sailors could have achieved such a feat.

Her resentment vanished like some evil mist when, two days after his return to St Germains, she bore a daughter in the presence of all those personages of Versailles who were not with Louis at the siege of Namur. In case the child proved a girl, a name had already been chosen, Louise Marie. But when her husband laid the little thing in her arms, he said of the last of that long line of children who had brought him so much sorrow:

'See what God has given to be the consolation of our exile.'

And henceforth Louise Marie was 'La Consolatrice'.

3

It was from this moment that St Germains became home to Mary Beatrice. While as ready as ever to venture his life in fighting to regain his throne, James was resigned to exile. He set the House-hold at St Germains on a permanent footing; as the river of exiles became a flood, French officials were replaced by English, Scots and Irish, familiar faces were everywhere. No distinction was made between Catholics and Protestants; here at least he could achieve his ideal of liberty of conscience. And though the salaries he could afford were small, he was as strict as of old in seeing that they were punctually paid.

For Mary Beatrice, St Germains became during these years almost dearer than St James's. It was the private nest she had built; there were no reminders here of Anne Hyde. And for the first time in all her years of wedded life, she could give herself up to the joys of motherhood. Against a background of revolution and acute anxiety, she had not been able to concentrate on her son; happy memories began with the birth of La Consolatrice. A child of exile, she knew nothing of the unhappy past.

A portrait hung at St Germains, painted by the Italian, Gennari, when the Prince of Wales was eighteen months old. Solemnly furious, he was perched upon a cushion, holding a stuffed bird in one hand and pointing to it with the other. Louise Marie was never solemn; she seemed to have been born with a smile. He was still in leading-strings, with the wadded cap called a black pudding on his head to save it from bumps if he fell, when his father displayed a rare anger with him. Lady Strickland, his Sub-Governess, reported his screaming in some childish fear, and he was lectured sharply by the King on the baseness of fear in one destined to fight for his inheritance. Louise Marie was not afraid of anything.

She was two when she was carried in her nurse's arms to witness the tremendous ceremony of her brother's breeching. He was grave as the tailor helped him into his first suit, while all the exiles crowded round to criticize and make suggestions; the baby waved her coral teething-ring and crowed with delight. It was only when his miniature sword was buckled on that he smiled.

From his birth he had been first and foremost the Prince of Wales, the rightful Heir of England, and with his own hand the King drew up twenty-eight rules to be observed in his management, for there was the constant risk of his being got at by some ill-wisher, either morally or physically. So there must be constant and wearisome surveillance; an embargo was laid upon presents of sweetmeats as a precaution against poison; there must be no whispering to him in corners, since St Germains was a happy hunting-ground for spies; all books and songs must pass his Governor's censorship, and no children might play with him unless invited.

Once he was out of the petticoats, he displayed far too much courage for his mother's peace of mind. His favourite game was soldiers; he sat entranced while Berwick, who had apartments at St Germains which he occupied when the French army was in winter quarters, described to him sieges and battles. When the Dauphin's boys came on a visit, the neglected gardens were noisy with toy kettle-drums and trumpets, shrill voices shouting orders. Much older than he, they were inclined to bully, and to sneer at a disinherited prince; when this happened, La Consolatrice rushed to his defence, beating the Enfants de France with her silver-bound hornbook. From the first dawning of intelligence she seemed determined to live up to her nickname.

Surely, thought Mary Beatrice, this little girl must heal the wounds inflicted by those other daughters, who were now at such savage feud that Mary had forbidden Anne to appear at Court. But the roots of James's love for them went back to his youth. He shut himself up in his own apartments when news came of Mary's death at thirty-two; he read and re-read with tears the ill-spelt, clumsily phrased letters of repentance from Anne. Not even Cordelia could compensate him for the desertion of Regan and Goneril.

'She seems a merry angel lent to us from heaven, rather than a human child,' remarked Lady Strickland, watching her charge, just freed from the leading-strings, dance along the terrace.

Louise was the picture of health in contrast with her delicate brother, who, in the bleak harshness of St Germains, was plagued by coughs and agues. From morning to night she sang and danced and laughed, interrupting herself in some game to rush and kiss her mother, tapping on the glass of her father's room where he worked at his memoirs, just to tell him how much she loved him. She was so enchanting in her pearl satin gown and the wired cornette set upright on her curls, when Largillière painted her with her brother, that the Duc de Berri, the Dauphin's second son, was rumoured to have lost his heart to her.

'It would be a great match for one in your daughter's unhappy circumstances,' observed Madame. 'Berri has not the brains of a louse, but he is Old Piety's pet, if that is any recommendation.'

Madame was now a frequent visitor at St Germains, and had shed the hostility which for a long while had puzzled Mary Beatrice. It was Lauzun, who knew everything about everybody, who explained that Madame had been furiously jealous.

'She cherishes a secret *grand passion* for our King, who remarked in her hearing that you were always a queen in prosperity, and in adversity are an angel. From this Madame leaped to the conclusion that he was enamoured of you.'

It seemed too ridiculous to credit, but Madame was a very strange character. Her hatred of Mme de Maintenon, whom she called Old Piety, the Manure Heap, and other opprobrious nicknames, amounted to an obsession, and indeed she appeared to loathe everyone at Versailles except 'the Great Man'. She had been known to box her son's ears in the Galerie des Glaces, and in general was so rude that she was referred to as the bear in its den. Red as a lobster from hunting, she now appeared unheralded at St Germains, in what time she could spare from writing her daily twenty or thirty letters to her German relations, on purpose, it seemed, to regale Mary Beatrice with the malicious tales which were meat and drink to her.

'I suppose you know that the retreats the King your husband makes at the monastery of La Trappe expose him to derision. He turns monkish, they say, for want of something better to do.'

Mary Beatrice made no answer, keeping her head lowered while she took tiny stitches in the gown she was making for her daughter's First Communion.

'The King your husband,' went on Madame, crossing one stout leg in a riding-boot over the other, 'would have won the Irish campaign had he taken the advice of Marshal von Rosen, my countryman, to force Londonderry to surrender by driving all civilians under the walls and letting them starve in the sight of the garrison. He is far too squeamish for a soldier; war must be all-out if it is to succeed. When his Deliction, my papa, regained the Palatinate, the countryside was so devastated that some cook-shops sold only human flesh. I have often wondered how it tasted. I have never really had enough to eat since I lived with her Deliction, my Aunt Sophy, in Hanover, for French food is detestable. I can see us now, feasting on a mammoth dish of sausages, just shown to the fire, while one of my aunt's husband's mistresses read aloud to us the spicier parts of Rabelais.'

Mary Beatrice reached for her stiletto to make a button-hole.

'I believe I was the only one at Versailles who truly mourned the Dauphine, with whom I talked German, though she had the accent of a peasant. Of course the Old Swipe made the doctors see to it that the Dauphine was never well after the birth of her third son. I cannot say positively that the Old Horror poisoned Louvois, though poisoned he undoubtedly was; and I would not put it past her to——'

'Madame!' Mary Beatrice raised a flushed face from her needlework. 'Although the duties of our station do not permit us to observe so strict a silence as the monks of La Trappe, we are not less obliged than they to govern our tongues in such a manner as not to offend our neighbours.'

Not at all put out, Madame twinkled at her with little button eyes, sinking her treble chins into her riding-stock which was twisted round under one ear like a halter.

'I am very frank and human and always say exactly what I think. Gossip and food are my two delights; and I suppose you have heard the tale I spread that while he was in Ireland your husband had two scarecrow mistresses. I made it up, my dear, just for the sheer joy of scandal-mongering. Now that I come to know this good King, I believe him to be the best fellow in the world, too good for it, maybe. As for you, I see you did not take the advice I gave you when you passed through France as a bride.'

'Not to fall in love with my husband, because it always leads to hatred,' murmured Mary Beatrice, with a secret smile.

'It has led to something even worse in your case,' pronounced Madame, 'extreme possessiveness, for which you will suffer by and by. But in the meantime you and I will learn to be good friends. I may be as square as a playing-dice, but there is a heart buried somewhere inside all this fat. When we are private, you may call me Liselotte, a pet name bestowed on me by my Aunt Sophy; its use I permit only to those I like, who may be counted on the fingers of one hand. And on New Year's Day, when I have a booth at the bazaar, I shall see that you have the costliest gifts.'

The ceremony to which she referred was a favourite one at Versailles. At his *lever*, Louis was handed by the Royal Treasurer a casket filled with gold pieces and another with silver, and during the day he presided over the distribution, bestowing the gold on great personages, the silver on his Household Officers. There was a lottery in which everyone had a prize, and a bazaar where there could be 'bought' for nothing such expensive trifles as lace aprons, a fan of peacock's feathers, perfumed gloves sewn with seed pearls, a scent-flask encrusted with table-cut rubies.

St Germains had its own pathetic imitation of this ceremony. All through the year, Mary Beatrice and her children put aside part of their pocket-money into a fund for the destitute loyal who, on New Year's Day, came up one by one to receive from the hands of King James five, ten or fifteen pistoles, folded up in small bits of paper with the name of the recipient inscribed. Poverty, that new and sordid background to her life, did not unduly distress Mary Beatrice; she had all the riches she could wish for in the beloved companionship of husband and children. A small incident opened her eyes to how mortifying it could be for the young.

The Prince of Wales had been invited to hunt with the Dauphin's three sons, who returned to sup with him at St Germains. She thought he looked tired and strained, as though about to have one of his feverish colds; but after supper she overheard a little scene which made her heart ache for him.

'The whole Court was laughing at you,' said the Duc de Bourgogne, 'because you were not able to give a pourboire to the huntsman.'

Louise came in shrilly before her brother could reply.

'And shall I tell you why, M. le Duc de Bourgogne? It was because when he was setting out this morning, the Prince of Wales met some poor soldiers who had fought for my father, and he emptied his purse for them. And if you are going to be King of France one day, as you are always boasting, you will have to learn better manners. It is rude to jeer at people because they are poor.'

'I had only twelve pistoles,' the Prince said wistfully. 'But I took their names, and I told them that one day I hoped they would find me no ungrateful king.'

'They will find you a better one than M. le Duc de Bourgogne!' declared Louise, getting the last word.

Unlike his grandsons, Louis increased if possible his delicate consideration for the exiles. Years of war had so drained his resources that the good of France necessitated a treaty, and inevitably one of the articles in it would be his recognition of Orange as King *de facto*. Unluckily the courier who brought the news that the Treaty of Ryswick was signed, arrived at Fontainebleau simultaneously with James and Mary Beatrice, invited for a week's hunting. Strict orders were issued that there be no signs of rejoicing for the peace nor was it to be so much as mentioned in the presence of the King *de jure*.

'Your Majesties may rest assured,' Louis told them in private, 'that I shall never consent to your leaving France against your wish.'

He added that an article in the treaty secured to the Queen her jointure, settled on her at her marriage under the Great Seal of England and confirmed by Acts of Parliament never repealed. He was confident, said Louis, that since 'M. le Prince d'Orange' had signed a treaty which included this article, he would honour it. She was not so sure. Orange had made no scruple of putting into his own pocket £50,000 voted by Parliament for the education of the Duke of Gloucester, Anne's only surviving child. But what concerned her most was Orange's attempt to get a secret article inserted whereby he adopted the Prince of Wales as his Successor, even though by doing so he brazenly admitted that he had slandered the boy at birth. She had not studied English history for nothing, and she shuddered as she thought of the fate of those other royal children, the Princes in the Tower.

James himself accepted the peace with quiet dignity; it was the duty of his Most Christian Majesty to consider first the good of his own subjects. That said, he published a formal protest against a treaty which denied him his just rights. As for Orange's cunning offer, whereby he could hold the boy as a hostage against further attempts to regain those rights, he observed that of two usurpers he would prefer an alien to his own son. Meanwhile, with all his old patience and thoroughness, he worked at an interminable correspondence with men who changed their political coats as frequently as those on their backs, at accounts which always showed a deficit, struggling to maintain a huge new flood of refugees, driven from England and Ireland by a Bill of Banishment which exiled every man and woman who had served him in any capacity whatsoever.

Yet occupied though he was, he never missed the daily promenade upon the terrace, where he loved to be surrounded by his own children and a host of small exiles, pausing in his play with them to gaze over the balustrade at that view which reminded him, he said, of the aspect from Windsor Castle. And to the joy of Mary Beatrice, he seemed to need her more than he had ever done before. Often unwell now, he seldom accompanied her on duty visits to Versailles, and when she returned she would find him watching for her; the time had seemed long, he said, while she was absent. Undemonstrative by nature, now he would take her hand

and smooth it; or again he would break out suddenly in praise of her, marvelling at her devotion to him in all his exiles and misfortunes, telling her he could never have weathered such storms without her love.

There was but one thing that troubled her, his visits to La Trappe. She begged him to forgo them, making his age and poor health the excuse. To kneel upright for hours in that cold church, to share the manual labour and herbal diet of the monks, surely these were austerities beyond him now. A shadow of his old reticence came over him; she had no sins of the flesh to expiate, he told her, and could not understand. He most carefully concealed from her the acts of mortification she guessed he practised even here at St Germains, and she had never known him more embarrassed than when, by accident, she saw his bloodstained discipline.

But secretly she knew that her dislike of his visits to La Trappe was an unworthy one. He went there as eagerly as a lover going to a tryst, and when he returned he gave her the disturbing impression that he, his essential self, had been in a realm from which she and her love for him were excluded.

4

So the sun rose and set, and rose and set again, over the great terrace of St Germains, where children, heedless of the grumbles and intrigues of their elders, played their merry games, as the seventeenth century drew near its end. The days passed tranquilly for Mary Beatrice, punctuated by small occasions.

There was her son's First Communion, when he was received by the Archbishop of Paris at Notre Dame as if he had been Louis in person, and the whole English colony, even those who had come over in the train of Orange's Ambassador, Lord Portland, flocked to cheer him. There was the day when she had to watch the tearing out of two obstinate back teeth, the small patient making never a murmur, while she wept with compassion for him. Even more alarmed and at the same time proud was she when her son, a sportsman of eleven, killed single-handed a *vieux solitaire*, the most savage of all boars. His father rebuked him; it was rash and irresponsible.

127

'Sir,' said the boy, 'we must not be backward in attacking our enemies because they are strong and stout, but take our hazard. Your Majesty has taught me that.'

He had few chances of such daring, for he was kept strictly to his books. To the ordinary curriculum was added English history; exiled almost from birth, he must never forget that he was England's heir; it was her language he had been taught from the cradle, though everyone round him spoke in French. He learned everything slowly but thoroughly, not least his father's strong views on religious toleration. A juggler came to entertain the children by throwing up coloured balls and catching them, while all the little voices chanted:

> 'He tossed his ball so high, so high,
> He tossed his ball so low;
> He tossed his ball in the Jews' garden
> And the Jews were all below.'

'I hate that song!' burst out Louise. 'St Hugh of Lincoln went to find his ball in the Jews' garden, and because he was chanting *Alma Redemptoris*, they cut his throat. I hate the Jews!'

'You must not say you hate anyone on account of his religion,' her brother reproved her sharply. 'The King says that nothing can be more contrary to Holy Writ.'

Louise had her occasions too. She was taken to the opera by her Governess, Lady Middleton, and caused some consternation by accompanying the artistes at the top of her voice. Very demure in her white gown and veil, she strewed rose-petals before the Blessed Sacrament on the feast of Corpus Christi. Very undemure, she climbed a tree, fell, and for some weeks had a black nose. She accepted with a pretty grace a wax doll with jointed wooden limbs and a whole wardrobe of costumes, given her by the young Duchesse de Bourgogne, whom everyone called Mignonne; but told her mother afterwards that she would always prefer her old wool lamb with bright red cheeks and tin legs, because it was made in England.

'The King my husband is perfectly cured of these troublesome carbuncles,' Mary Beatrice assured Madame, in the spring of 1699.

'Then it is no thanks to M. Fagon,' tartly replied Madame. 'He was named Premier Médicin du Roi on All Souls' Day, which was very apt, seeing the number of souls he has released from their bodies by his ferocious blood-letting. He owes his eminence to the Old Swipe when she was governess to the Great Man's bastards; she got him made physician to the late Queen, whom he killed by a massive emetic, just as later he finished off the Dauphine by bleeding her in the foot. I would not let Fagon come within a mile of me when I had the smallpox, but kept my windows open and took sweating-powders, and here I am, more hideous than ever, but alive.'

Both Louis and Mme de Maintenon were offended if those in whom they took an interest did not call in M. Fagon when ill. He had long thin legs like a bird, a humped back, and hanging lips which gave him a sort of perpetual sneer. Yet he could be very kind to those he liked, among whom was Mary Beatrice; after he had visited her husband one day, she decided to confide to him a discovery she had made while dressing.

He examined with care the hard lump, smaller than a hazelnut, on her breast, was glad to hear that it gave her no pain, and discreetly asked her age. She was forty-one.

'H'm, these indolent tumours often occur about the time when the menstrual flux ceases. They are common also in widows and celibates. Other causes are excessive fear, misfortune, blows, the pressure of tight garments, and cold. It is what we term a scirrhus, madame. Avoid the causes I have enumerated, and it will disappear.'

The tiny lump had worried her as something unknown and faintly menacing, and she was greatly relieved to hear it dismissed so lightly. She could not afford to be ill when James needed her.

For though she would not admit for an instant that he was failing, he required care, and death was visiting so many of those who had played their parts in his tragedy. The Pope was followed swiftly to the grave by Abbot de Rance of La Trappe; Fr Petre died at the College of St Omer, which he had ruled as Rector since his escape from England. Versailles put on mourning but secretly rejoiced at the death of King Charles of Spain, who had named the

Duc d'Anjou, the Dauphin's second son, as his heir. From England came a letter in a half-forgotten hand; Anne announced to her father that her only child, Gloucester, had succumbed to scarlet fever on his eleventh birthday. She declared her conviction that this blow was a visible punishment from heaven for her own treachery, and positively promised to use her utmost endeavours to effect the restoration of the Prince of Wales if ever she came to the throne.

The father who so often had mourned with her over the death of her other offspring, who had fretted lest she miscarry on her vile midnight flight, put his shadow Court into mourning, and bade his own son leave off all sports. There was some grumbling among the exiles; the death of so formidable a rival had enhanced the prospects of the Prince of Wales, and to mourn for Gloucester smacked of hypocrisy. Mary Beatrice herself was puzzled by her husband's attitude to Anne. Several times she found him re-reading that ill-expressed letter with tears on his cheeks, and he would repeat phrases from it.

'If wishes could recall what is past, she writes, she would long since have redeemed her fault. She hopes that I am as indulgent to receive her humble submission as she is ready to make it; she knows very well I am.'

'And you believe her sincere in swearing that she will accept the crown only in trust for our son?'

'Her good intentions must be proved by deeds, not words. But oh my poor daughter, how I grieve for her grief!'

She was silent, trying to digest the astonishing fact that love can endure when all trust is gone.

5

It was the evening of Good Friday, March 4th, 1701. In the chapel at St Germains, with its purple-shrouded statues, stripped altar and gaping tabernacle, their Majesties were assisting at Tenebrae. At the beginning of the office, fifteen lighted candles had been placed on a triangular candelabrum, but at the end of each psalm one was put out, and now the chapel was nearly in darkness. The voices of priests and hidden choir rose in a melancholy monotone;

the Queen, who had kept a strict fast since last night's supper, shivered with cold as she knelt at her prie-dieu, and drew her fur-lined hood closer round her head. They were beginning the Third Nocturn:

'*Recordare, Domine* . . . Remember, O Lord, what is come upon us; consider and behold our reproach. Our inheritance is turned to strangers, our houses to aliens . . .'

There seemed to be some odd confusion in the Sanctuary; a priest had risen and was making gestures which had nothing to do with this most solemn service. She turned to whisper a question to James; in the darkness, it was a moment or two before she realized that he was slumped forward on the ledge of his kneeler. Putting out a hand to touch him, she felt him cold and rigid.

A brief unnatural calm always came to her aid in crises. There were practical measures to be taken, and at once. He must be got to bed, his neckcloth removed, a hot brick laid against his feet, burnt feathers under his nose, and an express sent in search of M. Fagon. She recoiled for an instant from the gush of blood from nostrils and mouth which brought him out of his swoon, but reminded herself that the doctors had termed such a haemorrhage 'providential' in 1688. Panic threatened when she found that his right side was partially paralysed, yet Fagon assured her that a course at Bourbon L'Archambault, famous since the Romans for its thermal springs, would cure this. She hurried to take counsel with Mr Dicconson; what would such a journey cost? The sum he named was formid-able; well, it was an occasion for selling one of her major treasures, the string of pearls she had inherited from her mother.

But Louis, who for years had been obliged to let the exiles' pension fall into arrear, insisted on providing everything, funds, equipages, servants, Fagon himself. Because of the invalid's ex-treme weakness, they must travel at a snail's pace; by the second night they had got no further than Chaillot, where Mary Beatrice showed the nuns how well her husband could walk now. Yes, he still dragged his right leg a little, and there was a recurrence of that stammer which afflicted him under stress; but he was getting better even before he had begun the curative course at Bourbon, and he would return, please God, entirely well.

It was the longest journey through France she had ever made since she was here as a bride, and it curiously resembled that progress. Louis had given strict orders that they be received everywhere with the honours to which their rank entitled them, and there were civic welcomes in every town through which they passed. She tried to imitate her husband's patience as they sat through long speeches and gave receptions; but it seemed more like three months than three weeks before they arrived at a Bourbon decorated with the Royal Arms of England and the lilies of Este.

It was the season, and many visitors called. But Louis's foresight had included a private chapel opening out of the bedchamber, and a small walled garden where James could totter up and down on her arm in peace. Every few days came letters from the children, Louise still writing between ruled lines, the Prince already displaying an elegant epistolary style. She answered cheerfully; their father was eating and sleeping well, his leg was gaining strength, she was confident she would bring him back in perfect health.

She avoided asking Fagon his opinion; she would not admit that there was something extraordinary, almost supernatural, about her beloved's patience; her very love would keep him alive. The walled garden was their private paradise; he gazed with child-like wonder at the red-roofed turrets of the castle mirrored in a lake, the hedgeless fields in which heavy white oxen dragged harrows over the rich soil. How beautiful, he murmured, was God's world; he had never before had leisure to note these gentle, eternal things. His hand, with the skin stretched tightly over whipcord veins, arrested the fall of a red rose petal, and she choked at his clumsy, laboured compliment, 'It is like your lips'.

He wished to be back at St Germains for his son's thirteenth birthday, and towards the end of May they started homewards. As they neared Paris, Fagon was summoned in haste to St Cloud, the country seat of Monsieur and Madame. It seemed that after a violent quarrel with his brother, Monsieur had retired thither in dudgeon, and the very same evening had succumbed to apoplexy. St Germains buzzed with tales of Madame's behaviour. She had disturbed his death-bed with screams of, 'No convent! Do not speak to me of a convent!' She had been obliged to pocket her pride and entreat the

'Old Swipe' to plead for her that she might keep her apartments at Versailles, where alone she could be happy. Since Monsieur had left her nothing in his Will, she proclaimed herself penniless, though it was known that she had 40,000 livres of dowry money, and that her son, the Duc d'Orleans, was very generous to her. It all meant nothing to Mary Beatrice, absorbed in nursing her beloved back to health.

He was now so weak that shaving exhausted him, and he grew a beard, 'like a Capuchin', said Madame, a cheerful widow. Each morning he expended his tiny store of strength in dictating to his wife a paper he wished given to the Prince of Wales after his own death. He had begun this paper of advice after the disaster of La Hogue; his feeble hand could not complete it.

' "Remember no king can be happy without his subjects are at ease, and the people cannot be secure of enjoying their own without the King be at his ease also, and in a position to protect them. Therefore preserve your prerogative, but disturb not your subjects in their property nor conscience. Our Blessed Saviour whipped men out of the Temple, but I never heard He commanded any should be forced into it. You are the child of vows and prayers; behave yourself accordingly, never putting the Crown of England in competition with your eternal salvation. Keep your faith against all things and all men." '

'My dearest love,' she pleaded, 'your voice grows hoarse. Will you not rest a while?'

'I shall have good rest soon,' he said, with a joy that wrung her heart. 'I must give what advice I can to my son before my memory fails me. "Study the trade of the nation, and encourage it by all lawful means. And preserve the mastery of the sea, for without that England cannot be safe . . ." '

All that long hot summer she watched him, armouring herself in her duties as a nurse. It was time for him to take the decoction of tamarinds and liquorice; she would fetch another pillow, his head was not high enough; the evening was cool, if he felt he could manage a little promenade. She refused to see significance in the crowds who came from Paris and the village of St Germains to stare at him on the terrace, as though they would take their last look at an exiled king. Resolutely smiling, she diverted the attention of those who wished for a word with him, to the charming young son on her other side. With all her strength she pushed death away; the acceptance of God's will, that goal set her from childhood, was utterly beyond her now. Her prayers consisted solely in a petition, 'Take all else I have in the world, but leave me my dear husband'.

His weakness forced him to pause every few steps, and then he would lean on the balustrade and gaze in silence at the view. Did it still remind him of the prospect from Windsor Castle? she asked, supposing he still longed for dear England. No, he said; it was like that of some place he had never seen, and yet was strangely familiar. Then he would revert to the subject she dreaded, begging her to look upon death as a friend, trying gently to prepare her.

'I have always maintained with my Aunt Sophy,' said Madame, 'that the world will never be right until it is cured of this superstitious folly called religion. Yet I must confess, the King your husband is dying like a saint.'

'But he is not dying, Madame! I lie on a pallet in his room and know how well he sleeps; and this morning he was able to take some breakfast.'

On September 2nd, another Friday, he insisted on rising for Mass. The very same words from Lamentations occurred in the Gradual, *Recordare, Domine*, and this time he fell insensible into her arms. All but she knew it was the end; even Fagon did not have recourse to his lancets, but shaved the dying man's head and applied leeches. As soon as he recovered consciousness, James asked for Extreme Unction; then, looking death steadily in the face, requested the presence of his children that he might give them his last blessing. The necessity to soothe and quieten them when they saw the bed all covered in blood, kept Mary Beatrice in control of herself; but afterwards when, speaking in a strangely clear and forceful voice, he publicly forgave his enemies and bade his wife send his blessing to Anne, she flung herself upon him in passionate abandonment, kissing his hand, bathing them with tears, almost reproaching him; what would become of her when he was gone?

His hands did not respond; they began those curious clawing movements made by the dying when the sense of touch recedes. But he heard her; he said:

'God will take care of you.' And then with a kind of simple awe: 'Think of it, Beatrice, I am going, I hope, to be happy! And you who are flesh of my flesh, how is it that you are in despair?'

Fr Ruga remonstrated with her; immoderate grief was an offence against God and disturbed the serenity of the dying. She must not enter the chamber again until she had regained control of herself. At first she complied, creeping up a little circular stair to a closet behind the bedhead, where she could hear if he groaned or spoke. She pictured him lying there, patiently submitting to Fagon's ministrations which only added to his sufferings, a tired old warrior waiting for the order to sheathe his sword at last.

On Wednesday a note was brought to her from Louis, who had called three times already, alighting from his coach outside the gates to make less noise. He was coming again, this time with news he hoped would console her. She tried to attend to what he said. He had called a Council to debate whether, despite the Treaty of Ryswick, to recognize the Prince of Wales as King James III. The Grand Alliance had just been signed between the Empire, Denmark, Holland and England, and this was precisely the kind of gesture to involve France in another ruinous war.

'Monseigneur was the last to speak, and said with unusual warmth that it would be unworthy of the Crown of France to abandon a prince of our own blood, especially one so dear to us as the son of King James. I was of Monseigneur's opinion, as also was M. le Duc de Bourgogne; and I am come, madame, to impart this decision to the King your husband.'

What reason she still retained told her that it was a gesture worthy of le Roi Soleil, and her lips expressed gratitude. But when he led her into the bedchamber, she was aware of nothing but that face upon the high pillows, subtly changed since last she had seen it, august and aloof. His sight was gone, but he was still conscious, and began to murmur some broken words about his Most Christian Majesty's past kindnesses to him and his.

'Sir,' said Louis loudly, 'that is a small matter. I have something with which to acquaint your Majesty of far greater consequence. Let no one withdraw,' he commanded, as the attendants of both kings made to leave the room. A deep hush fell. 'I have come to inform your Majesty that whenever it shall please God to call you out of this world, I will take your family under my protection, and recognize your son as King of England.'

Forgetting that they stood in a death-chamber, all present, both French and English, burst into shouts of applause. But she, her ear laid close to James's lips, heard and repeated what he said. He begged as a last favour that no funeral pomp be used at his obsequies, but that the money destined for that purpose be given to his destitute followers.

'Sir, that is the only favour I cannot grant,' wept Louis, intensely moved by his own magnanimity. 'Adieu, my dear brother, the best of Christians and the most abused of monarchs!'

Throughout the remainder of that day, and the next, she fought for the control she needed to obtain Fagon's permission to sit up with her husband at night. Absurdly she clung to the hope that if she were with him, she could bar the door against death. Crouched by the bed, counting each laboured, shallow breath, wiping from his forehead a cold sweat, trying to interpret each groping gesture, she whispered:

'I am here, day and night, if you will allow it. I desire nothing but to be with you, and serve you.'

Very feebly, with long pauses, he spoke. He wished that Orange should be told of his sincere forgiveness; in her letter to dear Anne (yes, still 'dear' Anne), she must charge the Princess to atone to her brother for the injuries she had done their father. His Will, drawn up years before, was in a certain strong-box. By it, his wife was appointed Regent until his heir was eighteen; she would have a Council to assist her; he had made careful provision for Louise. He hoped very much that means would be found to have his memoirs published, in order that he might be vindicated in the eyes of his people. His body was to remain in the chapel of the English Benedictines in Paris, until it could be removed to Westminster Abbey.

In the small hours of the morning, the priest and servers came for Mass at the altar erected in his room; his lips moved, seeming to savour the familiar words. Afterwards he asked her what day this was; when she told him Friday, he smiled and said he had always prayed that he might die on this day of the week. Her ladies were about her, imploring her to take some rest after her night watch. Sure that the answer would be yes, she asked him whether he would not like her to remain at his bedside. But he was withdrawn now into the antechamber of a world in which she had no existence; almost it was as though she were no longer his concern. She said, placating God, attempting to bribe Him:

'Beg for me the grace of perfect resignation.'

She woke that afternoon from a sort of coma, to hear the great clock in the gatehouse hammer out the hour of three. There was a special little prayer she had always repeated at three o'clock on Fridays, the hour and the day of Christ's death on the cross. Dutifully she knelt and began it, but almost at once she froze. Footsteps were approaching through the anteroom, slow footsteps as of one reluctant to arrive. That old constriction of her throat prevented her from answering a soft tap on the door. She knelt there rigid as Fr Ruga entered, got down upon his knees beside her, and asked her to join him in some prayers. He began:

'*Subvenite Sancti Dei* . . . come to his assistance, all you Saints of God . . .'

It was a moment or two before she understood. These were the prayers for a departed soul.

She collapsed like a shot animal, sprawled grotesquely, her head hanging over the ledge of her prie-dieu. The old priest gathered her into his arms, hushing her, begging her to say in acceptance just one phrase, '*Fiat voluntas tua*—Thy will be done'. The words went echoing through her brain like those of a song which cannot be got rid of; what remained of her will could manage at last only the one word, '*Fiat*'.

'That is my dear good child. I think you have a saint in heaven; no purgatory for him who so willingly burnt in the fires of repentance here on earth. Never have I assisted at so happy a death-bed. The King died with a smile at the self-same hour as his Saviour.'

So he talked on gently, describing how the dying man had requested that his bedchamber door be set open, the curtains of his bed withdrawn, so that all, both friend and foe, might witness his end. She bit back the scream of her rebellious heart: I do not want a saint in heaven; I want my husband, the touch of his hand, the sound of his voice. My beloved, who, at the last, did not ask for me.

7

The King My Son

1

In the tribune at Chaillot, the Queen Mother knelt for some while after she had finished her prayers, bracing herself for the act of rising. Nowadays, any such movement was apt to rouse the alien thing inside her bosom; one day, she supposed, its teeth would find the vital spot it had sought for nearly eighteen years. Till then she must continue to appease it with all the painful and wearisome remedies prescribed by Fagon, so that she could be useful to the King her son.

Within the recess before which she knelt, a silver reliquary glinted under its thin crape veil. Strange how she herself had suffered in a nightmare the tearing as it were the heart from her body at the exact hour when, so she learnt afterwards, the surgeons were at their work at St Germains. By express order of Louis, no bells had been tolled, no prayers chanted aloud, when James's embalmed heart was conveyed here to Chaillot; yet she had known that it was somewhere near her; she was, as he had said, flesh of his flesh.

How many times since then had she kissed the cold silver, hoping that soon she would begin to feel his near presence, his continuing love. But it was not so; this was her last link with him, and it was just a dead physical organ encased in a silver urn.

She rose gingerly. The thing inside her at once responded; sometimes she thought of it as the hideous parody of an unborn child, beginning to quicken. Mère Priolo's hand slipped beneath her arm, gently kneading, as they walked into the cloister.

'We will not reopen the great wound by writing in our history of those days when your Majesty received it. I myself most carefully set down all that passed while you were here with us after the death of the King your husband.'

'I feel it, *ma mère*, not as a wound, but as an amputation. Indeed I cannot remember with any distinctiveness those few days I spent with you. I seemed to have no substance; I recall experiencing a foolish surprise to find that people did not walk straight through me. And yet at the same time I shrank from the lightest touch as though I were one open sore. But how selfish grief made me! I would have denied him heaven, I would have condemned him to years of pain and weariness, if only I could have kept him at my side.'

'But instead you said to me, here in this cloister where we walk, that it becomes us to shut the mouth and bow the head, to adore and approve all that God permits.'

'I am sure I must have added, "if we can". Oh I have sought for *abandonnement* all my life, but I practise it with so bad a grace, and so much against my will, that I have no reason to hope it will be acceptable to God. I have not regarded the warning given me when I was a child by Reverend Mother, to be on my guard against excessive attachment to creatures. Sometimes I fear——'

But she could not give utterance to that morbid terror. It was that God, jealous of such attachment, might take away her last remaining idol, the King her son. Shocking though it was, in those last days of her beloved's life, she had looked on God as a rival.

The return to St Germains had not been, as she imagined at the time, the sharpest ordeal of her life. The august ceremonies of death had sustained her; the deep-mourning which, usually modified after eight weeks, she was resolved to wear permanently, suited her feelings; tears brought relief because they were shared. Receiving visits of condolence in her mourning-bed, she found a sympathetic and attentive audience when she was seized with that compulsion, so common in the bereaved, to talk of her beloved.

There was a bitter-sweet joy in discovering that all had been done at his obsequies with loving care, to read the account for his embalming, full of strange substances, perfumed sparadrope, Indian balsam, rectifying spirits of wine tinctured with gums and rich spices.

The really cruel part came when she left her chamber, when visits of condolence ceased, when she must take up ordinary life again in a house empty of his presence. Looking back, she realized that it was then she had begun to rely, unconsciously, upon La Consolatrice. Almost their roles were reversed. It was the child of nine who knew when her mother was tired, and had a cushion ready for her chair, who noticed when a meal was left untouched, and who enabled her to face without flinching the first of many bodily ordeals.

The 'indolent tumour', the tiny hard but painless lump on her breast, had increased in size, with a protuberance in the centre; it gave her occasional shooting pangs when she moved, and the skin around it had become discoloured. Fagon, after an examination, scolded her; she had not observed his previous instructions, with the result that the scirrhus had developed into what he called an occult cancer.

'But your Majesty may prolong your life for many years, if you will enter upon a strict regimen which must be permanent.' He recited a whole list of medicines, warned against external bruising, advised a litter instead of a coach when she travelled, and begged her to use every method to divert her thoughts, since this malady was made worse by excessive agitation or grief. Then he added gravely: 'The tumour must be lanced for several days in succession.'

'Life is too wearisome to me to be worth the trouble of preserving it upon such terms!' she exclaimed. And then at once the old gesture of clapping a hand across her mouth. 'I beg your pardon, monsieur. I place myself in your hands.'

'In my opinion,' interposed Beaulieu, her own surgeon, who was jealous of his famous colleague, 'her Majesty should try a course of treatment with the doctress in Paris who has had remarkable success with herbs. Her Majesty's extreme slenderness makes lancings inadvisable.'

Fagon disposed of the doctress and her quackery in a few,

short sarcastic sentences, and an appointment was made for the first operation. He assured her she would scarcely feel it; she would be given a highly spiced caudle first, her ears stuffed with wool so that she would not hear the incision, and an ice-cold cloth clapped on her breast to numb it.

'It will take but two minutes. Your Majesty may time me.'

But much more effective than any of these anodynes was a little plan thought out by Louise. Beside the patient's chair she set upon a stand a portrait of her father, so that Mary Beatrice could look fixedly at it over her shoulder during the ordeal.

'For your Majesty has often told me that when you looked at my father in life, you had the power to confront every peril.'

She gave one convulsive shudder at the first incision, but afterwards sat unmoved, swooning only when she was in bed. She came round to see Fagon's assistant briskly towelling some leeches to make them suck with more avidity; and to feel a soft little hand stroking her forehead.

On her forty-third birthday she made a private retreat in her own apartments, setting herself as a penance a letter to Anne. Her stepdaughter's injuries to herself she could readily forgive; but Anne had broken her father's heart and virulently slandered her brother. Mary Beatrice wrote merely as one conveying a message.

'Some days before his death, the best of fathers bid me find means to let you know that he forgave you from the bottom of his heart, and prayed God to do so too, that he gave you his blessing, and prayed that you might be confirmed in the resolution you have several times expressed, of repairing to his son the wrongs done to himself. To which I shall only add, that I join my prayers herein to his with all my heart, and that I shall make it my business to inspire in the young man who is left to my care, the sentiments of his father, for better no man had.'

'I have written to the Princess of Denmark, Lord Caryll,' she informed the old gentleman, her secretary for so many years, but by the terms of James's Will ennobled and created Secretary of State.

'A difficult letter, madam. A lady of the Princess's temperament will not relish being forgiven; but I am sure your Majesty wrote with your customary graciousness and tact.'

She flushed. It was, she knew, a stiff letter. She neither expected nor received an answer.

One of her first duties on emerging from her mourning chamber was to hold a Council of Regency, seated at the head of the table with James on her right hand. Before she left for Chaillot, she had heard the heralds proclaim him at the gates of St Germains, and herself had performed the traditional gesture of a widowed queen, kneeling in homage to the pale-faced boy. But she had not been able to prevent herself from saying:

'I acknowledge your Majesty as my King, but I hope you will never forget that you are my son.'

It was an appeal of which she was slightly ashamed. She knew that he loved her devotedly, but first and last he was Heir to England, dedicated to the service of a country he did not remember, never allowed to be just Jamie, her boy. The strictness of his upbringing had made him prematurely grave; it was hard to remember that he was only thirteen, as he sat in the armchair beside her now, his great dark eyes, which had earned for him the affectionate nickname of the Blackbird, keenly intelligent as he listened to the proceedings. While she was Regent, he could take no decisions, but her awareness of his precocious judgment increased her nervousness. It was too late for her now to master the intricacies of politics; only too well did she know that the safety of her son would always matter more to her than the restoration of King James III; and she dimly foresaw a battle of wills when he attained his majority.

The question before the Council was whether or not to accept the Scots' invitation, brought over by Lord Belhaven, for James's presence among them. Upon this, as indeed on all policy, the Council was divided. The young King's Governor, Lord Perth, was for action and risk; Lord Middleton clung to caution; and old Caryll endeavoured to act as a sort of umpire between them.

'The Prince of Orange,' said Perth, 'is known to be near death, and it is of the very first importance that his Majesty should be at hand when that event happens. To his subjects he is but a name; his presence alone can inspire them to act, for it cannot be expected they should risk their lives and estates for an unknown prince.'

'But they invite him only on condition that he abjures his religion,' said Mary Beatrice quickly. 'That is not to be thought of.'

'I have already convinced Belhaven, madam, that there can be no question of it, and he is content that the King engages to make no attempt to alter the established religion of either realm. I am sure your Majesty would most readily make this engagement on the King's behalf.'

She looked appealingly at Middleton. An unkempt person, his upper lip stained with the snuff he took constantly, cynical, gruff, but loyal as a mastiff, he had suffered a long imprisonment in the Tower rather than take the Oaths to Orange. He at once reminded Perth of the very peculiar history of Lord Belhaven who, on the death of Charles II, had left Scotland, sent his servant back to say that he had perished while crossing Solway Moss, and reappeared under an assumed name as a market-gardener at Richmond whence, under colour of buying Dutch bulbs, he had made frequent trips to Holland, forming one of the most valuable media of communication between the Prince of Orange and the recipients of his secret bribes.

'He has changed his coat again simply because he despairs of a post under the usurper; I would have no dealings with such a rogue. Our best policy is to rely upon the promises, several times reiterated, of the Princess Anne, to use her utmost endeavours to effect the restoration of his Majesty if ever she comes to the throne. She is childless, and has no expectation of long life.'

'That is my opinion,' said the Queen. 'My son is far too young to be exposed to such hazards as Lord Belhaven proposes.' She was aware of a slight movement from the boy beside her, not of impatience, but of a kind of restrained frustration, and went on hurriedly: 'Moreover his health is delicate, and I remember well, from the years I spent in exile with the late King in Scotland, how harsh is the climate there.'

Perth muttered something about keeping him in leading-strings, but Lord Middleton, his fingers reaching automatically for his snuff-box, came to the rescue again.

'His Majesty would be better employed in finishing his education than in roaming about a wild country with rude Highland chiefs, from whom he might acquire habits of intemperance and ferocity. Let us trust to treaties and diplomacy, rather than expose him to such perils at his tender age.'

The perils to which James would be exposed in his native land were immeasurably increased by a vicious gesture made by Orange while his Court was still in mourning for the boy's father. By means of the extreme Whigs who formed a majority in Parliament, he forced through a Bill of Attainder, whereby 'the pretended Prince of Wales' could be put to death without trial if he set foot in Britain. As a preliminary, Fuller had republished his variation on the warming-pan story, appending a forged letter from Mary Beatrice, wherein she was made to consent to the murder of Mrs Gray, whose son had been smuggled into her bed at St James's. This, it was hoped, would be sufficient to attaint also 'the late wife of the late King James' (not 'widow', since that might have aroused sympathy), thus providing an excuse for withholding payment of her jointure, definitely promised in the Treaty of Ryswick. It was a matter of indifference to her that the Commons treated with contempt the Bill of Attainder against herself, throwing it under the table. Death by the hand of any chance assassin hung over her boy if ever he should appear in his native land; and once her Regency ceased, she knew only too well that he would go there.

In mid-March, St Germains went mad with delight, building bonfires and toasting the Little Gentleman in Black Velvet, the mole that had caused William's fatal fall from his horse. Mary Beatrice ordered the fires to be put out and forbade such unseemly rejoicing. She found something terrible in the descriptions she read of Orange's end. The nerveless hand trying in vain to sign the death-warrant of a child he had never even seen; the failing voice ordering a facsimile stamp to be affixed to it in his presence; the rude 'No!' in response to Anne's dutiful requests to visit him; the Dutch male favourites squabbling about his bed; his last cold words, 'I draw towards my end', without one expression of repentance or charity.

What a contrast between that death-bed and her beloved's! No dear children, no true friends content to be exiled for his sake, no

Sacrament, no one to succeed him on his stolen throne except a sister-in-law he loathed. A shocking gesture of hate, and the preparations for yet another aggressive war, these were the comforts William of Orange had turned to when his hour came. While here in France there was increasing talk of miracles wrought through the intercession of one who had publicly forgiven his most bitter enemies and died in such perfect charity.

She had always been cautious about miracles; but she could not help being deeply impressed when Lord Middleton, that confirmed sceptic, whose favourite *mot* was that no new light ever came into a man's head except through a crack in the tiles, electrified St Germains by announcing his conversion to the Catholic faith, claiming that it was due to a vision he had received of his old master.

'This is a greater miracle than the healing of bodies,' she wrote to Mère Priolo, 'and has given me more joy than I have known since my great loss, though not in my senses. The only susceptibility that remains in me is for pain. I miss him more and more in a thousand ways. In my first grief I felt something like an underlying calm, but now, though it does not appear so much, I feel a deeper sorrow within.'

She was ashamed to discover that since James's death all other losses affected her but little, and she could scarcely shed a tear for her childhood friend, Vittoria Montecuccoli who, with the exception of Molza, was the last of those who had accompanied her on her wedding journey. But then it had been the same while James was alive; the premature death of her brother Francesco in 1694 had caused her only a passing sorrow, as for a stranger. She prayed against selfishness; in the bitter cold of December she climbed three pairs of stairs to sit with an old dying equerry, who had ridden about Europe in the train of Lord Peter with his list of prospective brides. But the only comfort she could find was that solace peculiar to women, ministering to the beloved dead. More and more embarrassed for money though she was, she spent a windfall in the shape of the salt duties from estates left her by her mother, and grudgingly made over to her at last by Uncle Rinaldo, on rebuilding the dilapidated tribune at Chaillot. Mr Dicconson respectfully reminded her that the wages of her Household were sadly in arrear.

145

'The heart of my dear and holy King is in the tribune at Chaillot,' she said obstinately. 'And for anything which concerns him, I would give my chemise.'

2

The affairs of the living King, her son, remained summed up in that old question, should he or should he not answer the invitation of his Scottish subjects? According to the most influential among them, Scotland was ripe for a general rising; all she needed was the person of her King, French arms and money.

'His Majesty is keen to go. To thwart him, madam, you risk antagonizing him,' Perth warned her.

This, while it frightened, could not move her. She was unable to think of James as other than her child; it was as if the navel-string had never been cut, and he remained part of her very self.

'French arms and money will not be forthcoming,' grunted Middleton.

The War of the Spanish Succession had broken out, and France was suffering crushing defeats. Louis had even melted down his famous silver furniture to pay his armies; he worked ten hours a day in the apartments of Mme de Maintenon, directing operations at the front, where the Duke of Berwick commanded. It was largely through Mary Beatrice's influence that Berwick had become a naturalized Frenchman and was given the post of Generalissimo. Even Middleton had deemed this unwise, for he was the only man of military talent fit to command a rising on behalf of the King, when the right time came.

'But it would be so selfish to keep Berwick idle at St Germains,' pleaded Mary Beatrice. She would not admit, even to herself, that the company of Berwick had made her uneasy ever since he had criticized the flight of her husband from England, a flight for which she knew she was responsible.

It was about this time that her son became openly restless. Would she not ask permission of his Most Christian Majesty that he join the Duc de Bourgogne and the Duc de Berri at the front?

'I am sixteen; I need to learn the art of war as my father did at the same age.'

Yes, yes, of course he should go, she promised, but not while his health remained so delicate. Never a winter passed without his having the intermittent fever, which came on suddenly with vomiting and a profuse sweat. She had overheard whispers that he was consumptive; and the Low Countries, whither he wished to go, would be death to him. How could he take his Peruvian-bark regularly if he were at the front? She tried not to fuss over him, for she saw that he loathed and despised his weak health; the moment he was released from his sick chamber, he was out hunting boar or wolf.

Almost as it were to spite her, his health suddenly improved in 1705, the very last year of her Regency. She resolved to make the most of that year; once he was his own master he would go on a campaign or he would answer the call of Scotland. It began gaily; for the first time James and Louise were invited to Versailles for the feast of Twelfth Night, always a splendid occasion. Louise must have a ball-gown worthy of her loveliness. Among the precious things smuggled out of England at the revolution was a casket of rose-nobles, coined during the Lancastrian era and now very scarce. A superstitious value was attached to them because it was believed that the gold from which they were struck was the fruit of some alchemist's successful labours. The Queen had sold them one by one over the years, and had few left; but it was an occasion for parting with another to clothe Louise in an amber velvet gown, with an aigrette of jewels in her beech-brown hair.

For this one night, Louis laid aside his cares, and the festivities were on their old lavish scale. And as in the old days, he laid himself out to honour poor exiles, giving the Queen and her son an armchair on either side of his own, the Princess a *fauteuil* higher than that of the Duchesse de Bourgogne, now the First Lady in France. It was the custom of each couple, if specially honoured, to dance once down the room alone; and each time the young King of England led out his sister, Louis stood until they had completed this first measure.

It was an evening Mary Beatrice would never forget. Her children, partnered in the stately branle, were like figures from some old romance, gallant and beautiful and gay, the new little hoop Louise wore swaying gracefully as she curtsied or pirouetted, her elbow-length sleeves showing off to perfection her round white arms. It was her very first ball, but she was equally skilful in the graceful musette as in the rapid passepied, and it was noticed how often the Duc de Berri sought her as his partner. His brother Anjou having renounced all claim to the French throne when he was set upon the Spanish one by his grandfather, Berri stood next in succession after the Duc de Bourgogne.

At nine o'clock precisely, twelve tables were wheeled in, covered with moss and verdure, on which in compartments were all kinds of fruit and sweetmeats surrounded by flowers, so that when they joined in the centre of the dancing floor they formed a fragrant parterre. As they separated to be wheeled round the company, Madame refreshed herself instead with the malice that was her favourite diet.

'This throwing of Berri and your daughter together is the work of Mignonne,' said she, referring to the Duchesse de Bourgogne. 'The chit is a born match-maker, and thinks she can make the world as she likes it, just because the Great Man is so besotted with her that he lets her jump on his knee and tickle his chin. As for Berri, he is a fool. When he was sent to address the Parlement, he forgot his speech and sat absolutely dumb. It's true he can bring down pheasants with a pistol, but what recommendation is that for a possible King of France? I do not say a possible husband; Mignonne may match-make as much as she likes, but your daughter has no portion and no prospects. I am this evening as disagreeable as a bug,' Madame added unnecessarily.

Wakeful with pain in the small hours of next morning, the Queen heard her door softly open, and a pair of feet in satin slippers tiptoe to the bed. She had just looked in, whispered Louise, to see if her Majesty needed anything; had she taken her mercurial pill, was she sure the jolting of the coach had not been too much?

'The King and I danced till half-past two, and then Mignonne begged us to go with her to the Menagerie, which his Most Christian Majesty has given her for her own little chateau, and take a collation while we listened to the birds in her aviary, the finest in France. But all I wished was to come home to you,' and the flushed face was laid beside her mother's on the pillow, the tumbled curls, sweet-smelling, nestled against her cheek. 'I overheard what Madame said about the Duc de Berri. I do not want him or any husband, but to stay with your Majesty all my life!'

That ball heralded a year which, on looking back, seemed always summer to Mary Beatrice. Even her son put aside his longing to make a campaign, and threw himself into the round of festivities organized by Mignonne. Since her formal reception at Versailles, Louise was showered with invitations, to plays staged in the Cour de Marbre, to fêtes in the gardens, to masquerades that lasted all night, after which Mignonne would carry her off to hear Mass at St Eustache, and then to play at being dairymaids in the Menagerie, or for a donkey-ride in the park. Still fresh as an Aurora, Louise would come back to St Germains to kiss her mother good-morning, and to pour out an account of the fun they had had. A detachment of the Maison Militaire had turned out to salute her brother and herself as they took coach in the Place d'Armes; she and Mignonne had dressed up as beggars and walked the streets of Paris unrecognized; they had stayed till dawn in a gondola on the canal, listening to musicians hidden in the bosquets.

'But I am so glad to come home to dear St Germains.'

All that summer she robbed it of its melancholy, her laughter seeming to saturate its very walls. Her Majesty was not well enough to share in the fun at Versailles; very well, they would have frolic of their own at St Germains. She must come and see the little cere-mony Louise had arranged when the last of the hay was gathered.

'The hay-cock Lady Middleton and I built is neater and firmer than any other, and so we have the right to dispense the syllabub.'

A cow was a garland round its horns was led solemnly into the field by stout Lady Middleton, who milked it into a great china bowl in which were already wine and sugar. Louise, her white arms honey-coloured from long days out of doors, ladled the frothing mixture into glasses for all her rural company.

Sitting at her open window, Mary Beatrice heard the splash of oars and carefree laughter; James and Louise were going in their shabby barge to picnic at Pontalie, an old mill-house. Half-solemn chanting receded in the direction of the forest; they were on a playful pilgrimage to the shrine of St Thibault, who was said to cure agues. Mr Dicconson had an ague, and they were off to pray for him, while he sat with the Queen over the monthly accounts. Her eyes were beginning to fail, and she was obliged to wear spectacles, a sad blow to her vanity. Louis, delicately considerate as ever, had given her a silver-gilt case for them, with a butterfly on it, its body made of emeralds and diamonds, two rubies for its eyes. Dared she sell it, she wondered? Poverty was pinching worse than ever, and she sighed as she turned back to the accounts.

'The three-foot flambeaux must be dispensed with; white wax cost twenty-four sols a pound, and yellow tapers can be used instead. Could you persuade my gentlemen to agree to less than a pint of wine at dinner? Certainly I myself will dispense with the dish of cakes for my afternoon collation. I have not the heart to cut down straw and hay for the horses, but surely the kitchen does not need six livres a month for larding-needles and string. Do you think the scullery-boy could use a little less bran to clean the cutlery? At any rate, soup made from two chickens and a leg of veal must do without the veal.'

Mr Dicconson, making notes, showed by his expression how mortified he was. That a Queen of England should have to ask her scullery-boy to use less bran! Taking pity on him, she sent him off with some hastily invented message to the playful pilgrims; and presently Louise came flitting in, light as a dragon-fly.

'Oh madame, I quite ache with laughing! The Chevalier de Salle who was of our party would not join in our singing of the Litany, saying he had come for pleasure and not for devotion, so to punish him we made him sit by himself and wash all the glasses after our collation. And just as we had offered the last prayer at the door of St Thibault's chapel, who should appear but Mr Dicconson, quite cured of his ague, so we all cried, "A miracle! A miracle!" '

'M. le Duc de Berri called while you were absent, to invite the King and you to a bathing-party on the Seine next week, and afterwards to hunt at Fontainebleau.'

'The King will enjoy that, but I shall not go. Next week M. Fagon comes to perform another of his lancings on your Majesty.'

'The Duc de Berri seemed very disappointed not to see you.'

'I am not sorry to have missed him. He fancies he is in love with me, but I am never going to marry anyone.'

'My dear child, that will not be for you to decide.'

'Don't, pray don't make me ever go away from your Majesty!' begged Louise, suddenly serious and earnest. 'The King my father called me La Consolatrice, and that is all I desire to be. Just now I was in the forest only in body; my heart was here with you. And see what I have brought you.'

It was a cowslip-ball, made by nipping off the tasselled heads and stringing them on a ribbon which afterwards was tied up tight. Always there was some little present when Louise returned from her excursions, an apronful of wild strawberries, a carefully arranged posy of meadow flowers. And the constant refrain, Don't make me ever go away from you. Foolish, and selfish, to take comfort in this single-heartedness of a daughter who soon would be a woman. But Mary Beatrice leaned more and more upon La Consolatrice, as the day approached when her son would be his own master.

3

On that day, when she handed over to him the correspondence and the cipher-keys from her years of Regency, he said with delicate tact that he hoped she would continue to assist him with her advice.

She was not deceived. She could almost hear the sighs of relief of his advisers, while he himself got down to business with the zest of a starving man. There were no more gay excursions with his sister; he worked all day, wary of the fulsome promises she had taken at their face value, testing the sincerity of those who made them, writing with his own hand to announce his majority to the loyal in England and Scotland, and to foreign Courts, poring over news-sheets, inventing economies which made her own petty ones seem small indeed.

Early in 1708, he received an invitation to spend some days at Marli. She took it as an answer to her prayers, for Louise was down with a mild attack of measles, and she had an obsessional dread of her son's being exposed to infection. She was glad to see on his return how much he seemed to have enjoyed his little holiday, and was beginning to ask him about it, when he sprang a mine beneath her feet.

'His Most Christian Majesty invited me to Marli to give me the best news I ever received in my life. He has decided to assist me in regaining my inheritance; I am to leave at once for Dunkirk, where five French men-of-war, twenty transports and twelve battalions await me, under the command of Admiral Fourbin and the Comte de Gacé. At last I can answer the call from Scotland, nor will I steer back for the strongest winds and the fiercest enemies!'

She had known that sooner or later he would respond to that call, and had tried to adjust herself to the knowledge. But it was so sudden; in such bitter weather must he cross the sea for the first time since that nightmare voyage when he was an infant. She would not spoil his rapture; but the moment he was gone she was back in those days of agonized waiting for news such as she had suffered when her husband was absent. Even the now recovered Louise could not give her comfort; and her nerve was further shaken by Middleton's grumbles before he followed her son. Once again, said he, France was merely using the Stuart cause as a diversion against her enemies; Fourbin and de Gacé were known to be at loggerheads, and their quarrels were now causing delay which would give the English fleet time to intercept.

After dark on March 12th, David Nairne, Clerk of the Council, brought her news and a letter. All her careful excluding of James from contact with his sister had proved vain; he was very ill with measles, but had insisted on being carried aboard in a litter. His handwriting betrayed how seriously sick he was.

'The body is feeble,' he wrote, 'but the spirit is so strong that it will bear me up. I hope not to write to you again until I do so from Edinburgh, where I expect to arrive on Saturday.'

She took counsel with Fagon; what treatment should his Majesty have? The answer increased her anguish; on no account should a patient with measles be exposed to cold or light; he should drink ass's milk and take a very slender diet. And here he was, going to Scotland by sea in March, and when he arrived she knew from experience the kind of diet he would be offered, great bowls

152

of cocky-leeky, followed by every specimen of the baxter's art in the shape of scones, bannocks, venison pasties and turkey pie. She wrote him a long list of dos and don'ts, and sent Nairne back with a keg of elderflower-water and linseed, which must be drunk every hour.

Meanwhile she fled with Louise to Chaillot. It was impossible to wait in such dread at St Germains, whence all, even the aged Lord Griffen, had gone with her son. The lower servants grumbled worse than ever; she had overheard them complain that she fed her son's dogs, Missie and Folie, while they had to tighten their belts. At Chaillot she could live in a climate of prayer and unanxious poverty.

From two disabled French frigates which limped back to Dunkirk, she learnt that the fleet had encountered gales, that Admiral Byng was in hot pursuit with a vastly superior force, that a council had been held in James's cabin to decide whether or not to proceed, and that he, between bouts of sea-sickness, had insisted. She tried to join in the chorus of praise sung by the nuns; how brave he was! They recalled how his uncle, King Charles II, had breakfasted with them before his restoration in 1660, recommending his cause to the Community's prayers. Their monthly Communion had been offered for that intention ever since, and surely God was answering.

'Oh *ma mère*,' the Queen begged Mère Priolo in private, 'just pray that my son may be safe.'

And safe he was. On Easter Sunday she received a dispatch from him, written at Dunkirk. He said nothing of his cruel disappointment, blamed nobody, merely gave her the facts. Gales and the menace of the English fleet had decided Admiral Fourbin to retire while there was time; he himself had begged to be set ashore anywhere and alone, if no troops could be landed, but Fourbin's orders were to take the same care of his person as if it had been his own master's. One French ship had been captured, and James expressed his deep concern because Middleton's two sons and old Lord Griffen were aboard her. He was invited to Marli, where he hoped to meet her.

And that was all.

153

'Your hats, gentlemen,' Louis said to his guests, as the Afternoon began at Marli. It was one of the relaxations of Etiquette permitted here.

Mary Beatrice derived a secret amusement from the very small degree in which Etiquette was in fact relaxed. This morning Louis had dressed as usual in the presence of all those entitled to this supreme privilege; not the minutest bit of ritual was omitted down to the moment when the First Valet of the Wardrobe presented upon a silver tray three lace handkerchiefs for him to choose from. Afterwards he had hunted with James in the Small Park, changed his clothes completely in a rite called the *débotter*, dined *au petit couvert* with a chosen few, and now was beginning a promenade along the yew walks. Behind him a valet carried a sunshade and an umbrella, to hold over him in either contingency; and the Director of the Gardens bore upon a cushion a pair of silver shears, in case his Most Christian Majesty should choose to trim a yew into the fantastic shapes he loved.

But this afternoon he broke his rule never to speak of public matters at Marli. Taking Mary Beatrice by the finger-tips, he sat down with her upon a marble bench.

'For several years past, madame, the King your son has requested leave to serve in my armies as a volunteer, that he may learn the noble profession of arms. I was reluctant to agree while there was any possibility of assisting him to regain his inheritance; but he is so importunate that this morning, as we returned from the hunt, I granted his request. The late King, his father, would certainly have wished it.'

It was an argument to which she had no answer; and at least it was better than some rash attempt on his part to recover his throne without French troops. The remark in his letter that he had begged to be set ashore in Scotland, anywhere and alone, had horrified her; and now Anne, seizing the excuse of the late abortive expedition, had set a price on his head, and for the first time was styling him 'the Pretender'. The Queen listened with feigned cheerfulness to the animated talk of her son, and made a silent vow to acquit herself well in her new role of mother of a soldier on active service. He was going incognito to the front, and this, he said, would be an advantage, for he could mingle with the common soldiers and hear what they thought about every action.

'We must remember to refer to him always now as the Chevalier de St George,' she told Louise.

He wrote to her regularly and vividly, but with scarcely a word about himself, so that she was reminded of those journals of her husband she had read at St James's. It was from Berwick she learned of her son's gallantry during the battle of Oudenarde; Berwick's uncle, John Churchill, commanding the opposing forces, had praised his valour to the skies. Her Household complained because she sent him little hampers of food during a winter of such severity that there were bread riots in Paris, half the vines and olives were killed, and ragged skeletons of men and women dead from cold were found in the forest. News that James had contracted an ague made her break her vow not to fuss; she begged him to come home to be nursed. It would look bad, he replied, if he returned without his Most Christian Majesty's leave. She knew he was prevaricating; he did not want to return. She ordered Mr Dicconson to buy her some gold-leaf which must be dissolved in a rich cordial; Mme de Maintenon had advised her that this *aurum potabile* was a sovereign remedy for agues.

'The price of gold-leaf is quite beyond our purse, madam,' observed Mr Dicconson. 'And with respect, I think we should consider first how we are to feed the Household here, who are driven to poaching his Most Christian Majesty's game, as one of the keepers of the royal forests has complained to me.'

She could not believe that any of her servants would descend to such dishonesty and ingratitude, and appealed to the curé of St Germains who happened to be present.

'Madame,' said the priest, 'I verily believe that if I were dressed in a hare's skin, they would poach *me*.'

She gave orders that henceforth no game was to be allowed into her kitchens unless accompanied by a satisfactory account of whence it came; and decided that a more rigid economy could be practised if she retired for some months to Chaillot. She wrote to

155

the newly-appointed Guest Mistress, a certain Mère Bouchare, to have her apartments prepared; the reply, for all its courteous wording, was like a slap across the face. Since her Majesty was so deeply in arrears to the convent, Mère Bouchare had found a new tenant for the room formerly occupied by the Princess Louise, one Mme de L'Orge, who was already installed. The Princess's furniture had been moved to an upper storey; but Mme de L'Orge had signified her readiness to allow her Royal Highness the use of her old chamber when she herself was not in residence.

This blow from a quarter whence she least expected it moved Mary Beatrice to hot resentment. Had she not spent her windfall from the salt-mines in repairing their tribune? Had she not honoured Chaillot by giving into its keeping her beloved's heart? Tearing up a letter she had begun in this strain, she replied temperately to Mère Bouchare. Her daughter's old chamber adjoined her own; she could not accept it as a loan, and it would be most inconvenient to have the Princess so far away from her as an upper storey.

'But if you, my dear mother, or Mme de L'Orge, desire this arrangement, I pray you to tell me so plainly and with your usual sincerity.'

Mme de L'Orge, entirely ignorant of the trouble she had caused, wrote at once to relinquish the room; but for the first time in all these years, Chaillot was not quite the haven it had been. Still, it remained the only place where she could practise economy and attain to some resignation; observing the strict routine of the nuns, she made it a rule never to open any letters until the hour of Recreation. Sometimes she obtained permission for the novices and postulants to join the Community in her apartment where, seated on the floor, they listened with the most sympathetic interest to the news she gave them of her son.

He had been attacked again by a violent fever, and spent his convalescence under the roof of that very saintly man, Archbishop Fénelon, at Cambrai, who wrote of him in glowing terms.

'His firmness, his equability, his self-possession and tact, his sweet and gentle seriousness, his gaiety, devoid of boisterousness, must win him the favour of all the world.'

156

Still weak from illness, James insisted on returning to the front on a rumour of coming battle, and from Marshal Boufflers came an account of how he had behaved on that bloody field of Malplaquet.

'His Majesty refused to discard his blue ribbon of the Garter, which made him a target; he charged twelve times at the head of our Guards, despite a sabre cut in his arm, breaking the German cavalry. I never saw in action of the greatest danger a more intrepid courage, and I hear that all the English in the opposing armies drank his health openly afterwards.'

Torn between pride and anguish, she read aloud her son's lively letter describing how, attended only by three equerries, he rode to view the enemy outposts across a narrow stretch of the river Scarpe. Hearing them talk to one another in English, he called across to them, introducing himself as the Chevalier de St George. They had a long and friendly conversation, and on parting he sent an equerry over with some medals bearing his portrait, wrapped in a paper which bore the words, 'The metal is good, for it bore six hours' fire. You know it is hot, for you yourselves blew the coals'—a reminder of his repeated charges at Malplaquet.

'His Majesty exposes himself to unnecessary danger,' remarked Mère Bouchare.

'But gains in reputation, *ma mère*,' instantly countered Louise. 'It is just the kind of daring that appeals to the English, is it not, madame?'

Louise was something of an enigma to the nuns. Eighteen now, she was so radiantly beautiful and gifted that half Versailles was in love with her, but she showed no more inclination to marriage than she did to the cloister. Her vocation was to be La Consolatrice, she said. If anything happened to James, she would be Queen of England *de jure*; she merely shrugged her shoulders if anyone mentioned the fact; a throne was not for her, she said with a mysterious conviction. Her mother was mortified when the Duc de Berri married Mademoiselle, a stocky hoyden of fifteen, Madame's granddaughter, and the royal exiles must pay an official visit of congratulation. Berri's name had been linked with Louise's since they were children.

'While I am alive I never want to quit your Majesty,' La

Consolatrice assured her, as they returned in their shabby coach. 'I am never happy away from you; I can't bear the thought.'

The sight of all those piles of gold on the gaming-tables at Versailles had depressed Mary Beatrice almost as much as having to congratulate a bridegroom who might have been a son-in-law, and at supper she spoke with unusual asperity to Lady Strickland, her Keeper of the Privy Purse. Ashamed of herself, she said to her daughter when they were alone:

'I am sorry I spoke sharply to a lady who has served me faithfully for thirty years, but I was vexed that she should procure such costly dainties as those young partridges, when so many of my poor people at St Germains are in want of bread.'

'Madame,' said Louise, with her bracing common sense, 'you know that not all these people lost their fortunes in my father's service. Too many came over to be maintained in idleness out of your Majesty's pittance. These sort are more importunate than any other, and it is they who poached his Most Christian Majesty's game, for which you were blamed.'

James joined them at Chaillot for the anniversary of his father's death, and escorted Louise back to St Germains while their mother remained in that strict seclusion of mourning she always observed. She could find no sensible comfort in the conviction that her beloved's soul was in heaven; each passing year increased her sense of loss. She tormented herself by re-reading his letters, kept in a special drawer, nestling up to a past which, from this distance, seemed to have been cloudless. The present reached out hands to her in a hastily written note from Louise.

'I cannot refrain from writing to your Majesty this evening, being unable to wait till tomorrow. You will have the goodness to pardon this sad scrawl, but having only just arrived, my desk is in great disorder. I am here only in body, for my heart and soul are still at Chaillot at your feet, too happy if I could flatter myself that your Majesty has thought one moment of your poor daughter, who can think of nobody but you. Today has seemed like a year, as does every day when I am not with you; I can see nothing, nor attend to anything. I could write until tomorrow without being able to express half the veneration that I owe your Majesty, and if I may presume to

158

add, the tenderness I cherish for the best of mothers, but only my heart feels.'

It was almost like a love-letter, thought Mary Beatrice, adding it to a little pile in a certain drawer which contained pressed flowers, a sampler, a wool lamb with tin legs. When I am dead, she reflected, it will be a solace to my poor girl to find how I treasured all these little things.

5

As the year 1711 progressed, she began to hope that it would be her last. Beaulieu, her old surgeon, boasted that by his doses of quinquinna mixed with white powder of whalebone, he had arrested her cancer; she knew it was only hibernating. She had a poisoned finger, and Beaulieu's hand was so tremulous that he caused her agony when he lanced it. On her next visit to Chaillot, the nuns begged her to accept the ministrations of their own doctor, who came to treat sisters in the Infirmary; but she could not wound the feelings of her faithful old surgeon.

The Dauphin died very suddenly of smallpox, and Mary Beatrice, returning from a solitary visit of condolence, reported that even Mignonne, now Dauphine, had grown staid, occupying herself with her little sons.

'It would be just as dull for you at Versailles as here at Chaillot,' she told Louise. 'The Most Christian King has given up all attempts to keep his courtiers amused, and with so many of the young men killed during the late campaigns, Versailles seems inhabited by mourning mothers and widows.'

'A desert would not be dull for me so long as your Majesty was there,' declared La Consolatrice. 'And here is another letter arrived from the King while you were absent.'

Restless while there was no fighting, James was touring France incognito, while keeping up a secret correspondence with his half-sister. Anne, freed at last from slavery to her Mrs Freeman, seemed to be undergoing one of her periodic fits of repentance, and was reported by her new favourite, Abigail Masham, as often expressing concern about 'my brother'. His current letter was written from Lyons; keenly interested in all the arts of peace, he described with enthusiasm his visit to a silk factory, where he had been struck by seeing two thousand reels worked by one wheel.

'If ever it shall please God to restore me to my inheritance, I shall introduce these water-wheels into England. Meanwhile I was desirous of purchasing for my sister one of the most beautiful specimens of silk to make her a petticoat, but being uncertain of my own taste, I begged Mme L'Intendante to undertake the choice for me. So I hope she will have a petticoat of the most rich brocade to wear when she has left off her mourning for Monseigneur.'

'But when will you wear it?' sighed the Queen.

'Mignonne has promised to take me to my favourite opera, madame, *Thétis et Pélée*, as soon as we are out of mourning.' And she began to sing an aria in her true sweet voice.

Mère Bouchare pursed her lips. Of course her Royal Highness was free to sing in her Majesty's apartments, but yesterday she had been heard to do so on the staircase, which was a Place of Silence.

'But did not St Francis write that the Israelites could not sing in Babylon because their hearts were in their own land, yet in his opinion we should sing everywhere? And I shall never see my own land.'

Mère Priolo rallied her. Events were moving towards her brother's restoration, for the Princess Anne's health was failing. And was it not significant that a prosecution against the Faculty of Advocates in Edinburgh, on account of their receiving with thanks a medal bearing King James's portrait, had been dropped?

'For my part,' Louise said unexpectedly, 'I am delighted not to know the future.'

'It is a great mercy of God to hide it from us,' agreed her mother. 'When I came to France, I would have been in despair if I had been told I must remain here two years; I have been here for nearly twenty-three.'

Louise was looking out of the window and seemed unusually pensive.

'It seems to me, madame, that those who, like me, have been born in misfortune, are less to be pitied; never having tasted good fortune, they feel their unhappiness the less. And yet,' she added wistfully, 'it is sad to spend the best days of one's youth in so

160

hard a situation. What a day for a ride! I cannot understand why the King has so unreasonable a dislike of seeing women on horseback.'

'The King your father was the same. And necessity has settled the question for you; you have no horse.'

The rent for her apartments at Chaillot was due again, and she was trying to screw up her courage to make another appeal to Mme de Maintenon, due upon a visit. Pride was sinful, but it was so very humiliating to have to beg from a woman who was of the minor provincial nobility, even though she had acquired the air of the patrician. And as usual it was useless.

'Have not these nuns taken a vow of holy poverty?' inquired Mme de Maintenon. 'Then surely they ought not to charge your Majesty a sou. How well the Princess your daughter looks in these plain gowns she wears habitually. Of course if the Dauphine has invited her to the opera, she must go; but in this hot weather, the air of Paris is very unhealthy.'

'You cannot go to the opera,' the Queen told Louise later. 'The air is bad; you might catch some infection. And in any case I cannot afford to have that silk made up into a petticoat.'

She glanced away, unable to bear the disappointment on the girl's face. But after a moment came the constant refrain:

'I would far rather spend the evening with your Majesty.'

They were entering the chapel for Mass on St Ursula's Day, when a letter was handed to the Queen from the Duc de Lauzun. Suspecting its contents, she broke her rule never to read letters until Recreation, and turned into a side chapel, beckoning her daughter to follow. Lauzun warned her that peace was about to be signed at Utrecht, including an article, fiercely debated, wherein Louis repudiated the claims of her son and agreed to banish him from France. The blow was not less painful for having been expected, but she managed to retain command of herself during Mass. That evening at Recreation, Louise's red-rimmed eyes were so noticeable that her mother decided she must explain their cause to the Community.

'I shall impart to you, my mother and sisters, that the English have offered his Most Christian Majesty terms for peace which he must accept for the sake of France. The Princess of Denmark, so I understand, was reluctant to do her brother such grievous wrong as to drive him from French soil, but has been persuaded to it by her advisers.'

There were twitterings of dismay. Where would his Majesty go?

'The Duc de Lorraine has offered my son hospitality. There he will be at a convenient distance both from England and France.'

'But what advantage will your Majesty find in this peace?' inquired Mère Bouchare, plainly thinking about those arrears of rent. 'Surely there must be something stipulated whereby you receive your jointure, for so many years promised but unpaid?'

Mary Beatrice repressed a sigh. She had been having weary arguments with Middleton about the wording of a memorial to be sent to the plenipotentiaries at Utrecht. If she signed herself Queen Mother, it would not be allowed; if Queen Dowager, it would be of prejudice to James. She was absolutely resolved not to word the memorial in such a way as to deny her son's just claim, even if it meant forgoing every penny of the money owed her. She took refuge in platitudes.

'Peace is so great a blessing that it ought to be rejoiced at, and we have such signal obligations to France that we cannot but wish for anything that is beneficial to her. I have written to the Duc de Lauzun to send me any further information that may come to his knowledge. And now let us change the subject, for we are here at Recreation and should be merry. My daughter shall describe to you the day she had out hunting in the Bois de Boulogne.'

Louise gallantly did her best. Her dear Mignonne had arrived unexpectedly at Chaillot to beg for her this treat, and as it was such short notice, had brought a horse and a splendid habit for her, of scarlet laced with gold. All Paris had turned out to see the meet, and afterwards they had supped at the chateau of the Duchesse de Lauzun.

'I must confess,' said the Queen, 'I had a very sharp struggle with my pride before I accepted the Dauphine's offer. I cannot bear that anyone should give presents to my daughter, when she is not able to make a suitable return. And I know I should make a formal

162

visit to Versailles to thank the Dauphine, but I am getting to be so old and ugly that I affright myself and others.'

For once Louise did not hasten to assure her mother that she was still the most beautiful woman in the world. Her own lips trembled as she said:

'I am sorry I went, for the King my brother dislikes that I should ride, and soon I must bid him farewell.'

James arrived alone at the convent in November, having outdistanced his attendants. She was struck by his resemblance to his father when he too had been sent a vagabond about the world. There were no grumbles or recriminations; whatever happened, he said, he would preserve all his life a grateful remembrance of the kindnesses showered upon him by his Most Christian Majesty. As for the future, his chance of regaining his throne peacefully was excellent; the sick Anne had let him know by Lady Masham that she was well disposed towards him, whereas she detested his rival, George of Hanover, who had turned down the offer of her hand in marriage long ago.

As James was returning to St Germains that same evening, the Queen decided to go with him; every moment of his company was infinitely precious now. When next they parted, he would not be going on campaign or expedition; he would be leaving St Germains for ever. But at least she would have him for a few months yet; peace was not expected to be signed before the spring. And when that dreadful moment of farewell came, La Consolatrice would be there to sustain her.

6

In the new year, death swept the board at Versailles. Mignonne was the first victim of what at first was thought to be measles, but was in fact the dreaded smallpox. In the anteroom, Mary Beatrice sat with the stricken Louis for the whole of one night, while nine doctors constantly bled the patient, cursed by Madame, and the voice of Mme de Maintenon could be heard saying:

'You are going to God, my child. Today Dauphine, tomorrow nothing.'

Within a fortnight, Mignonne's husband and two of their

sons had followed her to the grave; and now the future King of France was a sickly infant of two, saved from Fagon's ferocious bleeding by his Governess, Madame Ventadour, who hid him in her bed. From the terrace at St Germains, Mary Beatrice watched the long funeral processions wend their way to St Denis, heard the solemn shock of bells. Thank God her own dear ones were safe; she had not allowed them anywhere near Versailles, and flinging economy to the winds, she had burnt all her clothes after her visits there.

These tragic deaths of the young seemed to her a warning that the end of her own weary pilgrimage was in sight, and she longed for the order of release. When James left, she would have to act as his factor once more; those incomprehensible public affairs snarled at her from the future, a maze of mysteries as baffling as an eastern alphabet. At any rate, she should set her affairs in order at once, since death struck where one least expected him. She sent to Chaillot for her Will and a bundle of papers she kept there, mostly bills; Mère Bouchare's hints about her unpaid rent and probings about her jointure had been very wounding. She sat up half the night alone composing a document, acutely missing the aid of good old Caryll, who had died last year.

'Having always intended to make arrangements for the good of the Convent of the Visitation of St Marie at Chaillot, in which I have been so many times received and well lodged for nearly four and twenty years, and wishing to execute this design better than it is possible for me to do in the circumstances under which I find myself at present: I declare that my intention has always been to give 3,000 livres a year for the hire of the apartments I have occupied there since the year 1689, till this present year, 1712, in all which time I have never paid but 19,000. It still remains for me to pay 50,000, which sum I engage and promise to pay on the establishment of the King my son in England.'

She sighed with pain and fatigue, longing for bed, for the soothing draught Louise would have ready, for those gentle but capable hands plumping up her pillows. Thank God there would always be Louise to read to her now that her sight was failing, to defend her from the swarm of duns and petitioners during the promenade, to stand up to Mère Bouchare, to nurse her when the hideous thing within her breast resumed its search for her vitals.

'And not having the power to do this while living, I have charged the King my son in my testament, and engaged him to execute all these promises, which he will find written with my own hand, and that before one year be passed after his restoration. I have left also in my Will,' she placated the absent Mère Bouchare, 'wherewithal to make a most beautiful restoration of the high altar of the church in the said convent, or a fine tabernacle, if they should like that better; and also I have left for a mausoleum to be made for the heart of the King, my lord and husband.'

She signed, impressed on the wax her diamond seal, and sat for a while turning the signet in her hand. It had been made for her coronation, the letters M.R. intertwined and surmounted by the Crown Matrimonial; perhaps even this treasure might have to be pawned soon; she could not let James set out on his wanderings without at least some resources, though he had assured her he could manage; he had no personal debts and was not extravagant.

James spent the next day hunting with the Duc de Berri, prospective Regent of France. Perhaps with his new importance, Berri could persuade the plenipotentiaries at Utrecht (where peace was still not signed) to insert an article phrased in so ambiguous a manner that Anne's successor might be either James or Elector George. She discussed this with Louise during their quiet day together, watching the girl's skilful hands paint a design on a big canvas, to be filled in with her needle afterwards. When it was made into a firescreen, she would send it to the King, said Louise cheerfully, sharpening her black lead and putting it fast into quills.

James looked tired at supper; he had a slight headache, he said, and then with his usual dislike of speaking about his health, hurried on to describe the chase. He gave so lively an account that his mother did not notice how little food he ate, or what a thirst he seemed to have.

She was dressing next morning when word was brought from his side of the chateau that he had a high fever and a rash on face and breast. Despite all her care to keep him from infection, he had caught smallpox, the disease she dreaded most.

She sat at his bedside day and night in the darkened room. He had the disease in its most dangerous form, the confluent; face, arms and breast were covered now in small flat spots with black specks, oozing with a thin watery ichor. A violent throbbing of the arteries in his neck, the brown crust covering his tongue, his bloody stools and the periodic grinding of his teeth, all made Fagon look very grave indeed as he inserted the inevitable lancet. Worst of all to Mary Beatrice was to hear that voice babble in delirium, betraying anxieties and fears ordinarily locked up by the key of reserve. The equable, firm and consistently cheerful son she knew had given place to a stranger, a poor helpless soul wrestling with problems too great for his years, tormented by hope deferred, by a temptation to despair. There were times when she felt she ought to send Louise out of the room; it was indecent that this girl, so passionately proud of her brother, should see him with his defences down.

But the dear familiar presence was her only source of strength during that week. With Louise beside her she could be steady; it was Louise who defied M. Fagon and insisted that the patient's linen be changed, and that sweet whey and not wine be given him for his thirst. Louise seemed to know without consulting her watch when five hours had elapsed and he must take a teaspoonful of poppy syrup to quieten him; it was she and not Fagon who thought of vinegar and currant jelly to moisten his poor cracked lips.

On the eighth day, Mary Beatrice was alarmed to see his face begin to fall in and his hands and feet to swell, but Louise was ready with encouragement.

'M. Fagon tells me, madame, that these are excellent signs. The pox, which before had a very threatening aspect, will rise and fill with what he terms laudable matter. Now the great thing is to prevent, by clysters and bleeding, the poison from the pustules being absorbed into the bowel. You see I have become almost a doctress!'

That night James slept for the first time without drugs, and in the morning asked for some tea. She turned to share her thankfulness with Louise, and not seeing her in the darkened room, asked fretfully where she was. Her Royal Highness was somewhat indisposed with a looseness, whispered Lady Middleton. But the next moment Louise came tiptoeing in; it was nothing at all, she said. She herself would make the marigold tea ordered by Fagon if the patient asked for drink, while her Majesty took some rest.

'If there is any change now, it will be for the better, madame. God has answered our prayers.'

The Queen slept for some hours from sheer exhaustion, and hurried back to the sick chamber. Her hand on his forehead encountered a blessed new coolness; he was trying to force down the extraordinary diet Fagon had prescribed, of roast apples and preserved plums. But being so delicate he would need careful nursing, she said to Louise; and there was no reply. Of course the poor child must be worn out, strong and healthy though she was. She could not at first understand what Lady Middleton told her, and had to ask her to repeat it.

'The Princess noticed a rash on her bosom when she was changing her dress. M. Fagon assures me that the symptoms are most favourable, and hopes that even her beauty may be spared.'

Louise did not look sick, lying there in her bed, her brown curls piled high as though for her portrait, her flower face only slightly flushed. She stretched out a hand to her mother, and smiled.

'You could not have kept me from the King's chamber, madame, unless you had locked me up, so don't, pray don't blame yourself that I have caught the smallpox. M. Fagon says he must bleed me in the foot, and give me a purge of senna and rhubarb, but by tomorrow I am sure I shall be able to take my turn at watching.'

It was said so confidently that the Queen was deceived. God did not send all sorts of afflictions at the same time, knowing her weakness. And meanwhile James was climbing slowly out of the abyss, but needing such constant attention that any anxiety she felt for Louise remained in the background. When she asked after her daughter, the answers were encouraging; she did not notice that they were also evasive. The Princess's fever was abating; she had been given something to make her sleep, and must not be disturbed. She would just look in on Louise, decided the Queen, before she lay down on her own bed for a while. The room was in darkness, and certain that Louise was sleeping, she was tiptoeing out again, when a voice from the bed spoke with heartening vigour.

'You see, madame, the happiest person in the world. I have just made my General Confession. It seems to me that I have made it as well as I could, so that if they had to tell me I was going to die now, I could not do it any better. I would like to live, because I think I could be of some comfort to you. But the King is safe.'

La Consolatrice! Of course she would live.

Dwelling for so long in semi-darkness, she had no idea what time it was when she awoke to find Fr Ruga standing by her bed. He carried a candle, and she saw on his face that same pitiful expression as when, long ago, he had come to beg her to join him in the prayers for a departed soul. Her lips formed the words, 'The King my son', but he shook his head.

'The Princess passed into a coma during the night, madame, and as there was no longer any hope, we would not disturb your Majesty. Come now and behold the peace of one who has just yielded her pure young soul to God.'

Death had been a visitor here for so short a while that as yet no marks of his coming were visible. Soon the room would be turned into a *chapelle ardente*, with tall candles of unbleached wax, windows and walls hung with crape, and a temporary altar erected. But for the moment it remained the room of the living Louise, full of the things which had made up her peaceful routine, her lute laid down as though she had just finished playing on it, her turtle-doves in their cage, the canvas she had been painting the day her brother went hunting with Berri, carefully spread out upon a table, with her little brass compasses, her badger brushes, sponge, pumice-stone and precious packets of ochre and vermilion, all ready for work to be resumed.

But she herself did not lie as though she slept. Rather the instant impression was that she had awakened somewhere else. Her lips were slightly upturned at the corners in a mysterious smile; her long dark lashes lay upon the youthful curve of the cheeks as though to hide a secret. 'She seems a merry angel lent to us from heaven, rather than a human child.' That remark of Lady Strickland suddenly had point. She had been lent, not given. The little candle of her life had not been allowed to gutter, nor had it been blown out in some passing draught, but by the breath of God.

La Consolatrice had fulfilled her vocation, and gone home.

7

The Queen is too prostrate with shock, said her ladies, to attend her Royal Highness's funeral. But it was not so. She desired to treasure the memory of a Louise lying as though she had awakened somewhere else. The comfort she had given was not wholly withdrawn; her mother felt it reaching out to her in most happy dreams of the dead girl, in sudden thoughts which only she could have inspired. For the first time, age and sickness appeared as blessings; it could not be so very long before she and Louise were reunited; and meanwhile she must live for James.

'The King is safe.' Louise's last words to her. He was recovering very slowly; as soon as he was strong enough he must set out for his new exile in Lorraine. Louis came to condole with his mother, and laying aside formality, shared her gentle tears for the way in which death had left the old and swept away the young. But that was Louis the man; to le Roi Soleil the interests of France remained paramount. James must leave France, and Louise was denied a funeral oration, for any public allusion to the Royal Family of England would be incompatible with the Treaty of Utrecht.

It was not till August that she paid her first visit to Chaillot since Louise's death, allowing herself this luxury because she could not bear to take farewell of her son at St Germains. He would call on her here before he set out on his wanderings.

'Where is the picture of my poor girl?' she asked instantly, as she entered her apartments in the convent.

The nuns had removed it, thinking it would pain her; she had it rehung, and often smiled across at a Louise who dimpled as she chased a butterfly in the gardens of Versailles. She had brought with her the length of brocade, never made up into the petticoat for which it was designed. The Vestiarian and her assistants were consulted; it would make the most beautiful cope. Mère Bouchare, with her usual lack of tact, repeated a tale that was going round. Fagon's insistence on bleeding the Princess in the foot had made her too exhausted to fight the disease, and the pustules had appeared prematurely.

'No, *ma mère*. The doctors did their best, but they cannot render mortals immortal. God took my daughter when it pleased Him, and I cannot doubt that what He did was best for her. And for me too if I knew how to profit by it, but alas I do not act as I speak.'

Alone with Mère Priolo, she said:

'Sometimes of late I have a strange fancy. In his talk of nautical matters, the late King my husband mentioned several kinds of anchor, but I can remember only the sheet-anchor, the last refuge in trouble. Mine is whatever service I can render the King my son.'

The nuns showed her one of their Circular Letters which would go the round of the other Visitation houses. It was a panegyric on Louise, and they were sure it would please her.

'The Princess was so entirely occupied at all times and places with the love of God, that even when she was at the opera, her whole thoughts were on Him, and she adapted the songs and music to His praise with internal adoration.'

She exchanged a smile with Louise's portrait.

'I am sure this would be very edifying, but it is not strictly true. My daughter was passionately fond of music and poetry, and took the delight in these amusements which was natural to her youth. Pray let that passage in the Letter be omitted.'

She was seized in the small hours of the morning with such pain in her foot that it felt on fire. The nuns' doctor, hastily summoned, diagnosed gout.

'This malady, madame, is usually caused by idleness and intemperance—have I said something to amuse your Majesty?'

'I am sorry, M. le Docteur. All my life I laugh in the wrong place. But surely there must be other causes for this malady?'

Yes, he said rather huffily, there were; night-watching and excessive mental agitation. On no account must she rise for early Mass; she must avoid intense thinking; and her foot must be encased in a large cocoon of flannel. It was in this state that she hobbled down the cloister to greet James when he came on his brief farewell visit. He, too, was limping; he had been bled so many times in the foot during his illness that the wound had not yet healed. They managed to laugh together as he described them as two old cripples. He did indeed look much older, his face faintly scarred by the smallpox, his manner tinged with melancholy, though resolute. Her heart ached to remember those babblings when fever had broken down the barriers of his self-command.

'Your Majesty,' observed an aged nun, 'very much resembles your late uncle, King Charles, who did us the honour of visiting us before he set out for England.'

'That journey, sister,' he said evenly, 'will not be yet.'

He left hurriedly after dinner, whispering to Mère Priolo to console the Queen. As soon as he had gone, she began to weaken in her resolve to make this a short visit; her courage was not equal to the terrifying solitude of St Germains, whence laughter and song had disappeared with Louise.

'Why should your Majesty return?' asked Mère Priolo. 'You have told me that there is but little business to be transacted there now; if your signature is required, surely documents can be brought to you here.'

It was a strong temptation. She wrote for advice to an old and valued friend, Cardinal Gualterio, and consulted also her confessor and chaplain. The Cardinal replied incisively: 'God designed your Majesty for the throne and not for the cloister, and it is necessary to submit to His will, even though thorns take the place of jewels in your crown.' Her priests sang the same tune; she ought not, in the present unsettled state of her son's affairs, to retire from the world. To make quite sure, she wrote to James himself; he replied that it would be a great presumption on his part to proffer any advice, but reminded her that St Germains was still a rallying-point for his friends and agents, and a sorting-house for his letters.

'I shall return in time for Christmas,' she told Mère Priolo. 'My sheet-anchor is there.'

She found St Germains rent with a new intrigue; Middleton was with her son at Bar-le-Duc, and in his absence the clique who hated him had revived an old slander that he had betrayed all secrets to the usurping government ever since the death of James II. Lady Middleton was hysterical with indignation; her husband, she raged, was resolved to retire, since such wicked things were said about him, and to spend his last years as a private person. Mary Beatrice wrote to him at once. If he was determined to resign his seals of office, would he not return to St Germains as her own adviser?

'I am grown so insignificant and useless to my friends,' she wrote, 'that all I can do is to pray for them, and God knows my poor prayers are worth but little. Yet weary as I am of the world, I am not so dead to it but that I strive, as best I may, for the good of my son's affairs. You told me in one of your letters that you were charmed with the King for being such a good son. What do you think that I must suffer, who am the poor old doting mother of him, and yet can do so little for lack of wise advice?'

Middleton replied kindly; so long as his Majesty trusted him, he would remain with the King. His rival Perth was mortally sick; a new generation had grown up at St Germains; of former counsellors none remained but Mr Dicconson, who was entirely preoccupied with the effort to make ends meet. Personages from Versailles continued to call upon the Queen, whose heart felt ready to burst when she was obliged to chatter to them on indifferent subjects, to hope, when she offered a flask of muscat, that they did not notice it had been watered down, to see the wolfish glares of her own people, who sometimes went for thirty hours without food, when she had to order expensive collations. She had lost all hope of ever receiving her jointure, and her French pension was eight months in arrear.

The evening was the hour she dreaded most. At Chaillot she wrote her letters in the morning when she had some energy and the light was good; at St Germains there was so much to occupy her during the day that it was not until after supper that she could write to James, in instalments because it had to be in code. He had a new 'in-and-out', a cipher-key in which she was 'Andrew' and he was 'Mr Jackson', a lawyer supposed to be engaged in some intricate litigation on 'Andrew's' behalf. She could never learn by heart the code names of his friends and agents, and each evening must search afresh through a list to find who was 'the bale of goods', and who 'the Hamborough merchant'.

But first there was the hunt for her spectacles. Louise had

made a jest of her constant loss of them, pretending to look up the chimney or out of the window. Her ladies regarded the mislaying as something tiresome.

'I suppose we shall have to ask St Anthony to find them,' sighed Molza, 'though really I am quite ashamed to pester him again.'

The draught from under the door made her shiver, and there was no Louise cunningly to arrange a screen; the china plates which ornamented her escritoire chilled her hands; Louise had made her a pair of mittens, now worn out. The kind-hearted Duchesse de Lauzun offered her a handsome new desk as a present, but she still had her pride, and said hastily that she was in the process of buying one for herself. It cost 45 livres, less than £2 in English money, and her sense of humour awoke as she surveyed it. She could not help contrasting the wretched thing with Louis's silver-gilt escritoire at Versailles, a large diamond at each corner, and a solid gold lion holding in its jaws a jewelled pounce-box.

Mme de Maintenon called; she had received the most charming letter from the Chevalier de St George, she said. Since the Peace of Utrecht, signed in May, no one was allowed to give James his proper title. Madame did so, loudly, to annoy the 'Old Swipe'.

'He combines in his writing the tenderness of a son, the elegance of an academician, and the dignity of a monarch.' She chafed her hands. 'Your Majesty's apartments are very cold; I myself suffer extremely at Versailles where, as you know, his Most Christian Majesty flings all the windows open as soon as he enters a room, and I have had a *tonneau* made, what you call in English a hooded chair. I strongly advise you to do the like.'

'If ever my jointure is paid, I will avail myself of your suggestion, Mme de Maintenon; meanwhile I have to go to the expense of buying a new portable chair for use when my little malady is troublesome. Lady Strickland and I have been looking at patterns for the lining; I understood that *gros de Tours* silk is hard-wearing and cheap, but I find it costs ten livres the ell, so we shall have to find something less expensive.'

'Your Majesty puts me in mind of St Thomas de Villeneuve, who disputed with his shoemaker about the price of his shoes, and a few days later gave one of the shoemaker's daughters 300 rials to enable her to marry. For your Majesty is parsimonious only that you may be munificent in your charities.'

Mary Beatrice flushed with annoyance, and tried for the hundredth time to hint, in a roundabout way, that Mme de Maintenon might call Louis's attention to the fact that her pension was in arrear.

'I certainly have no dispute about the price of my shoes, but I am obliged to get them for as little cost as I can. When I was in England, I always had a new pair every week, and new gloves every day, for I was told that as Queen I could not do with less.' She smiled wryly. Fantastic to remember the amount of perfectly good clothes she was expected to discard then; they were the perquisites of her Mistress of the Robes, who distributed them as she pleased, so that Mary Beatrice was for ever seeing her own gowns, worn only once, on someone else. 'M. de Lauzun once used an exaggeration in speaking to his Most Christian Majesty on the subject of my penury, when he said, "Sire, she has scarcely shoes to her feet!" Still, it is true that these shoes I now wear are quite worn out, and to buy new would cost ten livres. I think it is too much to pay, but they will not charge me less.'

'During my impoverished youth, I learned never to give a tradesman as much as he asks for his goods. It is a rule I recommend to your Majesty; these merchants expect one to cheapen the article.'

When she had departed to the luxury of Versailles, Mary Beatrice counted her daily ration of logs, decided she ought not to put another on the fire just yet, and summoned Mr Dicconson to their daily conference. James had the intermittent fever and needed to take the waters at Plombières; he made excuses for not going, but his mother knew it was because he could not afford the journey.

'I need to sell something which will fetch a good price, Mr Dicconson, and I have been reviewing my few great treasures. There are my mother's pearls, my diamond seal, and the little ruby ring of my marriage. With these I do not feel that I can part, not yet.'

'There is also the ring of your Majesty's proxy wedding. It is a very fine diamond.'

'I have already sent it to my son, reset with a curl of his sister's hair. To think of all those jewels I wore at my coronation! Only one small diamond, worth forty shillings, was lost during the ceremonies; if only I had that one little jewel now! But do you think I dare sell the silver-gilt toilette which awaited me here at St Germains when I escaped from England? His Most Christian Majesty calls seldom since he became indisposed; but someone might tell him, and it seems so ungrateful.'

They could say truthfully that it had been put into safe keeping, suggested Mr Dicconson. But what of their daily necessities? Tradesmen were beginning to refuse him any more credit.

'We shall just have to borrow from a common money-lender; I know the interest is high, but necessity has no law. And now for another particular purpose, I wish you to sell two of my smaller valuables, my tiny striking-watch concealed in a diamond ring, and my beautiful fur collar with head and claws in jewel-encrusted gold.'

James had begged her several times for a new portrait of herself; it would be a comfort to him during their long separation. She knew that at her age it was absurd to be vain; yet it cost her a sharp struggle to allow herself to be depicted as old, her hair and eyebrows turning grey, fine lines smocking her face. She was giving Gobert, the artist, a first sitting, when in waddled Madame. It was Sunday, and Madame at once announced that if there was to be High Mass in the chapel, she would not attend.

'This Gregorian chant—"A-a-i-i-i"! I would sooner hear a donkey bray. I have a chaplain who dispatches Masses in a quarter of an hour; that is quite to my taste. But if there is to be a sermon, I shall hear it; I find sermons better than poppy-syrup for my insomnia. Unfortunately I snore so loudly nowadays that at Versailles they have banished me to a tribune.'

She scrutinized the portrait, which represented Mary Beatrice as St Helena showing the True Cross, and said that it was most fitting; everyone agreed that her Majesty was a saint. The Queen was horrified, and immediately decided to be painted as herself, sitting by the urn containing the heart of her husband.

'You look ill,' remarked Madame, 'and much altered for the

worse in your appearance. For myself, I am cheerful. The hunting accident which befell that toad, Berri, last week will certainly be the end of him, for he broke a vein in his stomach, and then my son will be Regent when the Great Man dies, which will be soon. Fagon makes him sleep enveloped in feather-beds to induce sweat, and keeps his bad leg in a bath of burgundy. As for you, if only you would learn to eat in the true German style, you would feel better. I know perfectly well that your larder is bare, and so I have brought you a side of bacon, cured under my own eyes.'

She launched into an enthusiastic description of the curing, the amount of saltpetre to be rubbed in daily for a month, and the final smoking between layers of straw.

'Speaking of Germany, I think you may rest assured that her Deliction, my Aunt Sophy, will not dispute the English throne with your son at her advanced age. Of Duke George one cannot be certain; what is quite certain is that he murdered his wife's lover. Well, we shall know very soon; Brandy-Faced Nan, your stepdaughter, is drinking herself to death.'

Every post from England was full of the coming crisis, and Mary Beatrice was thankful to have Lord Middleton back at her side. He stuck to his old theme: trust the Princess Anne to do the right thing by her brother and thereby honour so many promises. But Anne was dying as she had lived, never able to make up her own mind, pushed back and forth between the strong Whig party who wanted Hanover, and Lady Masham who urged her to name her brother as her heir.

The threadbare, starving exiles at St Germains gorged like vultures on every shred of news. Anne signed a warrant for an instalment of her stepmother's jointure, an excellent omen! It was only for £11,750, whereas the arrears amounted to over a million, and it was at once swallowed up in payment to the more pressing creditors. But the very next day, Anne put her signature to a reward of £5,000 for James's arrest, styling him 'the person who pretends to pretend a right to my throne'. She fell into a rage when, as a sequel to this, the Whigs tried to bring in a motion to invite Elector George over to take his seat as Duke of Cambridge. To the fury of Madame, she gave £50 for a malicious doggerel on Madame's beloved Aunt Sophy's decease; and she wrote to the Duc de Lorraine that the more kindness he showed her brother, the more she would consider herself beholden to him.

'I can never think of her treachery,' said the severe Lady Strickland, 'without feeling disposed to invoke upon her the maledictions of the Psalmist on the wicked.'

'Never have I used such prayers, nor will I ever use them,' said the Queen.

To her there was something pitiful about Anne. What secret torment of conscience must she suffer that made her sit silent by the hour with her fan in her mouth; what flabbiness of will betrayed her into moaning about 'my poor brother' one moment, the next reverting to the odious mockery she had used at James's birth.

A note from James gave his mother the bare news of Anne's death; he was rushing in disguise to Paris to beg the aid of his Most Christian Majesty for an expedition to England, and would meet her at Chaillot. It was two years since she had seen him; he was as affectionate as ever, but it was the king and not the son who came. She tried to understand what he told her. Anne had left an unsigned Will, almost certainly naming him as her successor, since it was burnt unopened with suspicious haste by her Whig Ministers. Each of his own supporters on the spot had wanted the other to take the risk of proclaiming him, but there was no doubt that the nation at large was wild for his return, openly drinking his health, yelling 'Down with Hanover!', and throwing halters into the coach sent to receive Elector George. Yet Scotland remained his best hope; Lord Mar swore he could raise twenty thousand men there, if only he had the money to pay and arm them.

'I must find it somehow. His Most Christian Majesty has refused, but I have appealed to the King of Spain, King Charles of Sweden, and the new Emperor. I am not without hope that these appeals will be answered, though at present all his Imperial Majesty offers me is his sister for my wife. To talk of marriage at a time like this!'

She had *thought* of it for years. He was nearly twenty-seven; her cancer was increasing, and when she died he would be completely alone unless he had a wife. Wrestle as she might with that woman's heart of hers, it clung to persons and was indifferent to causes. A happy marriage for James would mean infinitely more to her than the regaining of his throne.

8

He seemed just about to regain it, during this year of 1715. On his twenty-seventh birthday, white roses entwined with oak leaves were boldly displayed in London, with the motto, *A New Restoration*. Louis, calling at St Germains, confided to the Queen that his conscience was troubling him. He knew perfectly well that he was dying, he said composedly, and he wished to make some restitution to 'my adopted son' whose title he had acknowledged on his father's death. He had written to his own grandson, the King of Spain, urging him to render all possible assistance to James, and he seriously engaged on his own account to furnish arms for ten thousand men and ships to transport them to Scotland.

But on September 1st, the great King died. She was not invited to be present at his death-bed, and heard from others of the violent scenes which disturbed his end, the Duc du Maine, Maintenon's pet, disputing with the Duc d'Orleans for the guardianship of the new child King. Orleans won, and her advisers impressed on her the vital necessity to court him, which entailed joining with the French Court in cold-shouldering Mme de Maintenon. She could not do it; she was incapable of fair-weather friendship. Her visits of condolence, paid with the ceremony due to the relict of a deceased Sovereign, gave Orleans a perfect excuse for repudiating the late King's engagements to James.

Her advisers at St Germains looked at her with reproach; she preferred integrity to diplomacy, and here was the result. The arms waiting at Le Havre were unloaded and carried to the arsenal at the very moment when they were needed in Scotland, where risings had broken out prematurely. And now here was Berwick, the only man capable of taking command there, excusing himself because, as a naturalized Frenchman, he must first obtain the Regent's permission, which everyone knew would not be forthcoming. And it was through her Majesty's influence, years ago, that Berwick had taken French nationality.

A line from James informed her that he was slipping over to Scotland in a small sloop provided by a new adherent, Lord Bolingbroke, and she must not expect to hear from him again until he reached his native land. She thought that surely after all these years she should have grown inured to hideous uncertainty, the daily waiting for news. She was not alone in her anxiety; most of her ladies had sons who had gone with James.

'The most common trial of women,' said Lady Sophia Bulkeley, who had lost her husband in the abortive expedition of 1708, 'has always been to sit at home and wait, unable to do anything but pray, and keep a good fire burning for their loved ones' return.'

She tried to keep up her mistress's spirits by singing to her guitar the Jacobite songs which were coming over. But though Mary Beatrice 'put on the courageous', as she termed it, in public, inwardly she suffered the same torments as in those days when her husband was in peril.

Now, as then, conflicting rumours tightened the screw. She knew it would be more sensible to leave unread the tracts and news-sheets which either gave false news or else were violently partisan, but to do so was beyond her. At Christmas, Lauzun brought her a melancholy gift in the shape of definite tidings; the English Jacobites had been routed at Preston, and the utterly incompetent Mar, who commanded in Scotland, had thrown away what might have been a victory at Sheriffmuir. Nothing was known of James himself, except that he had not been present at either battle. That evening she sat by her poor fire, dictating a letter to Lady Bulkeley. It was to Mère Priolo, but it was quite unlike her usual intimate notes. Only by being coldly factual could she retain any vestige of self-control.

'The Queen commands me to tell you that as soon as she receives any good news, she will not fail to impart it. She says, you are not to give credit to the report, which she understands you have heard, that the Scots wish to make peace with the Elector of Hanover, for it is not true, although their affairs are not in so good a condition as they were. The Queen orders me to tell you, dear mother, that she cannot write; and I am to tell you that she doubts not you will redouble your prayers for the preservation of the person of the King her son, and for the prosperity of his faithful subjects.'

Mary Beatrice put on her spectacles and read the letter through before signing it, repressing a smile as she did so. Lady Sophia had never mastered the art of orthography, and she herself described her handwriting as 'griffonage'.

'May I add a little postscript on my own account, madam?'

I know, thought Mary Beatrice, exactly what she will write. She will speak of my firm and lively faith in God, and how tranquilly I accept all that He may permit. If only she could see inside my heart! I would be content if I could say with Jacob, my son yet liveth.

Even her outward calm broke when, in January, a letter arrived in a dear familiar script. James had landed at Peterhead in December, dodging the Elector's fleet; he had, he admitted, nothing wherewith to begin a campaign but his own person, yet the affection of the Scots was beyond all his dreams, and he was resolved to hold Perth throughout the winter. He would not leave Scotland without at least one blow for his rights. The mere fact that he was safe made her ill with relief; she was just able to totter about her apartments again when another courier arrived. He had left the King in perfect health, and although the enemy far outnumbered his little army, the messenger was confident that by this time he would have been crowned at Scone. His chief lack was arms, and if her Majesty could find the money for these, he had instructed Lord Bolingbroke to arrange for their dispatch.

She would sell immediately her few remaining treasures, she told Mr Dicconson, who smiled sadly and said that these would fetch but a fraction of what was needed. She must throw her pride to the winds and beg. Not from the Regent, who had made it quite plain that his policy was to maintain friendship with Elector George; but perhaps his mother might consent to help, if only to spite him. Madame, who had taken it for granted that he would require her as his principal adviser, had been told very bluntly that he would brook no interference, and had retired in dudgeon to the Palais Royal.

A list of Madame's grievances had to be aired before she could be approached on the subject of funds.

'The Great Man must be turning in his grave if he can see

Versailles now. My son knows but one law, that of his own pleasures; he is surrounded by a crowd of nobodies, who dare to recline on couches in his presence. I would not stay under the same roof with his seraglio of opera dancers and *femmes de chambre*. So here I am exiled in detestable, pernicious, stinking Paris.'

'But could you not go to your dower-house at Montargis, Liselotte?' inquired Mary Beatrice, using the pet name as a preliminary to asking a favour.

'And what should I find to do there except walk? When the Great Man was alive, I could walk two leagues with him and not tire; now I have but to cross one room and I pant like a buffalo.'

Gathering her courage, Mary Beatrice asked baldly for a loan, and at once wished she had not. Madame treated her to a long rambling account of her own commitments and what she chose to describe as her poverty, ending with the spiteful advice to go and beg from Mme de Maintenon.

'The Old Hag having renounced the world and all its pomps and vanities, should have plenty to spare for one she has always regarded as a saint.'

A professional money-lender must be approached again, and everything she possessed pledged to the hilt. Bolingbroke, summoned from his Paris lodging to receive the precious funds, sent a rude refusal; he was much too occupied in courting the Regent on behalf of his master to come. She dispatched the money to him, heavily guarded, only to hear from Lord Middleton that he was squandering it on his latest mistress. In the act of writing him a heated remonstrance, she received a letter from James, written at Gravelines.

It was all over. The Scottish leaders had convinced him that his presence could only cause further suffering to their people; his person, on which was set the price of £100,000, was the chief object of the pursuing army, and once he was gone they could make terms. He was coming to St Germains on a flying visit, disguised as an abbé.

Without a periwig, she saw that his thick dark hair had thinned, and this aging was reflected in his manner. All spontaniety had gone for good, and while he refused to blame anyone, she sensed that the iron had entered into his soul. It was plain to her that the fatigues of a campaign and the rigours of a Scottish winter had taken their toll of his health, but she knew him too well to remark on this, and kept to practical matters. What would he do, where would he go? She understood that even his friend the Duc de Lorraine would not venture to harbour him now.

'My advisers tell me that I have no choice but to take refuge in the Papal States, though my last hopes of England might well be ruined should I be driven thither. Yet only His Holiness offers me asylum, and what is more important, funds for the loyal men I was obliged to leave in Scotland. Before I sailed, I sent the remnants of my slender resources to Lord Argyll for the relief of those villages my troops were forced to burn, so that I might at least have the satisfaction of having been the ruin of none, at a time when I came to free all.'

His self-control was cracking; his face worked.

'Our poor Scots have escaped into the hills, a death by slow starvation; God knows how they will exist; I have sent two ships in the hope of saving some of them. In England already the scaffolds redden. It is crushing to me who thought myself in a manner happy while I was alone in these misfortunes to which I have grown used. The deaths and disasters of the innocent, of which I am the cause, break my heart.'

He flung himself forward across the table, and for the first time since childhood she heard him weep. Gathering him into her arms, she murmured endearments, torn between compassion and sweet joy to find him her son again, her Jamie. But almost at once she felt him stiffen, ashamed that she had witnessed his collapse. She rose and turned away to give him time to recover; but she could not prevent herself from asking wistfully:

'Might I not come with you to the Papal States? It would save the expense of two Households.'

He blew his nose hard, squared his thin shoulders, and became the king again.

'And admit that my cause is hopeless? It is vital to my interests that your Majesty maintains friendly relations with the Court of France.'

She acquiesced immediately, shutting interior eyes to the bleak years ahead, the managing of public affairs for which she had never acquired the least aptitude, the constant need to be on her guard in what she said, the grinding poverty, the bitter loneliness. If it was vital to his interests that she remain at St Germains, at St Germains she would remain.

8

The Story Closes

1

The last sheet of cheap paper, covered in Mère Priolo's neat script, was read, and the Queen appended her signature. She had deleted much; there was more she had not told. It had been a painful task, sweetened with laughter, the thing she would miss so acutely when she returned to St Germains next week. The sonorous voice of the bell, Henriette-Marie-Phillipe-Augustus, called her to the window. Across there in the Chapter House, the Community were about to make the Annual Exchange; lots would be cast for cells, books, beads, crucifixes, a part of the Rule designed to destroy attachment to the least object.

She herself was so attached to things. Just before leaving St Germains on her present visit, she had lost her favourite holy picture, the card portraying Our Lady of the Visitation, given by Reverend Mother at Modena, and had fretted for it ever since.

'*Benedicamus Domino!*' sang out Mère Priolo, entering the room after dinner. 'Your Majesty has approved our little history!'

'Which has prevented me from finishing this seat-cover,' said the Queen, busy with her needlework. 'I hoped that I would complete Fortitude before I left.'

'A virtue your Majesty possesses to the most heroic degree. I have a favour to ask. Would you let me end our history with some sentences from a letter you wrote me last April? I have the letter here, but I scarcely need it, for the words are graven on my heart:

"Truth to tell, there remains to us at present neither hope nor human resource from which we can derive any comfort whatsoever, so that, according to the world, our condition may be pronounced desperate. But according to God, we ought to believe ourselves happy, and bless and praise Him for having driven us to the wholesome necessity of putting our whole trust in Him alone." '

'All my life,' sighed the Queen, 'I have made myself utter such good sentiments, but still I have not that detachment in my heart.'

The letter from which Mère Priolo quoted had been written after the dashing of a dear and tender hope. Driven from his new refuge at Avignon by the intrigues of the Regent and Elector George, James was making a slow progress towards Urbino in the Papal States, seeking a wife.

He mentioned the fact unemotionally in his first letters to his mother; all his advisers were convinced that the backwardness of many great ones during his expedition to Scotland was due to their reluctance to risk their all on the contingency of his single life, and therefore it was his duty to marry. But when he reached Modena on his travels, she could not prevent herself from indulging in a romantic dream. If only he were to fall in love at last, and with one of her own kin! He had been made welcome at the Court of Uncle Rinaldo, who was entertaining him *en famille*. Uncle Rinaldo was only a few years older than herself, had married very late in life, and had three daughters, all of them unmarried.

She read and re-read his letters, into which a note of animation began to creep. He wrote of his first impressions of her birthplace; he had visited Aunt Leonora at her Carmelite convent; 'She has very good health for seventy-five, and I am sure is a most holy nun, observing such perfect guard of the eyes that I do not think she once raised her eyes to my face.' He had paid his respects to the Visitandines at Modena, and was able to give her news of old friends there. Shame that for many, many years she had not so much as thought of Aunt Leonora, was overwhelmed in exasperation. She felt like shouting at him across the distance, 'What of Duke Rinaldo's girls?'

His next letter was almost as though he had heard her. It was dated from Bologna, and written with a pen which raced across the paper.

'I beg your Majesty not to be surprised if you hear of my betrothal to the Princess Benedetta, the eldest of Duke Rinaldo's daughters. I have proposed for her hand in writing to his Serenity, and though like the King my father, fate has used me to disappointments, I can't help but hope, from the encouragement he gave me, that the Duke will accept my suit. I am sure you will not disapprove my choice, but I shall await your written consent with anxiety.' And then a little heart-warming postscript: 'She is very like you.'

Mary Beatrice was ecstatic. She dashed off a note to him before writing to tell Aunt Leonora that if paper could blush there would not be a particle of white on this sheet, so ashamed was she of her long neglect. A letter to Rinaldo himself required time to compose; he had proved an extremely slippery character over the years. She devoted most of it to congratulating him on the proposed marriage of his son with the Princess Casimire of Poland, only adding at the end: 'I should have another point to touch on respecting what the King my son has written to me, and which surprised and delighted me to the highest degree, but I believe the time has not yet come to speak of it.'

Rinaldo replied evasively; she was misinformed about the marriage of his son; negotiations were in hand to obtain for him the Regent's daughter. As for the other matter, she must understand that it would be necessary to obtain the consent of his great ally, the Emperor. These tedious formalities! But it was cheering to learn that Pope Clement was so enthusiastic that he had offered to celebrate the marriage himself at the famous shrine of Loreto. She felt almost delirious with joy, an emotion to which she had been a stranger for years. It was just like a fairy-story, her son following his father's example and seeking a bride in Modena, their coming marriage at the shrine whither her mother had made her last pilgrimage, above all his falling in love.

Benedetta must have some really handsome presents; and once more the few remaining treasures were set out, but not this time, thank God, to sell for necessities. She selected three jewelled hairpins, a string of cornelians and lapis lazuli hollowed to contain perfume, and a parcel of the best French lace, given her just before she put on the mourning she had worn ever since for her husband. There would be sufficient in the parcel to make an entire wedding-gown, such being, she understood, the present mode. She longed to send all these gifts off at once, but that would be imprudent. Instead, she sent her diamond signet as a herald of the rest; engraved as it was with the Crown Matrimonial of England, it was a gift fit for one who yet might wear that crown.

A long silence, broken by a letter from James which pricked the airy bubble of her dream.

'His Serenity, the Duke of Modena, has sent me a dry and positive refusal of his daughter's hand. I must look elsewhere, therefore, for a wife, and I am resigned to marry any suitable bride, provided she be not horrible.'

Provided she be not horrible. Those poignant words had kept echoing in her mind as she started for her annual visit to Chaillot this May of 1717. But with poor James, she must struggle for resignation; princes seldom married for love, yet sometimes, as in her own case, arranged matches turned out so happily. And how curiously history was repeating itself! Like dear Lord Peter long ago, Lord Ormond was scurrying round Europe incognito, inspecting princesses, but alas, without the prospect of a throne or £20,000 worth of jewels to offer.

The Czar of Russia was willing to give his eldest daughter, but it transpired that she had been born before her parents' marriage. The Princess of Furstenburg had a red nose; the Princess of Baden was practically a dwarf; the Princess of Saxony was a stout widow, many years James's senior. But there was one who seemed promising, a granddaughter of the hero-king of Poland, Clementina Sobieska, a child not yet sixteen, gay and beautiful, with long fair hair reaching to her feet. Rumour said that she had played at being Queen of England when she was still in the nursery.

Mary Beatrice was musing about this child over her needle-work, after Mère Priolo left her with the completed memoirs, when an awed Portress announced Madame. Since Madame made no secret of loathing convents, the Community at Chaillot were astonished by her visits, while Mary Beatrice was apprehensive about her delight in shocking the sisters, and embarrassed by the fact that she was a kinswoman of Elector George. She opened the conversation with a dash of cold water.

'I hear that the King your son has an eye on the Sobieska chit. I would not wish her for my worst enemy, a spitfire and a perfect wild horse. In any case, how is she to join your son? It would be necessary for her to travel through the Emperor's dominions, who would certainly arrest her, ally as he is of King George.'

She did not expect a reply; nowadays she rambled on in a monologue, with noisy dozes in between.

'It being Friday, I have brought my own supper, a black pudding and bacon pancakes. My tame chaplain has given me a dispensation *in secula seculorum*. And I have presented the nuns with some cabbage seeds sent me from Germany for sauerkraut, though they do not deserve them. It is true I have a horror of Etiquette, but I know what is due to me, and Reverend Mother ought to have received me at the gate. And talking of marriages, as we were just now, it's a marvel to me how the Old Hag hood-winked everyone at Versailles into thinking that she and the Great Man were happy. I hear the wrinkled Old Swipe has cancer. That would be a rare bit of luck if it were true; if a devil would carry the Manure Heap off, I should look upon him as a man of honour and pray that he might be ennobled. I hope she will go to hell, whither may she be conducted by the Father, the Son, and the Holy Ghost, Amen.'

She went off into a fit of laughter, which turned into a choke.

'Each time I see you, you have grown thinner; I am sure that one day you will disappear into the air. I suppose you are fretting over the King your son, though why he wishes to be restored is a mystery to me. I have no confidence in the English, who hate kings and are eternally fickle. One day your son asked me, "What should I do to gain the good-will of my countrymen?" Said I, "Only embark thence with twelve Jesuits, and as soon as you land in Eng-land, hang every one of them publicly; you can do nothing more likely to recommend you to the English." Heigh-ho, what can I say to make you smile, you who used to be so easily amused? Did you ever hear the story of St Francis de Sales, of how a friend of his, when told of his canonization, remarked, "I am delighted that M. de Sales is made a saint, for it shows that there is hope for all of us. He talked so indecently and always cheated at cards——" '

'Liselotte, please stop. I detest stories which attack the reputation. But we will laugh together if you will come and see my coach, and give me your advice on what I am to do with it.'

It was among the many splendid gifts lavished on the exiles by Louis when first he established them at St Germains; since then it had become an increasing embarrassment. Its size was enormous, and so was the charge made for it in Virteau's mews here, which the convent patronized. If it were left in the street, boys played in it, and so it had been lugged into the convent courtyard, with a kind of barricade around it, but no shelter above, so that it was gradually disintegrating. The crown on top of the domed roof had been shied at by mischievous young hands and leaned drunkenly; the lamps were gone, and so were the poles; a door sagged on one hinge, mice had made nests in the decayed upholstery, and the royal coats-of-arms painted on its panels were now almost indecipherable.

'It cannot be taken to St Germains,' said the Queen, 'where there is room and to spare, because all my coach-horses have died. I suspect we ate part of the last of them at dinner yesterday.'

'And I know you are far too proud to accept new ones from me,' Madame declared happily. 'I heard the tale of your refusing a new writing-desk from the Duchesse de Lauzun.'

But at parting, Madame suddenly shed all her meanness and her spite, and caught the Queen into a warm embrace.

'Poverty-stricken you may be, and exiled and sick, and yet I envy you, Mary Beatrice d'Este! For you have had everything I lacked, beauty, belief in God, two children to be proud of, and a husband you respected and adored.'

'Yes, Liselotte,' said Mary Beatrice, humbled, 'indeed I do not sufficiently count my blessings.'

2

She returned to St Germains resolved to do better, in particular to make another effort to play her part as 'Andrew', her son's chief factor. In this she found an unexpected ally. Abbé Innes, once Rector of the Scots College, for several years past had been her Almoner, a gentle little man with whom she had collaborated in getting her husband's memoirs published. She was aware that he found it almost as difficult as she did herself to understand politics; but now he came to ask her opinion of an idea that had occurred to him.

He began by reminding her that, despite the disaster of the late rising, there was strong feeling for her son both in England and Scotland. Recently there had been riots against the usurper in both Universities; two soldiers were whipped almost to death for wearing oak-leaves on May 29th, and many were risking fines and imprisonment for adorning their persons and their homes with white roses on James's birthday. The King's chief supporters in his native land were the non-juring clergy, led by Bishop Atterbury, who had refused to take the Oath of Allegiance to George. But what of the Catholics? said Innes. Surely they could do far more than so far they had done to work for the restoration of a Catholic king, whose father had sacrificed his throne for the Faith, and who himself so many times had refused to barter his conscience for his birthright.

'My notion, madame, is to compose a circular letter to the Duke of Norfolk and other prominent Catholic noblemen, setting forth what benefits they would obtain if they would unite in striving for his Majesty's return.'

'But what a wonderful idea, *mon père*!' exclaimed Mary Beatrice, clapping her hands. 'Why did I never think of it myself?'

He begged her aid in composing the letter; he was not, he said, very skilful in such tasks. She actually began to look forward to the evenings which had been so lonely. She and the old priest shared little jokes ('If your Majesty is looking for your spectacles, may I respectfully inform you that they are upon your Majesty's nose?'); they asked each other's pardon for small criticisms; they decided after a long cogitation that this sentence might be imprudent, or to find a substitute for that word. Fresh inspirations kept occurring to them. What about reminding the English Catholics that they had fought for King Charles I in the field, alone had preserved King Charles II after the battle of Worcester, renounced their families and estates to follow King James II into exile? Then there should be an appeal to the personal history of each man to whom the letter was addressed, which entailed much searching for details.

Shivering in her black gown, now greenish with age, Mary Beatrice read the completed letter one cold spring evening, and said she approved. Ought they, perhaps, to show it to Lord Middleton before they dispatched it to the King for his opinion? No, on the whole she thought not. Age was making him very peevish, and he would be sure to criticize. And after all, she was 'Andrew', chief agent. Now the two harmless conspirators must apply themselves to making a copy in cipher to be sent to James. She had no doubt he would be pleased; he was always so appreciative of any service, and perhaps at last he might even be proud of 'Andrew', hitherto such a very unsatisfactory agent.

Weeks went by without an answer, but she was not unduly perturbed. He was absorbed, she knew, in the problem of how to spirit his affianced wife, Clementina Sobieska, to Italy, for Elector George had offered the Emperor a huge bribe if he would arrest her on her long journey from Silesia. And poor James had other worries; there were quarrels raging between Lord Mar, now his principal adviser, and the rest of his shadow Court. She thrust away the disquieting possibility that the letter had been intercepted by one of the spies who dogged his every footstep.

On a day in April she asked Fr Galliard to hear her confession preparatory to another operation on the tumour. She thought there was something oddly nervous about his manner, and in his little homily before he gave her Absolution, he stressed the necessity to receive all trials and injuries we suffer through the agency of persons as permitted by God to make us dependent on Him alone. It was almost as if he were trying to prepare her for some blow. But she put the thought aside; she needed all her courage and resolution to endure the physical pain she knew Fagon would cause her.

The tumour was now putting out claws like a crab, and was greatly enlarged. Neither the highly spiced caudle nor the ice-cold cloth could numb the anguish when he thrust in his lancet; she just had to clench her teeth and endure, gazing fixedly as she always did at the portrait of her husband, and remembering the loving thoughtfulness of Louise who had suggested this at the first operation years ago.

She spent the rest of the day in bed, drowsy from the infusion of belladonna substituted by Fagon for the hemlock which had lost its effect. But in the night she was wakeful and restless, and her imagination began to torment her. Fr Galliard knew something he had not disclosed; her son was ill, he was kidnapped, he was . . . That narrow escape from assassination before he left for Scotland in 1715. The English Ambassador in Paris had laid an ambush for him; only the wit and courage of a humble post-mistress had saved him from death . . . She must see Fr Galliard first thing in the morning; anything was better than uncertainty.

He came into her bedchamber with an opened letter; his nervousness had so increased that for one dreadful moment she saw not this middle-aged priest but old Fr Ruga, coming into this same room, begging her to join him in the prayers for a departed soul. She whispered:

'My son is dead.'

'No, madame, indeed no. His Majesty is very well.'

'*Laus Deo!*' she moaned, rocking herself backwards and forwards in a turmoil of relief and shame. 'Why do I always imagine the worst! All my life I have done it; never do I learn to leave my loved ones in the hands of God. I beg your pardon, *mon père*; sit here; I am calm now. Tell me why you look so troubled.'

She was almost gay. James was alive and well; nothing else mattered.

'His Majesty has written to me, madame, asking me to choose my time in explaining his views and sentiments regarding a circular letter composed by yourself and Abbé Innes. Would your Majesty prefer to read my decipherment of what the King writes?'

'By no means. He has expressed his wish that you should explain to me his views and sentiments, and his wish is equal with me to a command. But perhaps Abbé Innes should be present, since he was my fellow scribe.'

Fr Galliard licked his lips.

'It is his Majesty's pleasure, madame, that Abbé Innes be dismissed forthwith.'

She frowned in sheer bewilderment.

'Dismissed? But he is my servant, not his Majesty's. Oh my head spins round! It is the drugs I am obliged to take. Perhaps after all I should read what my son says, only I have not an idea where I have put my spectacles, and I am ashamed to ask my ladies to search for them again. Besides it is your letter. Pray, *mon père*, read it, and then I shall know what this is all about.'

'His Majesty writes of you in the masculine gender, madame, using your code name of "Andrew",' observed the priest, who seemed strangely reluctant to begin. She nodded with a touch of impatience, and he took the plunge.

' "The circular letter for which my approval is sought would prove most offensive to English Protestants in several passages. Andrew would force me to the same measures which were the source of my father's misfortunes. I know my duty, thank God; I am a Catholic, but I am a king; and subjects of whatever religion they may be, have an equal right to my protection. I am a king; but as the Pope himself told me, I am not an apostle. I am not bound to convert my people otherwise than by my example, nor to show apparent partiality to Catholics, which would only serve to ruin them later. I conjure you to persuade Andrew of the honesty and sincerity of my sentiments——" '

He broke off, for she had made a strange little gesture, raising and opening her hands. But as she said nothing, he continued:

' "He knows as well as I do that the qualities of a son and master are no wise incompatible, he knows that I have always allied them without detriment to my respect and tenderness for him. And as he is above all others, and has nothing in common with them, so I have the right to dispose of them as seems good for my service, without entrenching on what I owe him. I am sure he cannot but approve the dismissal of Abbé Innes, when he has examined the reason for it without prejudice." '

There was a long silence. She felt as though someone had read her a letter in an unknown tongue. Only the end was comprehensible, and presently she answered it.

'I neither approve nor disapprove. For nearly seventeen years he has been the King my son; and the King comes first. Would you do me the favour, *mon père*, to ask Abbé Innes to come to me?'

She waited, shaken now and then by an uncontrollable shudder, staring at the letter which Fr Galliard had laid down on the coverlet, so familiar in its handwriting, so utterly foreign in its petulance. When her old Almoner came in, she could rouse herself only to the extent of gesturing mutely towards the letter. He read it through twice; then he said with quiet dignity:

'The King is master, madame, and I, having the honour to be his subject, think myself simply obliged to obey his Majesty without saying anything for myself.'

'But where will you go, *mon père*? How will you live?'

'I will find a humble roof to shelter me somewhere, madame. It cannot be for very long at my age, and death is a welcome friend when we are no longer useful.'

No longer useful. Far from being of service to James, it seemed that she herself was a positive embarrassment to his cause. And perhaps had always been so; it was true that by her very nature she had often failed both husband and son. She had extracted a vow from the first to follow her to France, a vow that had proved fatal. In the same spirit she had kept her son in leading-strings throughout her Regency, obstructing every suggestion of his going to Scotland. She had urged the naturalization of Berwick and his command of the French armies; she had antagonized the Regent; she had allowed her feelings to overcome her tact in that letter to Anne conveying James's forgiveness. The old excuse that public business was beyond her; was it strictly true? Was it not rather what Madame had once described as her extreme possessiveness? She had disregarded the warnings of Reverend Mother at Modena, and of Fr Petre; she had given to creatures the adoration due to God alone.

Hot resentment had surged up in her just now at the treatment of Abbé Innes. It was overwhelmed by a flood tide of compassion for her son. She had a sudden clear vision of him, far away in Urbino, tormented by love crossed, hope deferred, squabbles, intrigues, penury. She heard him again, babbling in fever, betraying the hauntings of his mind, so desperately repressed; she saw him in that momentary collapse after the disaster of the rising, a tortured man, doomed from his cradle to fight for a lost cause.

Again she lifted her hands in mute question: What am I to do now? What is there left for me to do for anyone? But then she said aloud, and for the first time in her life she said it from her heart:

'My God and my all.'

3

May 1st was a perfect spring day, as befitted the commencement of Our Lady's month. It was also the feast of St James the Less, patron saint of her late husband, and she celebrated it in the village church of St Germains, keeping an hour's watch before the Blessed Sacrament, and staying on for Compline. She had refused the armchair prepared for her, and knelt motionless at her prie-dieu, incapable of vocal prayer, content merely to gaze at the Host enshrined in a jewelled monstrance above the altar. Last night she had had another of her curiously vivid dreams. She was back in the convent across the bridge of sighs; the door into the enclosure opened to receive her. There was a moment of blinding disappointment; it was not Reverend Mother who stood there. But though the face of the stranger was invisible, in her dream she knew it was that of motherhood incarnate.

She had no coach now, and was obliged to hire a voiture if she left the chateau. On the drive back today, Lady Strickland scolded.

'M. Fagon has said so many times that your Majesty should be carried in a litter. You must take a good rest before supper; all that kneeling when there was no need for it! As for the promenade, it is not to be thought of.'

'Not only will it be thought of, but performed. Have you forgotten that this is the patronal feast of my dear King?'

Lady Strickland folded her hands tightly in her lap. It was a gesture that said, I have served you for thirty-five years, and have learned the uselessness of argument.

At the entrance to Le Notre's famous terrace, a crowd had gathered to escort her Majesty on the evening promenade, old men, women and children, for the able-bodied were with her son at

194

Urbino. But there were some tradesmen from the village, come in the vain hope of dunning for debts, and a sprinkling of mere sightseers. The promenade was public, the evening was fine; even after all these years the Queen Mother of England was someone to see, still so extremely slim and tall and elegant, though so very shabby. The ermine trimming on her sleeves was rubbed bare, the black cloth of her gown was shiny, the only jewels she had left were the gold and ruby ring of her marriage, and the celebrated Modena pearls.

Like ancient watchdogs, the members of her Household on duty prepared to protect her from suppliants and duns. But the terrace was one and a half miles in length, a hundred feet in width, and the past winter had taken its usual toll in the shape of gout and rheumaticks, while her Majesty's step remained brisk. A girl, little more than a child, who had been watching for her opportunity since the start of the promenade, saw an empty space near the Queen, darted forward, hurriedly curtsied, began in a rush, 'May it please your Majesty', and was overcome by the glance of those large dark eyes, hollowed by pain, turned instantly upon her. She thought she heard a name whispered, 'Louise!'

'I beg your pardon, mademoiselle,' said Mary Beatrice, blinking once or twice. 'For a moment I mistook you for someone else. The drugs I am obliged to use for my little malady play tricks with my eyesight, and I thought you were my daughter, whose strong arm I miss on the promenade. Will you do me the favour of giving me your support on our walk? And then you shall tell me what it is I can do for you.'

Jealously watched by other petitioners, the child proffered her arm, but she was so overcome with pride that she remained silent.

'If,' the Queen prompted, 'it is the question of a dowry, I so very much regret that my circumstances prevent me from supplying you. But if you wished to enter Religion, I would be most happy to speak for you to Reverend Mother at Chaillot.'

'Oh no, madame!' cried the child, shocked. 'I would not presume to accost your Majesty for any favours. Ever since I heard that your Majesty had lost a holy picture from your prayer-book, I have been searching for it; and today I found it, quite by accident, near the grotto of Orpheus in the gardens here, which the late Princess, your daughter, was converting into a Christian shrine.'

Tears filled the Queen's eyes. La Consolatrice! How like her to have found a favourite little treasure. The child was prattling on beside her, nervousness overcome by enthusiasm.

'I never saw that picture of Our Lady before. Oh, what a gay smile she has, and how she seems to hold out her arms as though she were inviting you to heaven!'

'What did you say?' gasped Mary Beatrice. 'Quick, child, tell me, what did you say?'

But in that self-same moment, the malignant thing in her bosom found the spot for which it had been searching for nearly twenty years. The savagery of that bite made her stagger; the face of the child beside her whirled in a black mist. She waited until the pain became bearable, as the thing settled down to its last feed.

'Pray call my ladies. I am not very well. Don't be afraid, sweet heart, but keep this little card in memory of me. I shall not need it any longer.'

During the next few days she appeared neither better nor worse, but word was sent secretly to Madame, who came to visit her, scrutinized her with sharp little eyes, and ordered her coachman to drive her in haste to Versailles. Evidently she took a high hand with her son, the Regent, for that very evening he sent Fagon and another doctor, Mareschal, to examine the Queen of England and give him a report. They agreed that she had caught a chill by lingering on the terrace, automatically bled her, commanded her to stay in bed, and departed, promising to call again on Monday. They had scarcely left when the Queen asked that her pens and paper be set out on her cheap desk.

'It is useless to chide me, dear Lady Strickland. I have a letter to write, and at once.'

She frowned at the desk, not now because it was ugly, but because it had so simple a lock. For a long while past she had been sure that some spy extracted and copied her letters at night, for she noticed in the morning that her papers were not as she had left them. Well, there it was; she did not possess, had never acquired, the gifts of an *intrigante*; she did not know how to suspect.

196

She felt extraordinarily weak, and sat for a while fingering the small privy seal which was all that was left her since she had sent her diamond signet to James. Poor James; it was to have been a gift to his first, and perhaps his only love, Benedetta d'Este. She roused herself, conscious that she had little time, ruefully aware as she began to write that her once elegant script was now almost as bad as dear Lady Sophia's 'griffonage'.

'*Patientia vobis necessaria est.* Yes, in verity, dear mother, it is very necessary for us, this patience; I have felt it so at all moments. I confess to you that I am mortified at not being able to come to our dear Chaillot. I had hoped to pay you a visit soon, and indeed I think I shall, but not in life. Pray remember my oft-repeated request that my body be clothed in the habit of the Visitandines. There is nothing very violent about my sickness; yet I believe that in two or three days I shall be out of the turmoil, if it please God, and if not, I hope that He will give me good patience. I leave the rest to Lady Sophia, embracing you with all my heart. A thousand regards to——'

The pen fell from her hand, as once more those red-hot teeth savaged her. She waited, unable to move or cry for help, while the sweat broke out coldly on spine and brow. When at last she managed to ring, her ladies found her trying to unfasten from her string of pearls a favourite little crucifix. Pressing it into the hands of Contessa Molza, she repeated twice:

'I pray you, Molza, when I am dead, send this crucifix to the King my son.'

She asked that Fr Galliard fetch the holy oils and anoint her.

'But your Majesty is in no danger!' exclaimed Lady Strickland. 'M. Fagon assured us of that. And I never saw your Majesty look better, nor with a brighter air, than only last Sunday when you took your promenade upon the terrace.'

She did not argue. She must save her tiny reserve of strength for last duties; there was a message to be sent to James, a plea to the Regent not to let her servants perish for want in a strange land, thanks to be expressed to all her Household, down to the humblest scullion. But first she must be shriven; her eyes and mouth, her hands and feet and ears sealed with the holy oils; and she must receive Viaticum, the food for the journey. She seemed to be standing on a bridge, both familiar and strange. When she began to cross it, she would be quite alone.

'*Mon père*, tell the King my son that my mother's heart remains the same till death.' Yes, that was all she had ever had to give him, a mother's love. 'That as he has not ignored the pain I would feel at the last orders I received from him, I am so intimately persuaded of his affection that whatever comes from him, though it might be contrary to my ideas or wishes, it makes no contrary impression on my love.'

She was expressing herself badly; she was approaching the bridge. Sight was leaving her, but hearing remained acute. She could tell by the rustle of skirts, the whispering, the sobs, that her bedchamber was crowded; why, there must be almost as many persons present at her death-bed as at her lying-in when she gave birth to James. A voice close to her ear informed her that Marshal Villeroi, Governor of the child King of France, had come. She clutched at the flying remnants of her strength to recommend to him her poor servants, and to beg for aid for the King her son.

They were the last words she could articulate. She wished she could demur when she heard Madame inform the company that her Majesty was dying a saint as she had lived. But it did not matter; God was her judge. She lay listening with a smile to the prayers for a soul in its last agony; she was being sent forth in the name of the whole company of heaven; an august valediction speeded her to the foot of the bridge.

Narrow it stretched, and lonely; black flowed the waters under it; around and above there was only void. Her will gathered itself to make a last act of faith. Somewhere beyond, a door would open to receive her, and a voice would say:

'Come in, dear child.'